Readers love MA

Change of Heart

"…an incredible story filled with suspense, drama, love and family."

—Fallen Angel Reviews *Recommended Read*

"Mary Calmes has created an intriguing world that I would love to visit again and again."

—Coffee Time Romance and More

"The world built by Mary Calmes in this novel is amazing and refreshing."

—Reviews by Jessewave

Trusted Bond

"Mary Calmes' stories are always wonderfully written and full of drama, excitement, passion and hot steamy sex. And *Trusted Bond* is no exception."

—Night Owl Reviews *Top Pick*

"She throws her readers into a rapture with her engaging narrative and loveable characters. It's hard to take your eyes off the pages."

—Rarely Dusty Books

Honored Vow

"I think you should get this book and lock yourself in a room with a pot of tea and some chocolates and enjoy."

—MM Good Book Reviews

"*Honored Vow* earns 5 Fairies for a captivating book that had me biting my nails and crying tears of joy."

—Amethyst Daydreams

By MARY CALMES

Acrobat
Again
All Kinds of Tied Down
Any Closer
With Cardeno C.: Control
With Poppy Dennison: Creature Feature
Floodgates
Frog
Grand Adventures (Dreamspinner Anthology)
The Guardian
Heart of the Race
Ice Around the Edges
Judgment
Mine
Romanus
The Servant
Steamroller
Still
Three Fates (Multiple Author Anthology)
Timing • After the Sunset
What Can Be
Where You Lead
Wishing on a Blue Star (Dreamspinner Anthology)

CHANGE OF HEART
Change of Heart • Trusted Bond • Honored Vow
Crucible of Fate • Forging the Future

L'ANGE
Old Loyalty, New Love • Fighting Instinct

MANGROVE STORIES
Blue Days • Quiet Nights • Sultry Sunset

A MATTER OF TIME
A Matter of Time: Vol. 1 • A Matter of Time: Vol. 2
Bulletproof• But For You • Parting Shot

THE WARDER SERIES
His Hearth • Tooth & Nail • Heart in Hand
Sinnerman • Nexus • Cherish Your Name
Warders Vol. 1 & 2

Published by DREAMSPINNER PRESS
http://www.dreamspinnerpress.com

CHANGE *of* HEART

Mary Calmes

Published by
DREAMSPINNER PRESS

5032 Capital Circle SW, Suite 2, PMB# 279, Tallahassee, FL 32305-7886 USA
http://www.dreamspinnerpress.com/

ISBN: 978-1-61581-233-2
Digital ISBN: 978-1-61581-234-9
First Edition November 2009

Printed in the United States of America
10 9 8 7 6 5 4 3 2

This paper meets the requirements of
ANSI/NISO Z39.48-1992 (Permanence of Paper).

For my sister Melissa, who always believed.

To my family for their patience
in dealing with a zombie,

my friends for their generosity,

and the wonderful people at Dreamspinner
Press for taking a chance on me.

I cannot thank everyone enough.

Glossary

aset	(Throne) The appointed mate of a semel in the event of the death of their reah. An aset can only be chosen, made, by a reah.
beset	Companion of a reah.
khatyu	The soldiers of a semel.
maahes	Prince of a tribe, the emissary of the semel.
maat	Balance, harmony, correct action.
reah	True-mate of a semel.
semel	Tribe leader.
semel-re	Tribe leader blessed with a true-mate, a leader who has found his reah.
sheseru	(Flail) Enforcer of the tribe, guardian of the mate of the semel.
sylvan	(Crook) Teacher of the tribe, counselor to the semel.
yareah	A mate of a semel who is chosen, not the semel's true-mate.

CHANGE *of* HEART

Chapter One

I USUALLY didn't notice girls, so it was not surprising that Crane saw her first. Once he pointed her out and I noticed the men trailing behind her, I agreed that it was much too late for her to be out alone. The decision quickly made, we followed the woman and the four men down the empty windswept street. Her furtive glances over her shoulder let us know she was aware she had company behind her, stalking her. When she sped up, so did they, and from where we were, slipping in and out of the shadows, it all played out over the course of one block, from walk to jog to run. And maybe everything was fine. Maybe she was a master at Tae Kwon Do, or maybe she knew the guys walking behind her and it was a game, some weird kinky sex thing they had going on that my best friend and I were not privy to. The fact remained that she was out, seemingly alone, at two in the morning in a very bad part of town.

"Can I just go by myself?" I asked even though I already knew the answer. "It would be so much faster."

Crane shook his head before he darted away from me. Having known the man since we were kids, I knew better than to try and apply logic to the situation. With his whole affinity for damsels in distress, there was no chance he would let me go alone. All I could do was stay beside him, matching his stride as we ran.

"I wonder what she's doing out here," Crane mused, quickening his pace.

She was clearly demented. Two in the morning in a bad part of town all alone, the girl obviously had a death wish that I hoped she didn't drag Crane and me into. But whatever happened, the time to turn back passed the minute we saw she was in danger.

Taking a quick detour into an alley, we quickly stripped out of our clothes, dropping jackets, sweaters, jeans, shoes, and socks into a pile in a doorway. We had to shed all our clothes so we could shift and be scary. The fact of the matter was that the two of us would have inspired fear in no one. At five eleven, I was not big. I was built like a swimmer, with long sinewy muscles over a lean frame. My friend, Crane Adams, at six one and just over two hundred pounds, was more imposing than me with his heavily muscled body, but he would not have frightened anyone either.

Everything changed once we shifted. Once we became panthers, we became the stuff of nightmares, and I went from being smaller and weaker than my friend to stronger and faster in seconds. In my panther form, I was much scarier than any other I had met.

The scream reached me, and I listened for a second to make sure I knew where I was going before I took off running. It was like being shot from a gun, the burst of speed before my vision changed and my focus lowered. I went from being blind in the dark to having perfect sight in a heartbeat. My change always happened that fast. It would take Crane longer to catch up to me, his own metamorphosis coming at the cost of minutes, not seconds. I had been told many times that my transition was like watching a wave roll forward and then back to reveal a beast where a man had been. I had asked many fellow shape-shifters over the years what it felt like when they changed, and heard a great many descriptions. Some spoke of rippling power sliding over their skin, heat that infused limbs, while others said it was like an adrenaline rush or a euphoric high. I had never experienced even a moment of that kind of exhilaration because my body discarded one shape for another too quickly for my brain to register. One moment I was a man, and the next I was a panther. The change was so seamless that it could not be tracked with the eye. I could have done really well in a magic show in Vegas.

Bolting across the street and down a side alley, I emerged in time to see the woman running across an empty lot with the four men behind her. I flew after her, darting toward the chain-link fence that surrounded the property, clearing the six feet easily and landing on the other side without even a temporary loss of momentum. It was like I had arrived onstage, and I waited for the response.

I expected screaming, gasps and horror, panic and fear. I got nothing. Everyone froze. Even the girl stopped running and stilled. Nobody moved, nobody fainted. When had seeing a black panther materialize out of the night in the middle of downtown Reno ceased to be scary?

"What the fuck is this?" one of the men snickered, gesturing at me. "I thought you were alone."

No one was scared, and worse, they knew what I was; they were not mistaking me for an animal. I felt the knowledge in the pit of my stomach like a rock. Discovery was bad for those in another's territory without permission. I lowered my head for the coming fight.

"You think I would be out without a chaperone at this time of night?" the girl breathed, challenging them, walking backward, away from the men, toward me. "You better back off; this is only one of my bodyguards."

Only at that moment did they look hesitant. Nothing else scared them except the possibility that I was the vanguard of her tribe. They all moved back, darting looks back and forth before they suddenly turned and ran. I was exhilarated for the second before I heard them calling for the others, their growls carrying in the night.

"Oh God," she whimpered, stepping back, her hand clutching at my fur before she suddenly released me and started tearing at her clothes, stripping as fast as she could. Her eyes were huge, wild, and she was looking back across the lot as well as checking me, making sure I wasn't going to attack her. I would have shifted and told her she had nothing to worry about; being gay, I had no interest in anything outside of protecting her, but I wanted her to change as fast as she could, and I needed her to focus, not divide her energy.

As I suspected, her shifting took several minutes. Muscle and bone reformed as her body twisted and convulsed. I could tell that it hurt, her transformation, and my guess was she hated it. I did, too, for altogether different reasons. I heard the pad of paws in snow and was relieved to see Crane racing toward me. She huddled against my side, but the reassuring bump of my nose soothed her. When Crane stopped, frozen, in front of me, she slowly peeked around my side to get a look at him.

I saw him shudder, and had I been human, I would have yelled at both of them. They were having a tender moment when we should have been running. But between waiting through her change and not wanting to leave without him, the time for flight had passed. It was too late; cats were pouring over the chain-link fence to come and attack the three of us. We had to stand and fight instead of running for safety. Feeling a nudge on my shoulder, I turned and saw Crane staring at me, waiting for what I would do. The female panther was holding out for me as well, her desire for my protection overwhelming her instinctive urge to run. They were both scared, and when I bolted forward, they followed right behind me.

Huge razor-sharp claws came at my face, but I easily avoided the attack. Every cat I had ever met moved in slow motion in comparison to me, so I was able to veer out of the way without even being touched. The body that leaped at me I knocked aside with my lowered head, more bull than panther. I saw gleaming fangs and batted the face away, running over the fallen animal under me. I plowed through the pack, only vaguely aware of anything but getting my charges out of there. There were six or seven of them in all, huge male panthers trying to prevent our escape, but they came at me one at a time instead of working together to stop us. One at a time, my odds were better, and the glimmer of hope grew as both the female and Crane followed me precisely, intuitively knowing that we could not be separated.

Another of the panthers charged forward, and I leaped over him, landing briefly on his back before pushing off. He crumpled under me and the force of my jump sent him tumbling. As I turned to run, the female was suddenly grabbed and pulled away. I whirled around to face her attacker, who stood, unmoving, over her, staring at me. His teeth were bared; his lips drawn back over long, sharp dagger-like fangs and blackened gums. He could easily dip his head and inflict damage on her, so, hoping to intimidate him, I lifted myself up, lengthened my neck, and took in a deep breath, letting the growl gather in my throat. I knew what I looked like, as though I myself were a fragment of the night. As a black panther, I was different from the golden cat standing before me, and he had probably not seen one like me before. I was rare, more so than he could imagine. When his scent changed, I was relieved. I could smell the fear.

I watched in amazement as he stayed still as only an animal can be. When I dropped my head, my body bristling, he took the slightest step back. Pressing my advantage, I lifted my head and snarled loudly. He shuddered. My show of speed and strength had frightened him into waiting for what I was going to do next, made him apprehensive. When he took another step back, his teeth out of range of the female, I leaped forward, landing directly over her, and stood there, letting them all see me. My stance said that she was mine and that I had claimed her. If the leader wanted her, he would need to challenge for her, and that fight would be one on one. I knew the odds were in my favor in that instance.

When the leader of the pack did nothing, I was surprised. His hesitancy led me to believe he would sink to the ground before me, roll to his back and bare his throat. By the code we all lived by, he needed to make his show of submission, so I was stunned when he turned and ran, the others following.

Left alone in the now silent lot with the female, confused by their retreat, I was startled for a second by her movement under me. She rose with great effort, running her head up under my chin. When I gently enclosed her nape in my jaws, I heard her deep purr of contentment before she trembled.

Lifting slowly and gently, I had her on her feet and used my body to brace her. When the male panther had grabbed her, he had thrown her down hard, and she leaned heavily on me as we began to walk. Crane stood beside her on the other side, and we braced her between us. Seconds later, I heard the others and finally understood the real cause of the retreat. The lead male had known the cavalry was coming and, not knowing how much time he had left, had decided to run. I wasn't as scary as I thought.

The female's call was short, a brief cry to let her tribe know where she was and that she was well. I tensed and felt her teeth gently close on my shoulder to hold me there. Turning, I rubbed my chin over the top of her head before I nudged her, shifting her off-balance and away from me. I leaped away before she could regain her hold. She took a step forward, but I was already beyond her reach. They were close now, her tribe, her family, and she was safe. I growled at Crane, and after seconds of indecision, he bolted after me. I twisted around and ran back the way I had come. I heard her calling in short, loud bursts, the sound no longer of pain but of loss. I ran on, feeling my friend beside me, clearing the fence for the second time that night, across the road in a blur. Our clothes were where we had left them, and we were changed minutes later, having pulled and yanked on things now cold and damp.

"Why are we running?" he asked, visibly confused.

"How can you ask that?" I snapped. "We have no idea whose territory we're in, and we just got in a fight with God knows who. We need to get the hell outta here and back home fast."

"We saved that girl."

"Yeah, but who did we save?"

"Whaddya mean?"

He had no idea why I was worried. The fact that we had just had an encounter with a tribe of panthers, and that sooner or later they were going to come looking for us, was not a concern for him. It had been the right thing to do, saving the girl, so he was certain everything would work out. But I was a realist. I was worried about repercussions like who would come knocking on our door. The grateful tribe of the female panther we had saved? Or the very pissed-off tribe we had driven off? Either way, it was bad. I did not want to be involved, and, more importantly, I didn't want to be called before the semel, the leader, of their tribe or my own.

"What's really going on?"

He knew me, knew I was worried for a reason; he just had no idea what it was.

"Jin?"

I ran a hand through my hair. "Let's just go home, alright?"

"You're bein' all weird," he commented, but he followed me when I started walking back in the direction of downtown.

I was going to make a comment when he was suddenly illuminated by headlights. As it turned out, the opportunity to slip away into the night was not going to be an option.

Chapter Two

THE HUGE Lincoln Navigator rolled to a stop in front of us, and three men got out. That left the driver behind the wheel and two others I could see in the backseat. The girl was nowhere to be seen, and I wondered where she was. I slipped in front of Crane, and when he tried to move, I snapped at him.

"For crissakes, Jin, I'm the muscle, not you."

I ignored him as the three men closed in on us.

"Did you two just save a girl?"

He couldn't tell if we were panthers, which instantly gave me hope. The man was an underling; he had no station. He was a khatyu, a fighter, and nothing more.

"Yes, we did," I told him, offering him my hand palm up in a submissive posture of greeting.

He nodded, gave me a quick smile, and I saw the wave of relief wash over the group. They all relaxed, and I saw the respect on their faces.

"She is the sister of our semel and has been taken home to safety," he breathed, taking my hand with one of his before covering both our hands with his other. "We are in your debt."

"Then you'll forgive us being here without permission?"

"Of course," he said, like I was ridiculous for even asking.

"I told you," Crane muttered under his breath, bumping me with his shoulder.

"There's nothing to forgive," the man assured me, "and you can use my name, Andrian Basargin, as your shield whenever you're in our territory in the future."

"Thank you." I smiled wide, meaning it. "I'm Jin Rayne, and this is my friend, Crane Adams."

"Name your tribe," he ordered gently.

"Pakhet," I told him.

"Really?" His eyes lit up. "That's wonderful. I thought maybe you guys were from somewhere else, like visiting from wherever."

"Nope, we live right here in Reno."

"So then are you going to the mating feast in three months?"

"I'm going," Crane assured him, "but Jin's not much for that kinda stuff."

I had my reasons.

"I still can't believe it," Andrian smiled wide. "A covenant bond between our two tribes, how amazing is that? I mean, we'll basically be one big tribe."

The tribe to which Andrian and his friends belonged was Mafdet. The semel of that tribe was Logan Church. In two weeks, he was going to officially take Simone Danvers, the sister of our semel, Christophe Danvers, as his mate. In making her his mate, or yareah, as the "wives" of semels were called, he and Christophe would be making a covenant bond between their two tribes. It was a really big deal; everyone had been invited to the three-day celebration, which included hunting, drinking, and food, and was basically just one giant party that I was sure people would be talking about for years. I would not be caught dead there.

"I'm looking forward to checking out the hunting lands on top of your mountain," Crane told Andrian. "Other panthers from your tribe that I've met say it's beautiful."

"It is." He smiled at Crane. "At the feast, I'll show you."

"Thanks."

"You know, uniting two tribes, that's a great thing he's doing," I said sincerely.

"Yep." He smiled, and I saw how pleased he was. "The man's brilliant, and that was why we were all so worried."

"Whaddya mean?" Crane asked.

"Well, we want Logan to have a son. We wanna know that our semel's bloodline will continue, so we were all waiting around for him to take a mate. But then he didn't, and more and more time's passing and he's like thirty-two already and nothing."

"Thirty-two is still really young," Crane assured him.

"Yeah, but c'mon, most of us are mated by twenty."

Crane shrugged. "True enough."

"Yeah, so we were all gettin' a little worried, ya know, and then all of a sudden at our last gathering, he announces his mate, and it's Christophe's sister. So not only will we get an heir, but we get a tribal union out of the mating, as well. It's like winning the goddamn lottery."

My friend chuckled. "You guys wanna grab somethin' to eat with us? That's what we were doin' out here to begin with."

I could have killed him for suggesting we spend any more time with Andrian and his friends, but Crane missed the company of other panthers, and so his natural inclination had kicked in before his brain. He didn't even notice me glaring at him, as excited as he was. When he suggested a really good late-night burger place he knew, everyone was on board.

After calling the driver out of the car, there were introductions all around, and we decided to walk the two blocks to the diner. It soon became apparent that the others could not detect my presence at all. The realization that I was safe calmed me, and as usual, the minute I relaxed, the others felt it, completely at ease in my presence, each jockeying for position beside me as we walked. All my life, it had happened, and maybe it was the same with all reahs, but I had never met another one to ask. When I glanced over at Crane, he just rolled his eyes.

"So," Andrian said, sliding an arm around my neck, drawing me closer to him. I doubted he even knew what he was doing. It was simply the pull of a reah on a regular cat. "How long have you two been members of Christophe's tribe?"

"Six or seven months," I exhaled.

"Christophe's been away." He squinted at me, inhaling deeply. "Did he accept you and Crane, or did his sylvan?"

"Both his sylvan and sheseru were too busy to even meet with us." I smiled at him. "We were accepted by Christophe's yareah, Talon."

His mouth fell open. "Are you kidding?"

"Nope," Crane told him, laughing softly as the others joined him. "We've never even met the man; we wouldn't know him if we passed him on the street."

"That is fucked up," one of Andrian's friends said. "Our semel… he knows every person in our tribe, swear to God."

"Which is why you think he's great," I told him. "A leader that truly cares about his people is hard to beat."

"I agree," Andrian said, letting me go as we all filed into the diner.

Crane waved at the waitress, who told him to take his regular seat. I got a smile and a wave from her as well. At the table, Crane slid in beside me before anyone else could, and Andrian took the seat across.

"So lemme get this straight." Andrian smiled at me. "If Logan tells Christophe to commend two members of his tribe for saving his sister and gives him your names, he wouldn't even know who you guys were."

"Nope," Crane assured him before he explained that the mushroom burger and the Amarillo fire burger were the best things they served. The consensus was to trust him. No one even looked at a menu; they just ordered one or the other and drinks.

"Where were you guys before you got here?" Andrian asked a while later between bites.

"I was in Miami," Crane lied seamlessly, having told it so many times, "and Jin's been traveling for a while. We both work at Fusion; it's that nightclub on the strip."

"I've been there," one of the guys said. "It's a nice place. You've got that cool bossa nova lounge upstairs."

"Yep." Crane grinned. "That's it."

"What do you guys do there?"

"Jin bartends in the club, and I bartend upstairs in the lounge you like so much."

"I bet you make a shit load of tips." Andrian couldn't stop smiling at me.

"I do alright."

"What our boss would really like," Crane said, and arched an eyebrow for my benefit, "is for Jin to take over the night manager spot at his restaurant in King's Beach so he could run the club. I could work up there, too, and everybody would be happy."

"What's stopping you from taking the job?" Andrian asked.

I looked deep into his eyes until he got it.

"Oh, shit, King's Beach is our territory—you needed permission from Logan to come and go."

"Yep, can't be on your land without safe conduct."

"Well, shit, consider it done, Jin. I mean, you and Crane are heroes as far as I'm concerned, and Logan won't even care that you're there. I'll run it by our sheseru, but I really don't think it'll be any problem. Tell your boss you and Crane will take the job."

I nodded. It was a nice surprise for the evening. "Thanks."

"No, thank you, guys. It could've been a real bad night all the way around without you stepping in. Anything we can do to repay you, please just ask."

"Well, this'll do it." Crane smiled at him.

"Well, great." Andrian nodded, genuinely pleased as his eyes locked on mine.

It was four in the morning by the time we were dropped off in front of our apartment. I felt exhilarated as the car drove away. I had extracted a promise from Andrian not to let Logan's sister, Delphine, know anything about us, just to let her know that he had seen us when, and if, she asked. She would ask, he promised me with a smile, but he agreed to my stipulation. Alone on the street, I smiled at Crane.

"You lucky piece of shit," he groused, trailing after me toward the three flights of stairs we had to take to our place.

"What?"

"You know what." He snorted. "You dodge more fuckin' bullets than anybody I know."

"What are you talking about?"

"What am I… oh, I dunno, you get lucky and Christophe Danvers's yareah just so happens to come into our club one night with all those other women, ladies' night out or whatever, and you end up convincing her to let us into her tribe without having to appear before her semel."

I stopped on the stairs, turning to look down at him. "She enjoyed it. She didn't even know she could admit members into the tribe until I told her."

"Yeah, I know," he said, shoving by me to take the lead as we climbed the flights up. "And once you got her all pumped up about the idea, and you went all charming and seductive on her, she couldn't resist. I didn't know gay men could turn women into putty."

"She's a panther first, woman second, so I—"

"She's a woman first and you played her."

"I nudged her a little."

He groaned loudly, which made me smile as we reached our door. "I just hope that doesn't come back to bite you in the ass."

"And by me you mean you, of course," I clarified as I unlocked it and walked into the dark two-bedroom apartment.

"That's right." He yawned as I turned on the lights, and he collapsed onto the couch. "It's all about me."

"Well, I think we're good," I called out, walking around the back of the couch and through the door to my bedroom. "I'll tell Ray tomorrow that I'll take the job managing the restaurant, and we can move to King's Beach and not be around to bump into Christophe Danvers."

"And Logan Church won't bug us because Andrian will tell him that we're members of Christophe's tribe," he called back, making sure his voice reached me.

I shed my jacket and sweater and came back out in only my jeans, T-shirt, and socks. "So see, it's perfect. I don't have to meet any semels, and you can hang out with panthers like you've been wanting to since I got thrown out of our tribe and you followed me."

"What was I supposed to do? Let my best friend leave forever without a forwarding address?"

I sighed deeply. "You would have been sheseru someday if you stayed."

"Fuck that," he yawned loudly. "It's more fun to see what kind of bullshit you're gonna get yourself into with all your plotting and scheming."

"You're hilarious. I'm goin' to bed."

"Wait." His voice stopped me before I closed the door.

"What?"

He turned around on the couch to look at me. "You never miss it?"

"I don't know what we're talking about."

"A tribe, asshole; you never miss being part of a real tribe?"

"No," I lied flatly, and even knowing me for as long as he had, I knew he couldn't tell I was lying. Of course I wanted to belong to a tribe. I wanted it just as badly as he did, but since it was never going to happen, longing for the day when I would be accepted was futile.

We were silent for several moments before he suddenly cleared his throat.

"You know, it's too bad that Logan Church is giving in and taking a yareah to be his mate." He was changing the subject to some neutral topic that meant nothing to either of us, like he always did. "If I was a semel, I'd never do that. If I was a semel, I would wait forever for my reah. Who wants a fake mate?"

"Somebody you choose isn't a fake," I corrected, leaning against the doorframe. "Millions of people do it every day."

"I guess, but still, a semel is supposed to mate with a reah. That's how it's supposed to be. Settling for anything less goes against the nature of a semel."

"But if a semel never finds his reah, then he's supposed to do what? Just live without a mate, live and die without a family of his own?"

"I'm just saying—I would wait for my reah."

I nodded. "Sure you would."

"I would."

"Okay," I indulged him.

"Why are you being a dick?"

"It's just that anybody can say what they would do if they were a semel." I sighed. "And I'll bet you that every semel said the same thing before they took over leading a tribe."

"You're so cynical."

"I'm a realist. When you have responsibilities to no one but yourself, it's easy to say what you would and wouldn't do, but when your tribe is looking at you and waiting for an heir like Andrian was saying earlier about Logan Church… I mean, when your bloodline needs to be secured, no one can be strong under that kind of pressure."

He squinted at me. "So you're saying no semel can afford to wait for his reah."

"Realistically, no, they're too rare. The chances of finding one are too small."

"And yet," he said with a flourish, "there you stand."

I flipped him off.

"Oh, c'mon, Jin, all this talk about reahs and here you are, the rarest of all panthers, the one and only male reah in existence."

"I don't count."

"You count, idiot; you're a reah."

"I'm not a real reah. I'm not a girl."

"Who says a reah can only be female?"

"Oh, I don't know… everyone," I said, sounding bitter even to myself.

"Well, everyone's wrong—you're a guy and you're a reah—a real one, and that's not up for debate. You exist, so you're real."

"Crane—"

"Let's not have some weird, long existential debate, all right? I know you're a reah just like I know you're the only male one ever… period… end of story."

"But you don't know that. Not really."

"Oh, I don't know that?" He scoffed. "I'm thinking I know that, 'cause see, in all the traveling we've done over the past two years after we left college, neither one of us has ever seen or even heard of another reah, let alone a male one. I mean, a female reah is like one in a million… a male reah… gimme a fuckin' break. You're it, man."

"Whatever."

"I'm just saying… you don't ever want to tell anybody else but me?"

"My father knows," I reminded him, "and our old tribe, and our old semel who tried to kill me. I'm thinking enough people know already."

He turned around and slouched down onto the couch. I couldn't see his face anymore.

"You can go back, you know. They'd take you back, Crane."

"Fuck you. Go to bed. I don't wanna talk anymore."

I respected his decision because we were both beyond reason at that point. We both needed sleep, so I closed my door and fell into bed. I was so tired I didn't even dream.

Chapter Three

IN MY experience, people use the word "cold" much too freely. For instance, I have been in movie theaters and restaurants and even crowded grocery stores and heard people say that they were cold… freezing, even. The fact is that unless you've felt the blast of glacial air off Lake Tahoe at the end of January, you have no idea what you're talking about. This was why I never understood guests who wanted to sit out on the patio. Even with the heaters running and a coat on, even though the patio was covered, it was still damn cold out there. As I looked over at the cluster of people heading outside, I shrugged at the host on duty.

"So it's okay, then, Jin?" he was checking with me.

"If they wanna freeze," I said with a shrug, "who am I to say no?"

"Thanks, boss."

"Make sure you let Owen know that he needs to help Linda with the table. That's a lot of people, and it's cold as shit out there."

"Will do." He smiled at me.

"Tell them to wear their snow suits." I chuckled as I walked away.

I had to check in on my kitchen staff and was halfway across the room when a heavy hand came down on my shoulder. Turning, I found my boss, Ray Torres, looking at me.

I squinted at him. "What are you doing here?"

"Just my weekly visit up here to see how you're doing. As usual, everything's going great."

"And what else? You usually just call."

His smile was sly. "I was hoping you'd have an answer for me."

"Are you kidding? Ray, I haven't even had a second to—"

"Oh, c'mon," he chuckled, his hand moving to my neck, squeezing it gently. "It's just one more night. You've got three days off after this."

"And you act like I don't deserve it. I've worked fifteen straight days, Ray. I practically live here. I should just put a cot in the kitchen."

"There's the room upstairs."

"Oh, you're hysterical."

He smiled at me, reaching out to tousle my hair. "You're young. When I was twenty-four, I could go for days without sleeping or eating."

I tried to walk away from him, but his hand curled around my bicep, holding me up.

"You know, Jin, in the two and a half months you've been managing the restaurant, you've become absolutely vital to me. I hope you're giving my offer serious thought."

He had no idea how much thinking I'd been doing since he sprung his offer on me a week ago. He wanted me for the general manager spot at his restaurant—the position coveted not only by two other guys, but also by Crane.

Paragon was a lounge restaurant located right on the lake in King's Beach. In the summer, people could drop anchor and swim to the dock, paddle in, or step from the deck of their boat directly onto the back patio. In the summer, I was told, the place was a madhouse morning, noon, and night. In the winter, lined with lights, warmed by heaters out on the patio, it was the haven of the snow-packed winter retreat of Incline Village. Our clientele was made up of locals, tourists, and the vacationing wealthy elite.

"Jin." Ray's voice snapped me from my thoughts.

"Yeah?"

He stepped in front of me so that I had to meet his gaze.

"When you first came to work for me, I thought you were just some punk, but right away you stepped up and showed me your qualities."

"You thought I was a punk?" I teased, squinting.

"Jin," he warned.

"Ray," I said, using the same tone back.

He grunted. "Listen, everybody loves you and everybody takes orders from you. I need that."

"Ray—"

"Since you took over here, I'm actually running in the black."

I was silent.

"The marketing you've done, getting the tie-in with those clubs in Reno and working out the deal with The Lakehouse Inn to have private parties there… everybody's making money. Greg came by yesterday and said that the inn is doing well for the first time in years. He says you're a miracle worker."

"Oh, screw you, Torres."

His smile was huge. "He said that if I didn't offer you the general manager spot here, that he wants you there. He likes what he sees."

"And I appreciate that, but I dunno what I'm gonna do yet. Originally, I had plans to leave."

"I know you did, but I really want you to stay. We all do."

"I dunno… I'm not the only one who wants the job."

He shrugged. "The fact is, Jin, that when you're here, I don't hafta be. I don't worry when I leave you in charge. Everyone else… I worry."

"I appreciate what you're saying. Gimme some more time to think about it, okay?"

"Take as much time as you like." He smiled before he walked away.

Minutes later, in the kitchen, I was greeted with the usual round of loud affectionate obscenities before I was forced to try a new concoction of jalapeños, Pepper Jack cheese, and cranberry sauce all deep-fried together. It was disgusting, and I asked Ramon, the head chef, if he was trying to kill me or just make me really sick.

"Do all the girls here know you're gay?"

I could only guess at his train of thought, because it made no sense at all. "What does that have to do with what I just asked you?"

"Absolutely nothing," he assured me.

We were silent, just staring at each other, but I cracked a grin before he did.

"Okay, what about me being gay?" I sighed deeply.

"The girls," he repeated. "Do they know?"

"I'm gonna go with yes."

"Then how come they all talk about you all the time?"

"'Cause straight women and gay men go together like peanut butter and jelly," I enlightened him. "We're made for each other."

"No." He shook his head. "They talk like they wanna screw you."

But they didn't—he just didn't know the difference.

All the women I worked with loved me, and that was the reason for their appreciation. Whether I wanted them to or not, whether I had tried or not, none of that made any difference. I loved women; I just didn't make love to women, and they had always been crazy about me. They all complimented my light gray eyes, long black hair, and dark eyebrows. Girls noticed things like the perfect shape of your eyebrows, how long your eyelashes were, full lips and the curve of your nose. I was told that between my smoky eyes, hard body, and gorgeous skin that I should model. It was sweet, and so were the hugs and kisses I got every time I came into work.

"Hello."

I lifted my head and looked at Ramon. "No one wants to do me; they all want Crane."

"None of the girls are into your roommate—they're all into you."

But that made no sense.

"You're just too blind to see it."

I gave him an indulgent smile and turned to go.

Before I could leave, he took hold of my arm.

"What?" I returned my attention to him.

"We," he said, indicating the entire kitchen staff with a quick wave of the tongs still in his hand, "are gonna beat the crap out of that guy Ben if he's ever stupid enough to show his face around here again."

I smirked at him. If he only knew—there was no way that Ben Eller would ever come back near me on a bet. "I appreciate you guys lookin' out for me, but I'm not a girl. I don't need you to beat up that guy just because he messed me up a little."

"But he didn't fight fair, J. He broke into your place in the middle of the night."

This said more about my and Crane's crappy locks and how hard I had been sleeping than anything else. Crane had started dating a stripper, and of course she had a jealous ex-boyfriend who had stalked the two of them until he found out where Crane lived. The night he broke in, my roommate wasn't even home. I was the only one asleep in the dark on the couch, having collapsed there after a sixteen-hour shift.

"That asshole could've killed you."

"Yeah, well, live and learn."

"But it wasn't even your lesson."

There was that.

"You know you looked like shit after he hit you."

And I had. Split lip, black eye, and bruises on my throat from where he'd tried to choke me to death. Eller had broken into the apartment a week ago simply to threaten his rival, but, entrenched in the moment, adrenaline had overwhelmed him, and it went from scare tactic to attempted murder that fast. He had tried to strangle me.

Dazed, only half-awake, I had twisted free of Eller's death grip and then shifted right there in the middle of the living room. My hand had been forced by circumstances; I was not allowed the choice of flight, there was only fight, and so I had instinctively brought out the biggest weapon in my arsenal. He had run screaming from the apartment, but I wasn't worried. What was he going to tell the police? *When I was trying to choke this guy to death, he turned into one of those big cats from the* Discovery *Channel, right there next to the coffee table.* I was thinking that attempted murder made your eyewitness account less credible.

"Jin?"

"I know how I looked," I said quickly, rejoining the conversation. "I appreciate your concern."

"You should've pressed charges."

"Both Crane and I have a restraining order; it's all we need."

He shrugged. "Hopefully, your stalker goes away."

"He's not even my stalker," I chuckled, the irony not lost on me.

"Oh, yeah, that's hilarious." He scowled at me, leaning closer. "But off the subject, I heard Ray offered you the GM spot."

"He did."

"So take it already. We're all behind ya."

"Thanks."

He smiled at me, turning to get back to work. "Don't mention it."

Even though he never said it, I knew Ramon liked that I checked on him daily to make sure he was fine and had everything he needed.

Back on the floor, one of my servers, Linda Rice, nearly plowed into me.

"There you are," she sighed. "J, the party on the patio is loud, and one of those guys is drunk. I'm so not going back out there."

I nodded, turning to go.

Before I could slip past her, she grabbed hold of my wrist. "I'm gonna go get one of the bouncers from the lounge to go with you, alright?"

I smiled at her. "Don't worry about me, Linda, my love. I'm scrappy."

"Yeah, that's great, but a couple of those guys look like Russian mobsters."

"What did we say about too much *Law & Order*?"

"Yeah, you're so funny." She made a face like she'd bitten into a lemon. "Just be careful. You're not as big and bad as you think you are."

"No?" I smiled at her, and she giggled even though she was obviously flustered from her altercation outside. It was cute that she had to slap my ass before I got away from her.

On the patio, there were three tables pushed together, and everyone was drinking. It was really loud, even for outside, and my second server, a nice boy named Owen from Tulsa, was getting yelled at. The women wanted champagne, and as he was trying to ask which one they wanted, a huge man with massive shoulders suddenly stood and shoved Owen hard. He almost fell, but the guy grabbed the front of his sweater, shook him, and asked if he understood English. I moved fast and put myself between my server and the stranger.

"That's it," I said flatly, pointing at the door. "You're done."

"Oh, we're done," the guy said, poking me in my collarbone, hard. "Is that right?"

The second he touched me, I knew. He was a cat. He wasn't a semel, not a leader, but he was close, either the crook or the flail, sylvan or sheseru; I wasn't sure which. Either way, he was powerful and used to having people defer to him. I would have deferred as well, because I really didn't want anything to do with any cat, but Owen was there, and he was mine to protect.

"Yeah," I said, my eyes locking on his. "You're done."

He was drunk, or he would have never growled at me and bared his very human teeth to try to intimidate me. To anyone else, it just looked crazy, but I understood the gesture for what it was, him forgetting where he was because of the level of alcohol in his system.

"J," Owen said, and his voice was shaking as he laid his hand on my shoulder. "I don't think you—"

"Go inside," I told him. "Stay there, and don't send anyone else out. Everything will be fine."

He moved fast, used to obeying me.

As soon as the door closed, I stepped in closer to the massive man and smiled up at him, revealing not teeth, but my fangs, upper and lower. The second I did it, I regretted it. If I had been clear-headed and not sleep-deprived, my judgment would have been sound, and I wouldn't have acted so rashly. But instinct had taken over when my reason had failed.

My smile had the desired effect; the man stepped back, shaken. He wasn't like me; he wasn't a reah. He didn't have my power. He could be man or beast; he could not be pieces of either by choice. He could not take the form of a werepanther; it was the ability of only a semel or a reah.

"I… I don't…." He trailed off, unsure of what I was. I was not a semel; he knew that. There was no mistaking the power of a semel, and that kind of raw, primal energy didn't radiate from me.

What rolled off me in waves was different, warmer and gentler, because of what I was. A reah was the yin to the yang of the semel, each complementing the other, fitting together so that the reah gave softness and compassion to the semel, the semel bringing strength and logic to the reah. Every semel exuded strength and dominance, but I did not, so the man standing before me was at a loss as to what to make of me.

"How can this be?"

I understood his confusion. As far as I knew, I was the only male reah in existence. Maybe there were more, somewhere, but I had never come across one or even heard of one. And even though I liked to debate the existence of there being more than just me with Crane, chances were that he was right, and I was it.

"Reah," he gasped, louder now because he was finally certain. His eyes were wide as he stared at me.

Where there had been chaotic shouting only moments before, there was now only the wail of the wind off the lake.

"How dare you disrespect your tribe with a show of teeth to a stranger," I said with ice in my voice, hoping that if I could drive him out with my anger, then he wouldn't have time to question me. "Are you insane? What were you going to do next? Were you planning to shift right here in this restaurant in front of everyone?" I railed.

His eyes were glued to me.

"This is not *maat*. You are a disgrace."

"Forgive me," he said, sinking down to one knee in front of me, his face raised up to study my face. "Please, reah."

I nodded quickly.

"Take me to your semel so I can beg his forgiveness."

There was no semel to take him to, since I wasn't mated, but he didn't need to know that. "It's fine." I was curt, taking a step back. "Just get outta here."

His eyes narrowed. "What are you doing here?"

"It is not your place to question me," I snapped at him. "Take your friends and leave." After I gave the order, I turned away, purposely presenting him with my back and thereby showing him that I didn't fear him or even acknowledge him. The gasp of surprise was expected.

"Reah!"

When I had almost reached the door, there was a hand on my shoulder. Turning, I found myself faced with a pair of enormous sea-foam green eyes; a woman was standing there frozen.

"Hi," I said calmly, trying to breathe, running my tongue across my very normal human teeth. I knew my control was amazing, and for once I was glad. It wouldn't be good for me to go back into the crowded dining room looking like the werepanther I was.

"Hi," she barely got out, lifting a trembling hand slowly toward me, her fingers sliding over my chest. She was adorable standing there, mouth open, eyes wide.

It took me a moment because I was working on so very little sleep, but the woman was the one I had rescued in Reno two months ago.

"You saved me," she breathed.

"I did." I forced a smile, moving strands of light brown hair out of her eyes so I could see her beautiful face. I was vaguely aware that all movement had stopped around us.

"Oh," she whimpered, tears spilling out from under her fluttering eyelids. "I'm Delphine."

"Andrian told me."

"What's your name?"

"Jin," I said back.

She swallowed hard. "Can I… closer?"

I smiled and she flung herself at me, wrapping her arms around my waist, her face pressed against my throat. I held her tight, and the immediate deep tremble surprised me.

"You… you saved me. You were amazing…. I wanted to find you and talk to you and thank you, but they… they wouldn't… and now here you are, and you're even more beautiful than I thought possible."

"You were the one?" someone asked. "You saved the sister of our semel?"

Of course I had; that was the only way my luck worked. Andrian had told Crane and me those months back that she was the sister of the semel, but hearing the awe now in the voices clustered around me was almost frightening.

"We must thank your properly," Delphine said, her face still buried in my shoulder. "You must come and meet my brother."

"There's no need," I assured her, holding her out to arm's length. "It was my place, every male's place, to protect females. Those that attacked you should be punished."

"It's an old feud." She forced a smile. "One that I'm happy to see has not moved up this mountain. The hunting lands are here, though. You must join us."

I didn't hunt; it was not something reahs did. "Sure." I smiled back, scowling as the man who had bared his teeth came around to stand beside Delphine. "We'll see."

"Please, reah," the man said, going down to one knee again. "You have shown me your bravery by facing me, the sheseru of the tribe of Mafdet, and now I find that it was you who saved our sweet girl from the animals of the tribe of Menhit. Please, reah." He held his hand out for me. "Accept my apology and let us take you to meet with our semel, Logan Church."

The longer I stayed with them, the greater the chances of them realizing I wasn't a mated reah. A reah could only mate with the tribe leader, and if there was no semel I belonged to, then I could be forcefully taken to any semel to see, when our eyes met, if we were mates. I hated the idea of a mate, a person you were destined to be with; I preferred free will, so I steered cleared of all tribes and tribe leaders. It was why my greatest wish would never come to pass. A reah could only truly belong to the tribe that their mate led. Since no semel would ever take me, a male mate, I would never have a home anywhere.

"Please, reah."

I gave him my hand and heard his exhale as he placed it on his face, holding it there.

"Your name is Jin?" he asked, looking up into my eyes, leaning into my hand.

"Yes."

"Jin what?"

"Rayne."

The eyes that had been so combative and angry had become warm, soft, and heavy-lidded. He was a sheseru, and because I was a reah, his place was to stand as my champion. Instinctively, he wanted to be my shield, as I was supposed to be the mate of a semel. The longer I was around him, the more protective he would become. It was all hard-wired into him, and I saw it sliding across his face, the turmoil and the conflicting desire. He wanted to throw me over his shoulder and take me to his semel so from there, beside his leader, he could watch over me. "You'll stop feeling like this as soon as you leave," I assured the sheseru.

He shook his head just a little. "Something's wrong. I can sense it."

The man was scrutinizing my face. I had to get them out of there before he put it together and read the lie on me. I didn't have a mate, and he'd know that any second. "You need to go."

"Please come with us to meet our semel and receive his thanks."

Absolutely not! I shook my head, trying to pull my hand away.

His fingers tightened instantly, digging into my wrist, holding on. Our eyes met, and I saw him studying me. He was not a stupid man, and his instincts were good, or he would never have been chosen to be sheseru. If I struggled, if I showed any fear, he would simply drag me out of there and take me to his semel by force. Once there, the truth would come out. Logan Church would know instantly that I had no mate.

I couldn't be taken to him, so I stalled for time. I dropped my eyes to stare at the ground, hopefully looking penitent. "I would go with you, but my semel would be displeased. It would not be *maat* for me to go without him."

Through my lashes, I saw him nod and rise slowly to tower over me. "Of course. I understand. It would not be *maat*, right, for you to be in the presence of another semel without your mate. Forgive me for suggesting such impropriety."

He thought I was concerning myself with archaic rules that meant nothing to me, but that was fine. Whatever got him out of there worked for me.

"Reah," he breathed.

When I lifted my eyes, I saw the muscles in his jaw clenching. He wanted to take me to his semel so badly, almost sure I was lying about who I was but not quite able to know for certain. And if he was wrong and took me anyway… his life could be forfeit over a mistake like that.

"I have never met or even seen a reah."

"We're rare, so you know my value to my tribe."

"You're a value to all of us, not just your tribe."

I nodded even though it was a load of crap.

"It is said that a semel who finds his reah is favored of Ra."

Uh-huh, whatever.

"A semel who has found his reah is semel-re, the seat of the eye. It's a blessing."

"Blessing" was not the word I would have chosen. No freedom to choose who you wanted to love, chemistry and genetics and fate making the decision for you. I wanted no part of it. If I had been born a regular cat, I could have been with whomever I wanted, but because I was "blessed," any semel I came across could potentially be my mate.

"A reah knows their mate as soon as their eyes meet."

"Yes, I know," I said quickly, taking a breath. "Please give your semel my best."

"Give me the name of yours."

I gave him the only name I had. "Crane Adams," I said softly.

He nodded, looking me up and down. "And who gave you and your mate safe conduct?"

"Your man Andrian Basargin gave my semel and me his name the night we saved Delphine," I coughed, "but he had no idea who or what we were."

He just stared at me, studying me without saying a word. I stepped back, and since he didn't seem quite ready to leave, I asked him his name.

"My name is Yuri, Yuri Kosa."

"It's been a pleasure meeting you."

"The pleasure was mine, reah… really, all mine."

I thanked him before I asked him again to leave, as it would not look good for them to stay after so grievous an exchange with me. Everyone agreed to go except Delphine. She wanted to talk with me further, but I explained I was working, after all. They left after paying the bar tab, and Ray came and found me a half hour later, impressed that I had handled yet another explosive situation so deftly and quietly. He told me I was definitely management material. I got more brownie points with the servers for coming to Owen's rescue so quickly, and the man himself thanked me a good hundred times for saving him. He had been really scared, especially when the psycho snarled at him. I agreed that it had been creepy.

Chapter Four

I WAS walking to the apartment with Crane, both of us having left work early, and he was giving me every reason he could think of to keep us there instead of leaving on the next available flight out of Reno.

"Why are you freaking out about this?" he asked, keeping pace with me. "So the sheseru of Logan Church's tribe met you, so what?"

"Shit."

"So you might hafta go see the guy, so what? You'll look at him, you'll see he ain't your mate, and that's the end of it. I never get why you don't just tell every semel we come in contact with about what you are and just get it over with."

"I'm not a normal reah. What if they try and hurt me?"

"What if they don't?"

"I'm just supposed to take that chance?"

"You're supposed to have some balls."

"Fuck you," I snapped at him. "You didn't have to live through it."

"Didn't I?"

The way he was looking at me, furious and pained at the same time, I felt terrible.

"I know I didn't take the beating, but watching it was no picnic either."

I winced, the memory a brutal one because of the aftermath of my announcement that I was not only a reah but gay as well. Beaten, stripped naked, and left on the side of the road, only Crane coming in secret to hide me, had saved me from death. My semel had allowed my public torture for being gay, my own father applauding and participating in the act. I was exiled when they learned I had lived. I had not spoken to any of them again, not my parents nor my brother nor even one member of my tribe except Crane. My best friend had chosen to be an outcast with me. When there had been no one else who cared at all, there had always been Crane. I owed him so much, because after he saved my life, he had needed to keep me sane and not wallowing in grief. If I had killed myself, that would have made them victorious over me, he said, and we couldn't have that.

"Crane," I said softly, the lump in my throat making it hard to breathe.

"Forget it," he grunted. "What I don't get is why in the hell you showed that guy your fangs in the first place."

"I didn't mean to." I exhaled sharply, calming, regaining my normal composure. "I screwed up because I'm tired, and I'm tired because I'm working too hard, and I'm working too hard for what? I'm just gonna end up leaving here anyway... shit!"

"You're an idiot," he passed judgment on me.

"Yeah, I know."

"What the hell were you thinking?"

I was so angry I could barely think straight. How in the world had I made such a stupid, idiotic mistake like showing my teeth to Yuri Kosa? He had done it first, and I had even thought it was brainless. Then I had gone and done the exact same thing!

"Lemme see."

I squinted at him. "What?"

"Your fangs, lemme see... your hands too."

"Why?"

"Because it's been a long time since...just lemme see."

I was going to do whatever I could to restore things between us to normal. He was my touchstone, and I needed him, so I parted my lips and showed him my fangs, upper and lower, before lifting my hand so he could see the claws where my fingers should have been. I had a middle form—the part-man, part-animal werepanther form that he did not. We said "werepanther" or "shape-shifter" to describe ourselves and the change, but only a semel or a reah had the horror-movie form that was both in one. There could never be a mistake about what I was.

"Shit."

"What?" I asked, returning instantly to my fully human form.

"That's amazing, you know. Just seeing you do it is really something."

We were silent for several breaths.

"Do you regret leaving with me?"

"No, Jin," he said quickly, matter-of-fact.

"You don't miss your family?"

"They called for your blood just like everyone else. I had no idea that they would turn on you like that, or me. I don't miss anyone, but I would have missed you, my friend."

He blurred, and I realized I was really much more tired than I thought.

"Oh, don't cry for fuck's sake," he grumbled at me. "Ya big girl."

I smiled through my tears.

"A male reah," he said as he smiled back at me. "How the fuck did that happen?"

"Your guess is as good as mine."

He took a breath. "Okay, so seriously, whaddya wanna do now?"

"Now I gotta get outta town."

"Why?"

"'Cause Yuri Kosa is a sheseru and he knows I'm a reah. Logan Church is gonna want to see me as soon as he finds out."

"Why?"

"You know why. To see if I'm his reah."

"Maybe he's not gay."

"It doesn't matter."

"Really?" Then he nodded. "'Cause it would matter to me. I don't care how hot the guy is, I ain't fuckin' him."

"You're not a semel. You have no idea, the pull on your body and your mind. There's no way you could ever understand."

"Okay, so why don't we just tell Logan Church or any other semel that wants to meet you that you've already got a mate."

"I did. I told Yuri Kosa you were my mate. I told him you were my semel."

He gave a snort of laughter. "Good job, idiot."

"It's all I could think of."

"And when they check us out and ask Andrian where we came from… it's all gonna get out about us belonging to Christophe's tribe, and then we're really screwed."

"This is why we gotta go."

"Shit, Jin, why didn't you just say that you were mated to someone else? What's wrong with just lying so we could stay here?"

"Because any semel would know I was lying."

"See, I've never understood that. How do they know?"

"They just do."

"But how? That makes no sense. How would Logan Church know that you don't have a mate?"

"He just will."

"That's crap; tell me how he'll know you don't have a mate."

"The way I smell, the mark the—"

"The mark." He was frowning at me.

"Yeah. It's…." I took a breath. "See, when a semel and reah mate, which they do for life—"

"Cats don't mate for life," he said smugly. "They can choose each other just like everybody else, but they don't mate for life."

"Semels and reahs do."

He gave me a look.

"They do, I swear."

"They do?"

"Yeah, they're the only ones that do, but it's more than just taking a mate and speaking the vows. It's forever from the moment they see each other."

"Are you kidding?"

"No, I'm not kidding. Why would I be kidding?"

"Shit."

I nodded. "This is what I'm saying."

"Tell me about this mark."

"Why?"

"'Cause you never talk about this with me, and I kinda like it."

"Can we walk at the same time?"

He started down the sidewalk, answering me with his action.

I followed quickly. "Okay, so when a semel finds his reah, the reah is marked with a bite on the back of the neck." The bite, I understood, was as brutal as it was orgasmic and left a scar that could never be mistaken for anything but the brand of the leader on his mate. I never wanted one.

"One bite, big deal. I can just do it and it'll look the same. We'll tell them your semel did it, and we're good to go."

I shook my head. "Thanks, but no. I'm never letting anyone put a mark on me."

"But if it'll help us out, why not?"

"No." I was adamant. I would never let anyone brand me. It seemed hypocritical.

He threw up his hands, annoyed with me. "So fine, then, just don't let him check for a mark. I'm thinking he can't do that within the rules of hospitality anyway. Where does he get off doubting that another semel has marked you?"

"Because he'll be able to tell that we're lying to him, and if he says, 'prove it, show me your mark,' then we're really screwed."

He shook his head. "I don't think he'll make us see him. We saved his sister, after all."

"You still don't get it," I sighed heavily. "I'm a reah and—"

"So you actually told that guy Yuri that I was your mate?"

"Can we focus, please?"

His smile was huge as he shook his head. "You're such a dumbass. All they hafta do is look at me to know I'm not a semel."

"But hopefully they won't get the chance to see you."

"I see, so you were just stalling for time."

"I was."

He nodded. "You know, I was told once that maybe one semel in a thousand ever finds their reah. You're so rare, Jin."

"Yeah, great. Can we go?"

"Don't you ever wanna find your mate?"

"No," I said before I started jogging.

He kept pace with me as we headed home.

"Can I ask you another question?"

"Can I stop you?"

"What are you gonna do someday if one of the guys you meet is your mate?"

"Never happen." I sped up so he had to work to keep up with me. I didn't want a mate, so God willing, I would never find one.

When we finally reached our apartment, we were stopped as Crane almost tripped over a guy crouching on the second-floor landing.

"Oh," he said as he stood up. "Sorry."

"It's okay," I said, seeing his badge, wondering what a policeman was doing in front of our apartment. "Can I help you, Officer?"

"Are you Jin Rayne?"

"Yeah. Is there a problem?"

"No, Mr. Rayne, we're just out here following up on a complaint from your neighbors."

My neighbors were complaining about me? How was that even possible? I was never home. "Am I in trouble?"

"Or me?" Crane asked.

He squinted at us both like we were stupid, and his tone suggested the same thing. "No, neither of you are in trouble. I'm from Animal Control."

I saw the badge more clearly and saw the words on it, actually looked at what was embroidered on the parka he was wearing. Not a policeman, not there to cite me for God knew what, instead he was investigating some kind of animal concern.

"You see these?" he said, moving aside to point at the ground. "How long have you guys been seeing the tracks around the stairs here?"

"Tracks?"

He scowled then. "You have noticed the tracks, haven't you?"

I must have looked as lost as I felt, because he let out a quick breath.

"They're all over your stairs here, Mr. Rayne," he said as he knelt down.

"I guess I'm not crazy after all. I told everybody that I've been hearing something out here at night," I said to the officer. I had to come up with something plausible before he started thinking I was acting weird, which I was.

He looked up at me from his crouch. "So you've heard noises, but you haven't noticed the tracks? How is that possible?"

"These are the first tracks I've seen." And I wasn't lying. I had never noticed anything out of the ordinary, but there, outlined in the snow right outside our apartment, were paw prints—huge paw prints, which could only have been made by a very large, very heavy panther. There were claw marks, urine stains, and traces of hair where it looked like a cat had been rubbing up against our front door. From coming and going only in the dark for the past few weeks, I had missed seeing my place in the light of day. I realized now that my feline visitor was not new but had been watching Crane and I for a while.

"Well, everyone else has reported seeing the paw prints before."

"That's funny."

"Funny is not what I'd call this, Mr. Rayne. As far as I can tell, you folks have a serious cougar problem here," he explained, rising to stand in front of me. "And it looks like he's marked your apartment as his territory."

The news just got better and better.

"Okay," I said, starting to get cold. "What should I do?"

"Well, unfortunately, there's not a lot you can do. I haven't seen a cougar around here for years, so.... I mean, we'll watch it; I'll come by when I can, but...just, if you see it, don't do anything but call us, and stay inside," he said, pulling a card from the inside breast pocket of his parka. "Don't try and be a hero, Mr. Rayne, because from the size of the prints, we're looking at a full-grown male cougar, and you don't want to mess with that."

"No," I agreed. "I really don't."

"Alright, then," he said, turning back toward the stairs, casting a glance at first me and then Crane. "You both take care, and call if you see anything at all."

"Yes, sir."

I watched him take the two flights of stairs down to the ground before I turned my head to look at Crane. "Is it time for us to go yet?"

"The sarcasm is not lost on me, but this doesn't mean anything."

"How have I missed the fact that you're an idiot all these years?" I asked as I unlocked our front door and went inside.

He tried to defend himself, but I cut him off as I wondered aloud how fast we could pack.

Chapter Five

TWENTY MINUTES later, we were walking back to the restaurant. We had decided to go and say good-bye to Ray before we left. Leaving without an explanation was just not an option. The man had treated us like members of his family, me even more so than Crane, and running out on him was bad karma waiting to happen. I wasn't looking forward to the scene where I would have to be purposely vague and he would press me for answers. I was so involved in thinking about what I was going to say that I didn't hear someone calling my name. When I finally registered a voice, I turned and saw Yuri, Logan Church's sheseru, standing beside a car with blacked-out windows. He tried to wave me over. When I didn't move, another door opened, and a man I had never seen before climbed out.

"Jin?" he asked, starting toward me, his black dress shoes crunching in the snow as he walked down the sidewalk. His heavy wool trench coat flapped around his legs in the wind. He was shorter than Yuri but still taller than me, with brown-black hair and dark cobalt blue eyes. He was a handsome man, and his smile was warm.

I took a step back, but he lifted a gloved hand, asking for me to wait. "My name is Mikhail Gorgerin; I just need a moment of your time," he said, coming to a stop in front of me, the laugh lines in the corners of his eyes crinkling. He looked at me and then studied Crane before offering him his hand. "I'm Logan Church's sylvan, and you are?"

"Crane Adams." He smiled quickly. "Pleasure to meet you."

"And you, Mr. Adams," he said before he turned back to me, slowly extending his hand. "Jin."

I took his hand, and he instantly tightened his grip so I couldn't pull away.

"I have never seen or even met a reah," he said slowly, the awe there in his voice. "I don't know anyone who has."

I nodded.

"And Yuri says you have a mate."

I looked at him, and his eyes didn't leave mine. It was one thing to lie to the sheseru—the muscle, the flail, the enforcer of the tribe—and completely another to lie to the sylvan—the crook, the shepherd, the teacher of the tribe. Everyone lied to the disciplinarian to get out of something. No one lied to the man who spoke on your behalf in tribal matters.

"I had no idea that reahs could be male." His eyes narrowed.

"Yeah, well." I forced a smile, shoving Crane forward so we could walk away. "Would you excuse us?"

"Wait."

"Give our best to your semel."

"Please, wait."

Ignoring the "please" was dangerous, so we stopped.

Mikhail Gorgerin, sylvan of the tribe of Mafdet, did not even look at Crane. Instead, he stepped in front of me.

"Jin, Logan Church needs to see—"

I took a step back. "I can't. We hafta go; you heard my semel."

His brows furrowed. "This man is no more your mate than—"

"We really need to—"

"You misunderstand—"

"I'm freezing out here." I smiled at him. My thick wool sweater, the parka over it, my beanie, my jeans, my hiking boots—I was dressed for the snow, but none of it was keeping the wind from slicing through me.

"Jin, I only need you to listen for a—"

"We saved your semel's sister," I cut him off. "Is this how we get repaid? We get forced to see him just because you can make us?"

That stopped him, his eyes clouding. "I think it would be in both your best interests."

I smiled quickly. "I don't. There's no purpose for him to meet a mated reah."

"But you're not a—"

"I need to go. Give your semel my apologies."

He tried to argue, but I was already walking away, Crane close behind me.

Halfway down the street, I had to duck inside one of Crane's favorite pubs because he wanted to say good-bye to his drinking buddies. The man had always made friends so easily, and I was always the one who made him leave them. I felt bad, so I trailed after him and didn't say a word. The place was packed, and I was forced to inch my way toward the bar. When I was suddenly grabbed and shoved up against the glass window, for a second I was too surprised to react. My head snapped up so I could see the face of the man who had me pinned there.

"Jin." He smiled at me.

I just stared. He was handsome, and at any other moment, I would have found him tall, dark, and definitely my type, but he had his hands on me without benefit of permission or introduction.

"I'm Domin Thorne," he said softly, his eyes intent. "And you're going to be my reah."

While it was easy to see his innate beauty, it was also simple to see the lack of conviction in his dark brown eyes. It was a game, and I was sport, nothing more.

"Take my hand," he ordered, taking a step back before thrusting his hand at me.

I didn't move.

"Remember your manners." He smirked.

I took another step away, because I knew exactly who he was. "You're the semel of the tribe that attacked Delphine."

"So what?" he chuckled, and his eyes seemed almost liquid. "You have no ties to Delphine or her tribe. You don't care. I would have known."

"What do you mean?"

"I know everything about you."

The hair on the back of my neck stood up. "How?"

"I watch you."

Apparently Crane and I both had stalkers, the stripper's ex and this guy; how lucky were we? "You watch me?"

He nodded. "All the time."

"When do you—"

"At night, while you sleep… I watch."

I was suddenly furious. "And were you watching the night that psycho nearly killed me?"

"Yes." He smiled wickedly. "Had he overpowered you, I would have interfered, but I wanted to see how strong you were. I wanted to see if you could save yourself."

"Asshole," I growled, shoving him back, turning away quickly, headed for the door.

He caught me outside in the alley. "You have terrible manners, reah," he said as his hand closed around my neck, choking me as he gripped my throat. His eyes held no trace of anything but menace. "It was like this… he cut off your air like this."

I couldn't breathe, but I didn't panic. I didn't frighten that easily.

"Perhaps I will drag you to my car and make you mine."

"I won't let you."

"Then I'll make you."

"You mean you'll rape me."

"Rape you, mark you… yeah, it'll be fun."

"Never happen."

"There are others there. They could hold you down."

His tribe obviously respected no rules, no laws; he was the leader of a gang, not a nurturing, loyal family. I had come across many of those. "You know nothing of the law."

"I know what I want."

But he said it without any conviction whatsoever.

"And I want a reah."

He wanted a reah, not me specifically. Any reah would do.

"You smell amazing."

When I looked down his body and saw the bulge in his jeans, I realized that having me seemingly at his mercy was a big turn-on for him.

"Even with everything else around us… all I can smell is you."

I could move so fast, and even though he said he'd been watching me, he had apparently missed that. Before he could react, I had my claws buried in his wrist. He gasped as he released my throat, pulling his hand back like he'd been burned. His eyes were huge as he looked at me.

"Keep your hands off me," I warned, my voice low, full of gravel, not yet my own.

He held his bleeding hand against his chest so no one could see. "I beg forgiveness, reah." He smiled slowly, his eyes dancing. I had hurt him, and he was having a good time. The man was twisted in ways I didn't want to know about. "Give me another chance."

I squinted at him. "Why?"

"I know you don't have a mate… it's my right to bind you to me."

"You really do need to read the law," I told him, turning away, deliberately shunning him. "Only the reah chooses the mate, and you are not mine."

He moved quickly, stepping around in front of me, still clutching his injured hand. It would soon heal, but it hurt, I knew it did. "Look again, reah. Are you sure I'm not your mate?"

"Yes," I said flatly, staring into his eyes. "We're done, and you know we are."

He had no retort, no snappy comeback; he'd played his hand and lost. He wasn't my mate, and that was the end of it.

"Jin," Crane called as he reached my side, looking back and forth between Domin and me. "Did this guy hurt you?"

"Do I look hurt?" I asked irritably, my body starting to ache with the need to lie down. It was still early, not even nine, but I was exhausted. I was looking forward to sleeping on the plane. "C'mon, let's go."

Crane stepped in close to Domin. "You stay away from him."

"Don't threaten me. I'm semel of my tribe, and you're nothing."

Crane was going to say something back, but I grabbed hold of his shoulder and dragged him after me.

"Why'd you—"

"I don't wanna stand around and argue with him. I wanna get outta here."

"I think it's a mistake."

"What is? Leaving?"

"Yeah," he said quickly.

"What are you talking about?" I yelled at him.

"Jin, we should stay!"

"Are you kidding?" My voice rose. "Did you hear that guy?"

"Yeah, but—"

"He's the one that's been creepin' around our place. We need to—"

"Careful."

I had gotten to the end of the alley, turned left, and walked into someone. "Sorry," I mumbled, trying to move by.

"Hello."

I looked up into the face of what I'd always imagined an angel would look like—blond hair, bright turquoise blue eyes, that alabaster skin you hear about but never see in real life.

"Are you Jin?"

"Who wants to know?"

"I'm Christophe, semel of the tribe of Pakhet."

"Oh, shit," Crane groaned beside me.

"Oh, yes." Christophe smiled slowly. "It seems that you two joined my tribe without me even knowing it."

"No," I said quickly, seeing he was not alone; four men had appeared and fanned out around us. "We didn't join your tribe."

"Oh, I think you did." His voice was trying to be sultry but missing it completely. The man was not a smoldering volcano of lust, but merely sort of vanilla. I liked vanilla; you could do all kinds of things with it when it was ice cream. But as far as men were concerned, sexy and hot was mandatory for me, and the man standing in front of me was definitely not. "You and your friend belong to me."

"All you guys that don't know your law," I said flatly, scowling at him. "An unmated reah has no ties but to the semel who is their mate, and any tribe that is not that of their mate has no claim on them."

His smirk was instantly erased. "I don't understand."

Of that, I had no doubt. "Look." I softened my tone, taking the bite out of it. "All reahs have to be free to find their mates and so may belong to many tribes in the course of that search. All reahs, as well as their beset, their guardians, are free to leave any tribe at their discretion."

"I don't… no one can leave a tribe unless they're released by their semel."

"Unless they happen to be a reah," I said, pointing to myself, "or belong to a reah." I pointed at Crane. "It's how it works. You can call your sylvan and have him check the law. I'll wait here while you do it."

He was stunned. It was all over his face. He thought he had me, but he didn't. No one ever would. I knew my law too well, backward and forward. The surge of relief and certainty mixed with pride burst through me.

"Christ, Jin." Crane shivered at the same time he cracked a wide grin.

"What?"

"I can always tell when you're happy."

"How?" I asked, smiling.

"I feel it." His eyes were soft as he looked at me.

"That makes no sense."

He shrugged. "I don't know what to tell you… but I can."

I was going to tease him, but again there was a hand on my bicep. When I turned my head, one of the men with Christophe was smiling at me.

"So a reah makes you feel like this?"

"How do you feel?" I asked him gently.

He swallowed hard. "Just… good. Drunk, almost, or stoned."

"You smell different," another man said before clearing his throat.

"Is 'different' good or bad?"

"Good," he coughed. "Like musk and pine and grass after you cut it."

I looked back at Crane, who shrugged.

"Jin."

My attention returned to Christophe before he suddenly grabbed me and walked me away from the others, halfway down the street. I rolled my shoulder when we stopped, and his hand slid off me.

"Sorry."

"It's okay." I forced a smile.

"Jin." He cleared his throat. "You're a reah."

We had already established that.

"I never considered having a male mate."

"You have a mate," I reminded him.

"I have a yareah; I don't have a reah, and any semel may leave his mate if and when he finds his true-mate, his reah."

"I think that's bullshit."

"But Jin, if I couldn't leave my yareah, how could I claim you as my—"

"Oh, you're not my mate," I said matter-of-factly, trying to go around him. "And Crane and I need to go."

"No, Jin." He reached out and stopped me with a hand on my shoulder before I could go. "Please, reah, I—"

"I'm not your mate," I snapped, my patience gone. "We both know it. Why waste time talking? Just move."

"But I would still like you to stay with me, reah… with me and my tribe. I will take care of you, protect you, give you shelter."

"That's very flattering." I stepped by him. "But no."

He grabbed my shoulder yet again. "I need you."

"No, you don't," I said, peeling his fingers off me, moving faster so he couldn't reach me a second time.

"Please, reah, stay."

I sped up, jogging away from him.

"Why?" he called after me down the street.

I didn't look back. The desperation of the man was overwhelming, his desire for me palpable. He was weak, not physically, but inside. Strength was missing from his eyes, from the way he carried himself, even from the tone of his voice. And weakness would never do.

"Jin." Crane caught up with me. "Is it like that with all semels? Even if you're not their mate, they wanna keep you?"

I looked both ways before I crossed the street.

"Jin?"

"I guess," I answered.

"You guess?"

"I dunno." I got to the other side of the street and kept moving.

"But all your meetings go that same way?"

"Pretty much," I breathed. "They meet me, I explain that I'm not their mate, and then they try to talk me into it anyway."

"And have you ever been hurt in the process?"

"Once or twice," I admitted without explaining any more.

"When we were in Santa Fe that time… you came back to the hotel room all cut up. Was that what happened?"

"Why are we talking about this?" I asked as I sped up, walking faster.

"I just wanna know."

"Fine, yeah, that's what happened. Sometimes when I say no, it's hard for a semel. Think about it—they are tribe leaders; the ego that comes along with that has gotta be huge. They're not used to hearing 'no.'"

"It's more than that."

"How much more can it be?"

"Well, maybe even though you're not their mate, you're still a reah, and they know you're probably the only one they're ever gonna see."

I didn't feel like hypothesizing with him.

"It's a big deal, Jin, meeting a reah. I don't think you get it, 'cause you are one, and I don't think I get it, 'cause I've known you all my life, but I think to everybody else… I think seeing you is like a religious experience or something."

I gave him a look.

"I didn't tell you that I thought it was. I'm just telling you that I think that's why semels lose their minds when they meet you. They just can't believe they're actually seeing you."

"Okay," I indulged him.

"Don't be a dick. I'm being serious."

"Jin!"

I looked over my shoulder, and there was Mikhail, Logan Church's sylvan, again. I just stood there on the sidewalk looking at him, and he stared back. After a few moments, when I was sure he wasn't going to move, I turned to leave.

"Jin!"

I looked back over at him.

"Please don't force my hand."

He looked like he had actually meant the "please," so I gave up and jogged over to him.

"What do you want?"

He shrugged. "It seems only fair that since you have met Domin Thorne and Christophe Danvers that you should meet Logan Church as well."

I scowled at him.

"I know you're an unmated reah. I am the sylvan of my tribe, after all."

I sighed out my irritation.

"You're calling him a liar," Crane shouted.

"You're his friend," Mikhail soothed, his voice kind, the hand on Crane's shoulder gentle, "so I understand."

I watched my friend look at the sylvan of the tribe of Mafdet.

"Jin lied, and you're going along with it because you think to protect him from the wrath of our semel. It's not necessary; there is no anger to fear. You both saved Logan's sister and have conducted yourselves honorably while on his land." He just barely squeezed Crane's shoulder. "Please, if he has to hunt you both down, he'll be annoyed. It would be better if you could simply come and meet him, and it would be done."

"I don't see why he—"

"It's okay with me." Crane shrugged, chiming in. "We can just leave tomorrow instead, or…."

"Or what?" I asked when I realized he wasn't going to finish his sentence.

His eyes were back to Mikhail. "What if Jin comes and sees your semel, and if they're not mates, then can we join your tribe anyway and be granted protection from Domin and Christophe? Could that be on the table? I mean, we live up here on your land anyway."

Mikhail nodded. "Of course. Having a reah and the beset of the reah in our tribe would be a great honor."

"Do you think your semel would protect us even if Jin isn't his mate?"

"He would, and I speak for him when I make you that promise."

Crane looked at me; hands raised like all our problems were solved. "That's what I call a win-win situation."

Of course it didn't matter to him; it had nothing to do with him. There were no ramifications for him if Logan Church turned out to be my mate. Being dragged in front of semels was scary business. I didn't want a mate, but what if I ended up with one anyway? I didn't want to be a slave to my senses, be bound to another and belong to them; I wanted to be free. Didn't I? "I just don't want to have—"

Mikhail's hand came up to stop me "You should listen to your friend, Jin; you have nothing to lose by coming with us, and everything to gain."

I had everything to lose if Logan Church was my mate, namely my identity and my freedom and any semblance of choice.

"Fair is fair. I simply want him to have the same chance the others did."

Mikhail was not going to let it go.

"Domin and Christophe have both met a reah; Logan should have that honor as well."

I rubbed my eyes because they had started to water.

"The house is packed with people; we're celebrating Logan's mating ceremony in three days, so the feast is going on as we speak."

I had my out. "Wait, if he's being mated anyway, why do you even want me to meet him?"

"You're a reah," he said, like that was all the explanation I should need. "He should be allowed to at least meet one in his lifetime."

There had to be a way out of getting into the car.

"There are at least a hundred people at the house."

I was silent.

"You're quite safe."

"I'm not worried about my safety."

He nodded. "So what do you say? Come now, or insult him instead?"

When he put it like that.... "Fine," I said, shoving Crane toward the car. "I'll meet your semel, but the second we're done, I—"

"Excellent," he said, smiling first at me and then Crane. "Will you follow me?"

"Sure." Crane grinned at him, slipping by me to follow the sylvan.

The man would follow the devil right into hell if I weren't there to watch over him.

"Are you coming?" Mikhail asked.

I moved, and he led me toward the curb where the car was parked.

"You know this is a giant waste of everyone's time, right? Did you see how fast I met and rejected Christophe?" I pointed back over my shoulder.

He chuckled. "I did, yes. I saw you meet Domin, as well, and I can't wait to tell Logan."

"Can't wait to tell Logan what?"

"That neither semel was your mate."

He was missing the point.

"Jin," he said, smiling at me. "Do you have any idea how much I like you already?"

I tried another tactic. "I'm a guy. Don't you care about that?"

"You're just meeting with my semel. That does not make you his mate."

He was right, of course. I was probably worrying for no good reason. The odds were definitely in my favor.

"But," he said, his tone gentle, "if fate has seen fit to give my semel a male mate, who am I to argue? A reah, in whatever form, is a blessing for a semel."

His faith was exhausting. "Whatever. Let's just go."

The relieved smile made me sigh in spite of myself.

Crane and I walked to the same car with the dark windows from earlier, and I was surprised at how I was treated, not just by Mikhail but by Yuri as well. I apologized for lying to him earlier.

"I understand your reasoning," he said gently, holding open the door to the backseat. "Perhaps I would have done the same in your place."

Once Crane and I were seated, he closed the door and slid into the driver's seat. As Yuri pulled the car away from the curb, he and Mikhail started talking. I tuned them out, lost in the sound of the hum of the tires on the road, the steady rocking of the car, and the miles of moonlit scenery that ran past my window. The drive was long but relaxing. I had no idea anyone lived so high on the mountain, and as we passed a glassworks, I wondered who owned it.

"Our semel owns the glassworks," Mikhail answered my silent question.

I nodded, and, when I looked up, noticed his worried eyes in the rearview mirror. Nice that he was concerned about me, someone he barely knew. It showed his character.

"What's your story?" Mikhail asked, and I realized he was talking to Crane, not me.

It was nice to have the focus off me, and I slouched down into my seat and closed my eyes.

I listened as Crane talked, telling the two men all about our adventures together, the list of the jobs we had held over the past two years, the many, many women he had seduced and how one of them had even been the mate of a semel.

"How did you become the beset of a reah?" Yuri wanted to know.

"We've been friends since first grade." Crane grinned wide. "We grew up together, and when Jin was exiled from our tribe, I went with him. We finished high school together, went to college together, and we've been doin' the traveling thing ever since."

"You don't miss having a home?" Yuri asked.

"I do. Jin doesn't."

"Is that true?" Mikhail looked at me in the rearview mirror.

"What's to miss?" I yawned.

Everyone fell silent as Crane leaned against me. After several long minutes of silence, Crane started up with a new topic of conversation. It was one of the things I found most endearing about the man, his ability to just start talking about something, anything, to fill uncomfortable silence. I drifted in and out, listening as Crane asked the two men more questions.

"Everybody's got, like, a Russian name around here, and then there's Logan Church. What's up with that?"

"Logan's grandfather was Vanya Chernishoff, and he changed the name to Church."

"Why?"

"I'm sure there were many reasons to do so forty years ago."

"So Logan—"

"Logeen," Mikhail chuckled, "if you want to say it correctly."

"Whatever. Logan's family and his tribe, most are Russian?"

"Just Logan's family, mine, Yuri's, and Andrian's, but then there are many others, like the Chings and the Browns, who don't hail from the old country."

"I dunno," Crane said, and I could hear the smile in his voice. "I'm thinking China qualifies as a really old country."

"Indeed."

"Okay, so I have another question. How come Domin Thorne and Christophe Danvers are creeping around on your semel's land? Do they have permission?"

"Logan allows both of them to come and go as they like," Mikhail answered, "as long as they never bring more than five attendants with them."

"That sounds risky to me."

"And I would agree," Yuri said pointedly.

Mikhail sighed deeply; it was obviously an ongoing argument. "As for the reason that both semels are suddenly around, my best guess would be Jin."

"Jin?"

"Yes. You've spent too much time in the company of a reah, Crane; you have no idea what it's like for the rest of us. A reah is a miracle, plain and simple. I cannot tell you how much I hope that Jin is my semel's mate."

"Jin doesn't want a mate," he said irritably.

"That is not for Jin to say."

I loved being discussed like I wasn't there. "Could we change the subject, please?"

"Yes," Yuri told me. "Let's hear more about Crane's conquests."

My best friend was always up to talking about that.

As we rolled through the huge wrought iron gates, I took a deep breath. When the car stopped, everyone got out but me. When Crane tried to get me to move, Mikhail told him to give me time. It was nice that he and Yuri weren't trying to rush me. They just waited until I was ready. When I finally climbed out and looked around, I smelled wet earth, smoke, and pine. It rolled through me, and I calmed.

"You come up to the house when you want, okay, Jin? We'll take Crane up with us."

Funny that they were all so familiar suddenly, like they were friends.

"Is that okay?"

I nodded at Mikhail and leaned back against the car.

From where I was, I could see all the lights, and, closer to the house, all the cars clustered in the large circular drive and parked on the snow-covered ground farther on. The place was teeming with people, and since crowded places were always best for awkward meetings, I realized that standing there a moment more was just stupid. I was putting off the inevitable.

The front door swung open when I pushed against it, and I stepped inside the living room. Immediately, my senses were flooded. The aroma of the food, the warmth of the air, the hum of dozens of conversations, and the reflected glow of the fire in hundreds of crystal glasses was mesmerizing. I had worried briefly that I would be underdressed, having been to many black-tie feasts, but this one was casual, so I relaxed and took a breath.

"Can I take your coat?"

I turned to the voice and found the darkest, clearest emerald green eyes I had ever seen in my life. They were beautiful, and so was the man who had seemingly materialized out of thin air.

"Thanks," I managed to get out, unzipping my parka and passing it to him.

He took it and then stepped in front of me, offering me his hand. "Hi. I'm Ruslan Church, but everyone calls me Russ."

"Jin," I said, taking his hand.

He tightened his grip, not letting me go.

"So," I began awkwardly. "Are you Logan's brother, or a cousin?"

"I'm his brother."

I nodded, slipping my hand from his. "Well, it's a pleasure to meet you."

"And you. Do you know Logan or Simone?"

"Neither, actually." I smiled at him. "I'm a guest of Mikhail's."

His eyes swept over me, but he didn't say anything. The silence was awkward.

"So do you like his yareah?" I said quickly, making conversation as I took a quick step back from him.

He smiled suddenly, which made his dimples deep and visible. "It's not my place to question his choices. He is the semel, after all."

"No, of course not. I was just interested."

He nodded and then gestured for me to follow him. "I think it's the right thing to do for the tribe, but not for him."

"How do you mean?" I asked as he started leading me through the crowd.

"Well, his yareah, Simone, she's the sister of Christophe Danvers, a semel of one of the other tribes here. So when she and Logan mate, then we have a covenant bond between us."

It was old news, but I let him explain and kept my mouth shut. "An alliance is always good."

He shrugged. "It makes protecting everyone easier, and that's important."

"That is," I agreed.

"So like I said, it makes sense. It just sucks for Logan."

"Why?" I asked, my eyes scanning the huge room. Everything was dark and opulent, with a gothic feel I really liked.

"It just would have been nice to see my brother happy for once."

"How do you mean?" I said slowly, distracted by the tapestries on the walls, the flames roaring in the enormous fireplace, and the polished wooden floors. When there was no answer after a long moment, I looked over at him. His expression made me smile. He looked so confused. "What's wrong?"

"I dunno, I just… why am I telling you all this stuff?"

It was part of being a reah; most cats were at ease in my presence, so they spilled the vault of their secrets almost immediately. They couldn't help it.

"I feel like I've known you forever, but we just met."

I shrugged. "Tell me more about Logan."

He shook his head like he was trying to clear it and then continued talking. "Well, see, Logan just always does the right thing, the best thing, but he never does anything that makes him really happy. I haven't seen him really smile since we were little."

"But that's how it is when you're the leader of a tribe. Your own happiness comes after that of the tribe. He has to put himself second."

"No, I know, but with his mate, I thought he'd at least find one he loved."

"I think for a semel, duty comes before happiness."

"I guess you're right."

"I usually am," I teased, warm suddenly, flushed with a feeling of ease and excitement at the same time. Something was different. I never felt this good.

He opened his mouth to speak.

"Russ."

We both turned to the man who had appeared beside us.

"What?" Russ said softly, almost reverently. "You look weird, Logan."

I looked back and forth the between the two men who were so obviously brothers. They had the same towering height, the same profile that should have been stamped on coins, and the same dark gold hair. But whereas Ruslan Church's eyes were green, as I looked at Logan Church, I saw that his were a deep, burnished gold. He was stunning, heart-stopping, and since I didn't want to stare, I looked back at his little brother.

"Don't look at him. Look at me."

I did as I was ordered and realized I hadn't been seeing things—the man's eyes were actually gold, after all. They were the color of honey, flecked with gold and brown, almost amber. They were breathtaking, as was the man, and with his entire focus on me, it became hard to breathe. There was almost a rippling energy that flowed off him that I could feel.

"Find Koren," he told Russ, his voice deep and husky.

"What?"

He turned his head to look at his brother. "Go find Korneiley now."

"But—"

"What do your senses tell you?" Logan said, his voice low, a hint of warning in it.

Russ went completely still, and then his eyes widened like he was startled.

"Tell Koren it's off unless he wants to do it."

"Logan," he gasped, eyes flicking to me, to his brother, and then turning his head to look around before looking back at his brother. "That's it? All this time and then… it'll be my fault because I stopped to—"

"No," Logan said, smiling warmly as he reached out and squeezed his brother's shoulder. "When Mikhail and Yuri came in, they both smelled like… him," he said, looking back at me. "I was on my way to the car to talk… to be sure before… and I am, now, so with or without you being here, talking to him… it was done."

"Swear?"

He nodded, looking me up and down, turning quickly to give his brother a final pat. "Now go. Find Koren and let him know what's going on."

"But what should I—"

"Excuse me," I said quickly, grabbing my parka out of Russ's hand, turning to leave, feeling like an idiot for standing around while they were trying to talk, obviously being careful because I was there.

"Wait."

I looked up at Logan, who stepped in closer to me.

"Go away, Russ," he said, and his voice was more growl than anything else. "Please… I don't want to hurt you."

"I need to go," I said, turning fast, slipping through the crowd to the front door. Outside, on the porch, I felt like I could breathe again. I had my jacket on, zipped up, and was down the steps before I remembered that I had to go back in and get Crane.

"Shit," I muttered. That was the problem with the quick exit. If it wasn't coordinated in advance, it wasn't clean.

"I told you to wait."

I froze where I was.

He walked around me, but his wingtips in the snow were all I could see, because I was looking down instead of up.

"Please look at me."

He took a step closer as he gave the gentle demand so that I had to tilt my head back to meet his golden gaze. He was much taller than me, easily six five, with broad shoulders and a wide chest. His thick blond hair was streaked gold from the sun and was longer on top, shorter on the sides and in back. The open collar of his shirt under the V-neck cashmere sweater he was wearing gave me a clear view of the smooth golden skin at his throat. He was probably gold all over. As soon as the thought crossed my mind, I found myself trembling with barely controlled need. I hated feeling that way; he was to be mated, after all.

"Mr. Church, I—"

"It's Logan," he said, and I saw the muscles in his jaw clench. "And you?"

I needed to get it together. I had seen a lot of gorgeous men in my day, slept with plenty, and knew even more who were much better looking than Logan Church. And my brain understood that even as it shut down. "Jin—Jin Rayne."

"Jin." He repeated it, crossing his arms over his chest. "You're shaking."

"I'm just cold."

He nodded, his eyes locked on mine. I felt the sliver of heat run straight to my groin. No matter what I tried to tell myself, I had never met a man like Logan Church before. He had all my senses on full alert.

"You already knew my name. Why make me repeat it?" I asked to have something to say; then I took a deep breath before stepping away from him, hoping that by putting a little distance between us, I could clear my head. I felt like I was drunk.

"To hear it as you prefer it spoken."

Which was nice, except my name was easy. No way to mess up Jin. "So you're to be mated."

"I was," he answered, taking a step forward so he was back to where he was, just inches separating our bodies. "I'm not anymore."

"Why?" I licked my lips because they were dry. He wasn't looking into my eyes anymore. He was staring at my mouth.

"You're a reah. She is not," he said, his eyes back on mine, locked there.

I stared up into them and watched them slowly darken until they were absolutely molten.

"Come back inside. I want to talk to you." Out came an undignified snort of laughter before I even realized it. His smile was huge and made his eyes glow. "Don't believe me?"

"No, I—"

"Please come inside," he cut me off gently.

"I should really just go," I said, taking a few steps away from him. "My buddy and I didn't mean to intrude on your party. It's just that your sylvan was so insistent, and—"

He laughed deep in his chest. The rumbling sound was warm and rich and filled me with an absolute ease that had been missing seconds before. He was bigger than me, stronger than me, all solid muscle; he could overpower and hurt me, and yet fear was the furthest thing from my mind.

"Listen." He cleared his throat softly, again closing the space between us. "You don't know me, and I'd like to fix that. Come inside and let me feed you. My mother and my aunts have been cooking for a week for this party. Everything's good. You should eat."

I cleared my throat. "Actually, Mr. Church, I should just go, because I'm tired and I need to go to bed and I have unpacking to do and—"

"Logan," he corrected, staring deep into my eyes. "Please."

"Logan," I heard myself say, the sound of his name feeling right somehow. What the hell?

"Look at me."

I did it without even questioning him.

He cleared his throat. "Come on, my family's inside, and Mikhail, and Yuri, and your friend. Just eat; you'll feel better. You look like hell."

I smiled then. "Yeah, I'm beat."

"Okay, then." He smiled back. "Food will do wonders."

"Alright," I agreed, feeling better suddenly, more normal because we had agreed that I looked like crap.

He put his hands in the pockets of his dress pants and tipped his head toward the front door. "C'mon."

I walked beside him back across the huge porch, telling him how gorgeous his home was.

"You like it?"

"What's not to like?"

"It's way up here."

"Which is nice," I exhaled. "Secluded is so nice."

"It's far from everything. I get snowed in a lot."

"Yeah, but all you need is a horse to get down to the glassworks."

He nodded. "That's right, and I do have horses."

"Well, see? There ya go."

His smile made his eyes glitter. "You get it. Of course you get it."

"What's not to get?"

The muscles in his jaw clenched. "Maybe I'll give you a tour of the house before we eat."

"Oh, no, you—"

"I want to, if it's okay."

"It's okay."

He grabbed his trench coat from the hall closet and walked me back outside, showing me the grounds first, pointing as he explained where the stables were, where the garden was, and how far up the mountain his property went. My eyes couldn't take it all in. I judged him rich, and he laughed at me. He made enough to take care of his family, his land, and his business. There were no luxuries beyond the house itself. Inside, he walked me from one end of his huge home to the other.

"Whaddya think?"

"I think it's great," I told him, standing at the bay window that looked out toward the tree line.

He took a deep breath, and when he smiled at me, like he was just so pleased, I couldn't help but smile back.

"Let's eat," he said quickly. "My mom's a great cook."

The kitchen was bustling with activity on one side, a quiet haven on the other. Apparently there had been a huge spread I had just missed, but there was still some left over from the buffet. Yuri, Mikhail, and Crane each had a plate piled with food.

"Is it good?" I teased, coming to stand behind Crane, my hands on the back of his chair.

He said something, but his mouth was full.

I couldn't contain my laughter. "Chew your food."

He took a long swallow of his glass of iced tea and then smiled up at me. "Come sit down and eat. You look like shit."

The hand sliding across my back drew my attention.

"Jin," Delphine sighed, leaning into my side. "It's so wonderful to have you here. Let me introduce you to my mother."

I met Logan's mother, Eva, and her smile and eyes were both warm. He had two other siblings besides Delphine and Ruslan, whom I had met, and Korneiley, or Koren, whom I had not. He and Logan's father, Peter, were missing from the warm gathering in the kitchen. Nice that even though the room itself was huge, the people in it made the space seem small and intimate. I felt the earlier tension rolling off me.

"Logan."

He turned to look at his mother.

"Does he know?" she asked.

"Yes," he answered quickly, "and no."

"Russ came in here first," she said, her eyes returning to her son. "Are you sure?"

"Yes."

She let out a quick breath. "Well, I'm glad, more than you know."

He smiled warmly at her. "I know."

"The timing is terrible, though."

"I could care less."

She laughed. "Well, I'm sure that's true."

They were talking about me, but exactly what about me, I had no idea.

"Well, Jin," she said as she smiled at me, "come here, you beautiful thing, and get something to eat. Take off your jacket and stay awhile."

She made me a plate of Russian delicacies with names I couldn't remember, even though she named them as she served them. I had never had rabbit stew, but it was really good when I tasted it, so I sat and made myself comfortable next to Mikhail.

He lifted a pitcher off the table. "Can I pour you a glass of tea?"

"Sure."

"Mikhail."

His eyes went to his semel, and Logan held his hand out for the pitcher. There was no missing Mikhail's stunned expression as he passed his leader the tea. Logan filled my glass, and I thanked him before I took a sip.

"Jin."

I turned to look at Delphine.

"Tell me all about yourself."

"There's not much to say," I assured her.

"No, there's a ton, I'm sure. For starters, where were you born?"

Not on her life was I answering personal questions. "How 'bout you tell me what you were doing all alone on the streets of Reno at two in the morning, instead?"

There was instant silence as all eyes went to her.

"Note to self: kill Jin," she muttered under her breath.

I couldn't contain my grin.

"You know, that's an excellent question," Eva said, arching a brow as she regarded her daughter. "What were you doing out so late?"

As she stammered, shooting me a look before launching into a long, halting, very contrived story, I ate. As odd as the circumstances were for getting me there, listening to everyone talk, laugh, and just be a family was nice. I could get used to it.

"Jin."

I almost came out of my skin, I was so surprised that Logan had leaned in close to me and whispered my name. His warm breath down the side of my neck sent heat straight to my groin.

He inhaled deeply. "You smell like burning firewood and rain."

I had to swallow down my heart. "Do I?"

"Yes," he growled, and the sound, the deep, sexy, very male sound made my cock rock-hard. When he turned his head to look at me, I was swallowed in gold.

My breath caught.

"You're trembling," he said, his voice low, husky.

He was possibly the hottest man I had ever met in my life. I needed to run.

"Tell me where you're from, Jin."

"All over. I travel a lot."

He nodded. "You're traveling with your friend, keeping him safe."

"We look out for each other."

"I suspect that you take better care of him than he does of you."

"Well, then, you would be mistaken."

"I doubt it."

I cleared my throat. "No one needs to take care of me."

"I'm sure that's true," he said slowly, "but it doesn't mean no one should."

I would have argued with him, but he rose suddenly and excused himself from the table. It made sense that he couldn't just sit with us; he had a whole house full of people who had basically come to see him.

"He'll be back," Eva said, reaching across the table for my hand.

It felt like an electric shock ran through my body. Why was she trying to reassure me? What must my face have looked like that she would be compelled to say that to me? Why did Logan's leaving mean anything to me?

"We should go," I snapped at Crane.

"Did he give us permission to go?" He looked confused as he gazed around the table. "'Cause if he did, I missed it."

"I doubt he cares one way or another," I muttered under my breath as I stood up. "And unmated reahs don't need permission to do anything."

Crane sighed deeply and looked up at me. "Can I finish eating?"

I looked over at Eva. "Ma'am, would you mind making us a plate to go?"

"You might not need permission to leave his tribe," Mikhail told me, "but you do need permission to leave his home."

I nodded. "Fine. Would you please go make him aware that we're leaving while I make a call?"

"Who do you need to call?"

"Someone needs to pick up me and Crane."

"No, Jin. Yuri and I brought you both here. We'll take you back."

"But we're leaving now," I said, smacking Crane's shoulder to get him to stand up, "and I don't want to take you guys away from the party."

"Jin, I doubt that there's still going to be a—"

"Should I call someone or not?" I asked, all my attention on him.

"No." He sighed deeply, rising from his seat. "Give me a moment to find Logan."

I nodded before I walked to the sink with my plate.

"Jin?"

I turned and looked at Delphine.

"Can I have one dance with Crane before you guys leave?"

I really just wanted to go.

"Please."

My eyes flicked to Crane, and I realized all his attention was on her. He liked her. She liked him. Crap. "Sure."

The way he bolted up out of his seat made everyone smile. They liked him, but that had been inevitable. Everyone did. Crane and Delphine disappeared hand in hand through the kitchen door after he threw his parka at me.

"Hey."

Yuri was smiling at me.

"Why don't you go upstairs and wait for Crane? There's a really nice sitting room that's quiet."

I squinted at him. "Do I look like I need a quiet room or something?"

"Kind of," he said softly. "And I can sort of feel it… like you need everything to just stop."

I let out a deep breath. "Are you always so perceptive?"

"No," he said flatly. "Never, actually. I think it's just you."

"Why don't I take you up there?" Eva said as she reached across the table again and squeezed my hand. "Give Delphine and Crane a little bit of time together. She seems quite smitten."

My second mistake of a very long night was having gone to Logan Church's home in the first place. The first had been smiling at his sheseru. Would my third now be to let Logan's very sweet mother have her way?

"I'd love to see the room," I said to her, surrendering. "A little quiet would be great."

There were two ways out of the kitchen. One door led to the hall and then upstairs to the second floor, and the other, the one Logan had disappeared through, led back out to the living room and then on to the great room where the party was raging. The crowd, from what Eva explained, was supposed to be drinking and dancing all night, and there was a hunt scheduled for midnight in the moonlight. This was the feast to celebrate the mating of a semel; the debauchery and reveling had to be of bacchanal proportions.

"You don't like a party?" I teased Eva as I followed her up the huge mahogany staircase.

"They seldom end well," she sighed.

I had to agree.

"Here we go, darling."

It was a small room with polished wooden floors, one wall lined with books, a fireplace, a big thick rug in front of it, and overstuffed furniture that looked soft and comfortable. I felt all the tension run out of me just looking at it.

"Why don't you relax here in front of the fire, and I'll bring you up some chamomile tea?"

"You don't have to do that," I told her.

She shook her head. "I want to. I would love to take care of you just a little."

"Thank you."

"I'm going to pack up food for you and Crane to take."

I grabbed her and hugged her tight. The gasp before she clutched me back made me smile.

"Oh, Jin, why does such a small gesture touch you so deeply?" she asked, more herself than me. "Who hurt you, angel?"

When I let her go, she put her hand on my cheek, staring up into my eyes. "I've never seen such dark gray eyes before. They're just beautiful."

Her own green eyes were like pale pieces of jade. "You're not so bad, yourself."

"Go sit down," she said gently, her hand slipping from my cheek as she walked to the door. "I'll be right back."

I watched the door close behind her.

Crossing the room, I dropped our parkas on the wingback chair as I passed it and then sank down onto the couch that faced a loveseat. I didn't want to lie down because I was afraid to fall asleep. I had to be ready to leave as soon as Crane joined me.

The click of the door behind me was expected; the man was not. I thought it would be Eva back with the tea, but it was Logan carrying the steaming cup.

I stood up, hands in the pockets of my jeans.

"Sit." He smiled gently. "I just came to bring you this."

I cleared my throat but didn't sit. "Is Crane ready to go?"

"Shouldn't you be asking me if you and Crane can go?"

"Unmated reahs do whatever they want."

"Is that right?" His eyes narrowed, and I felt my mouth go dry. "You don't have to observe any of the rules of hospitality?"

I did, and we both knew it. "Fine. Can we go or not?"

"You can do whatever you want, but when you're fully conscious, I would like to talk to you."

Probably my surly tone had made him sarcastic. It was my own fault. "You didn't answer my question," I pressed.

"You can go whenever you want."

That was clear.

"Alright?"

I nodded.

"Can I sit with you for a minute?"

His voice was like a caress.

"Sure."

He moved fluidly for such a big man, his body graceful and powerful at the same time. I was sure people watched him constantly, utterly spellbound.

I took the saucer and cup from him and sat back down. It was surprising when he took a seat beside me and not across from me—even more interesting that he didn't talk to me, just stared at the fire. He was actually just going to sit with me. When I felt my eyes getting heavy, I asked him if he was going to be missed downstairs.

"Drink your tea."

I sipped it because I wanted to and not because I was ordered to. He was definitely a semel, used to demanding things instead of asking for them.

"Look at me."

I lifted my head, and he stared deeply into my eyes. I could barely hold his gaze.

"Do you have any idea how badly I want to hold you down and mark you?"

I couldn't breathe.

"I've never felt anything like this."

Me, neither, but I wasn't going to share that with him. "You don't want me. You just think you do," I said slowly.

"I know myself well," he assured me as he stood up. "And you're going to be mine."

I was flushed with heat, and my eyes were riveted to him as he got up and headed for the door. I was so confused. He made wild declarations and then left me. What was that? "Wait."

He stopped right before he closed the door behind him. "What?"

"How can you just say stuff like that and then leave?"

"How can you want to leave?" he countered, his tone sharp.

We stood there, staring at each other, and I realized there was no air in the room at all. When he left, he slammed the door behind him. It was a mistake to stay a second longer. I had his permission to leave; I just needed to find Crane and go. Grabbing our parkas, I was almost to the door when it opened and I was faced with Christophe Danvers.

"I thought I saw you," he said, walking forward.

"I need to go." I tried to maneuver around him.

He lifted his hands, blocking me in. "What are you doing here, Jin?"

"I met you and Domin, so I had to come up here to meet Logan as well."

"And is he your mate?"

I couldn't answer him because I wasn't sure myself. While I had never had a reaction like the one I was having to anyone else in my entire life, I wasn't ready to say for certain that the man was my mate. I needed time to think, to process, and I definitely needed to be left alone so I could do it.

"Jin?"

I withdrew to the fireplace, leaning my forehead against the ice-cold marble mantel. I was freezing and overheated at the exact same time.

"Listen, maybe I should take you home. This might not be the best time for you to—"

"Don't touch him."

I lifted my head and saw Christophe beside me, his hand frozen in midair, Logan beyond him, standing by the open door.

"Did you hear me?"

"Logan," Christophe began, turning away from me.

"Get out."

"Logan, I'm here for the party," Christophe chuckled, moving toward him. "I can't just leave. My sister's going to be your yareah, after all."

His eyes were flat as he closed in on Christophe. "Your sister and I are done. You know that."

"Logan, you can't," he gasped, suddenly ashen. "She'll be shamed and—"

"Enough!" he roared, and his voice filled the room. "Every part of me wants to rip you apart right now because you're standing so close to him. Please just fuckin' move."

"Logan, you—"

"Listen to me! Listen instead of whining to me about your sister," he said, taking a shaky breath. "He's my mate, but he's not yet marked. And I know you won't try to... my head tells me you won't, but the rest of me... all I want to do is tear your throat out."

"What are you saying? Logan, you can't have a male mate any more than I can."

"Chris," he said, his eyes narrowing, darkening, a warning in his voice and stance. "Please just go."

"Logan, have him in private if you must, but don't call off the mating ceremony. You need a yareah to continue your bloodline. You can't just have him alone. That's mad—"

"Get away from my mate, or I'll bleed you where you stand."

His voice was chilling, filled with a snarling, savage, primal threat. At that moment, all he wanted was for Christophe to get away from me. If he didn't move, I had no doubt that Logan would kill him. I had no idea how long the two men had been friends, but Logan would slaughter him without a second of hesitation. To come between any cat and his mate was scary. To come between a semel and his reah was simply suicide.

A semel and his reah... instinctively, I had thought the words. There was suddenly no air in my lungs. I felt light-headed and dizzy, my legs unable to support me. I held on to the mantel for dear life and willed myself to breathe.

"Logan," Christophe began. "You—"

"Get out!" Logan thundered.

Christophe bolted for the door without another word to either of us.

"I'm not your mate," I said quickly, turning back to the fireplace.

"The hell you're not."

I took a deep breath, trying to calm down.

"You can't run from me. I won't allow it."

I didn't turn around. "I'm not running."

"Look at me."

But I couldn't. Looking at him made me dizzy. "I need to go."

"I thought you weren't running."

I had no idea what I was even saying anymore.

"Turn around," he ordered, and I realized how close he suddenly was.

I did as I was told.

"I want to see your face."

I lifted my eyes to his, seeing and hearing his sharp intake of breath as I was swallowed in his smoldering gaze. The deep topaz eyes were locked on mine, the dark gold eyebrows furrowed, and the muscles in the chiseled jaw were working. His stare should have made me burst into flames, as searing as it was.

"Did Domin hurt you when you saw him earlier?"

"No."

"Lucky for him." He exhaled slowly, his breath warm as it ghosted across my face.

"Listen, I should really—"

"Tell me where your tribe is."

"I don't have one."

"Why not?"

"Who cares? I just need to go. That guy Domin creeping around my place just—"

"What?"

"You should see my place," I said, raking my hands through my hair. "I totally missed the tracks and the rub marks. He might as well have put up big neon signs saying 'Domin's territory.' It's crazy, and because I've been working so much I just…." I trailed off, losing my train of thought as he took the last step so he was in front of me, looking down at me. "I can't stay here. I hafta go."

"Why?" he asked, lifting his hand toward me. "Make me understand what makes you want to turn your back on a sacred bond."

"Because I don't want anything to do with tribes or semels or anything else. I just wanna be a regular guy and live without all this bullshit."

"You're a reah," he said softly, his fingers almost touching my cheek but stopping, hovering, holding still. "May I?"

"What?"

"I want to touch you."

I had never been asked. Everyone just grabbed me or manhandled me or tried to make me submit. No one had ever made sure it was okay before they put their hands on me. I knew the smart thing to do was to say no; the smart thing was to get out of there and run as far away from Logan Church as I possibly could.

There was no way I could ever be a member of the man's tribe. I would end up begging him to take me to bed.

"Jin?"

I felt like I had swallowed my heart. "You can touch me."

His smile was so slight, just the corner of his full lips and a glow in his eyes. His fingers were featherlight on my skin, barely touching my cheek. I saw the slight shudder run through his powerful frame, just that much contact overwhelming for him. Not that I was unfazed myself. I wanted to lean into the caress, into the warmth of his hand, and tell him to do whatever he wanted to me.

"You know that since you're a reah, there was never going to be 'normal' for you."

My vision blurred as the wave of emotion rolled through me. The man was my mate; there could be no mistake. His scent, the sound of his voice, the heat in his eyes—it was all too much. I had always been told that when I met the semel destined to be my mate, I would know. I would feel it, the reaction visceral. Standing in front of Logan Church, feeling like a slave to the animal within me, my only thoughts primal and carnal, the overwhelming desire to beg him to mark me, take me, fuck me—I knew I had found my mate. There was no lie in my throbbing, aching desire.

"You knew the minute you saw me. Why fight it?"

"You should go back to your party. You'll be missed."

"Right now, Christophe's telling everyone that I'm claiming my mate. I won't be missed."

"How can you? You don't even know me? You've got your whole life planned out, and—"

"My life belongs to you, my reah."

I swallowed hard, closing my eyes, struggling for control of a body that was slowly starting to burn. "You can't just change everything because of me."

"I can and will. Kiss me."

I bolted for the door instead.

"No."

Just the one word, a word no louder than any other, interrupted my flight. I froze where I was.

"I just found you. Why would I let you go?"

Domin wanted me as a possession, Christophe as a companion, but Logan wanted me to be his mate. “Shit.” I groaned under my breath.

“I like you.” He chuckled, pressing his hard chest against my back as he came up behind me, wrapping me in his arms. He buried his face in the side of my neck as he hugged me tightly but gently. “You’re not at all what I expected.”

“Well, then, you should just mate your yareah and—”

“Stop,” he mumbled, cutting me off, nuzzling his face to my shoulder under the collar of my sweater. “We’ll have no more talk of yareahs.”

“Don’t.” I tried to pull free.

“Just gonna taste you.... Your skin smells so... good.”

I gasped as his teeth closed down on the spot where my neck joined my shoulder. My knees buckled, and I would have fallen without the arms wrapped around me, one across my chest, the other my abdomen. It didn’t hurt. His mouth was hot, the bite slow and sensual. It felt like heaven.

“You’re mine.”

It was terrifying, and yet I couldn’t shake a feeling of rightness. “Lemme go,” I said without any conviction whatsoever.

There was snort of very deep, very masculine laughter. “Why would I do that?”

I turned my head, trying to look over my shoulder to see his face, struggling in his arms. “You should let me go because you’re about to be mated.”

“Yes, I am. To you,” he promised before licking a line up the side of my neck from my shoulder to behind my ear. “You’re my reah, my mate, and I will teach you to love instead of fear your heritage.”

The certainty of his words nearly undid me.

“You’re mine.” His voice sent heat all through my body. “Make no mistake.”

I opened my mouth to argue, to tell him I wasn’t his mate, but before I could get the words out, he whirled me around to face him.

“I’m not your mate,” I lied.

His eyes locked on mine. "You can feel the truth roaring through you just like I can. You belong to me, reah, and I will put my mark on you."

He was right. I belonged to him. Everything about the man drowned me in a torrent of need. Never had I felt like this. "You can't mark me."

He chuckled, and the deep, rumbling sound made my cock so hard it hurt. "The hell I can't. It's like you're calling me—your smell, your voice, your skin… you're mine."

I kept my eyes on him, watching, staring up into his eyes as he ran the back of his fingers up and down my throat. It felt so good to be touched; I wondered what his hand would feel like stroking over my cock. The sound that tore out of me made him smile.

"You say you should go, but you shiver when I touch you. Does that make sense?"

Nothing made sense anymore.

"You know," he said, his eyes narrowing, "all my life I've known about reahs, but I never heard… no one ever said that they could be men. Where did you come from?"

"You don't want me. I'll mess up everything for you."

He grunted, smiled. "A reah mates for life."

"I know, and that's why—"

"Were you thrown out of your tribe for being gay?"

Of course I was. My tribe thought I was an abomination. I was a reah, and reahs only mated with semels. Never had there been a female semel, so… it was wrong, I was wrong, and I was cast out. Just looking at me made my mother sick; my brother thought I was a perversion. When I was sixteen, my tribe, all of them, stopped speaking to me, and my father, my sylvan, the teacher of our tribe—he wanted me dead. He said it was his duty to kill me, to make sure no other semel was tempted to give up his life, his family, and his bloodline just for me. It still hurt. Even after eight years, it still hurt.

"Look at me."

But I wouldn't, instead taking a breath and bending my head, my eyes open and staring at my shoes.

"You're a gift, reah, and anyone who told you different was a liar. You need to learn your value."

I swallowed hard but couldn't contain the moan as his hand slid around my throat, his thumb under my chin tipping my head up.

"You are… precious." He took a quick breath before he smiled.

I knew he meant it. The man didn't just want me in his bed; he wanted me in his arms, at his side, forever. "You're scared," I accused him.

"Hell yeah, I'm scared." He took a breath, the muscles in his jaw cording. "You're my mate, so there's no hiding anything from you. Everyone knows pieces of me, but you… you're gonna know everything. That's scary as hell."

I felt the same. "What if once you get to know me, you hate me?"

"I don't think that's possible," he sighed, bending his head to kiss the side of my throat.

I pressed my skin against his mouth, hoping to feel his teeth. His hands slid over me, one moving slowly down the groove of my spine to my lower back, the other pressing over the inseam of my jeans. I arched up into him, my breath catching in my throat.

I wanted to be under him on the floor, wanted to slide my thighs over his hips, have him lift me up, put my knees over his arms and have him buried inside me deep and hard. The vision filled my mind as his hand cupped me through the denim.

"I would like nothing more than to strip off all your clothes and be buried inside your warm, willing body," he said into my hair. "But you are my mate and precious to me. I will not have any say that I was seduced or lured away from my yareah. I will announce to everyone that I have found my reah and claim him for my mate."

I just needed him. How it looked wasn't important to me.

"I need you to listen to me now."

I opened my eyes slowly to gaze into his, and the way the man was looking at me, full of desire and heat, made my blood race, even more so because of the longing. In his gaze, mixed with the passion and need, was tenderness.

"I am the leader of my tribe, the semel, and I wasn't nominated or made. I was born to it, meant to lead, to take care of others, and—"

"I know all—"

"Stop," he chided gently. "Let me speak. A reah is born to your place in the tribe, same as me. You're born to only be the mate of the strongest, the other half of only a semel, the only one who can truly be. Without a reah, a semel can never have *maat*—balance, harmony. Reahs are so rare, no one I know has ever even met one, and then here you are. I waited for so long, but my family and my tribe all thought it was time I took a mate. I guess I thought so, too, but... I almost made a mistake. What if I'd missed you?"

The way he was looking at me—with wonder—no one had ever looked at me like that.

"I waited all my life for you," he said, his hands sliding up under my sweater. The feel of his warm skin on my own chilled flesh was making me dizzy. "My mate, you are my mate. It was done the second I saw you... looked into your big, beautiful eyes."

The tears came, and I felt stupid, but it was too much. The emotion was overwhelming.

"Your skin is like silk, warm silk... I want to feel it all."

The man was the sexiest thing I'd ever seen in my life, and he was trying to kill me by talking like I was all he needed.

"Stop fighting, reah." He smiled, sliding his hands up both sides of my neck, making sure I couldn't get away. "I want you."

"It's a mistake. You should send me away... I'm bad for you."

"Having my heart cannot be bad." He bent and kissed me hungrily, roughly, devouring my mouth. It was like being dipped into liquid heat. I felt it rolling through my body, consuming me. When he leaned back, the whimper of need could not be helped. "There you go... need me more, reah. Want me more. Put your hands on me."

I lifted up and wrapped my arms around his neck, pulling him back down into a scalding, claiming kiss with lots of tongue. I sucked and bit, the kiss hot and wet and deep. When he had to breathe, my name came out in a gasp. It was surprising to hear it from his lips, my plain, ordinary name spoken as it never had been before, with awe, like it was sacred, like treasure. Like I was a treasure.

"Logan," I breathed. "You don't want—"

"You?" He cut me off, his mouth hovering over mine. "I don't want you?"

There had to be something I could say to make him stop, to make him go away. He was risking too much if he took me for his reah. Even in so short a time, the man's happiness was important to me. He was my mate, after all.

"Oh, hell yeah, I want you." He smiled. "And I'm keeping you."

Before I could answer, argue, protest, his mouth was back on mine. His tongue slid over the seam of my lips for a second before I parted them. The reaction was instant. I felt a hand fisted in my hair so I couldn't move, an arm around my back holding me against him, his mouth grinding down over mine. His tongue swept inside, into the hollows of my cheeks, over my teeth. The kiss was hard and scalding, pulling whimpers and whines out of me that made the man in my arms shudder.

"God, I could fuckin' eat you," he growled in my ear before pressing his face into my neck, breathing me in. "Where the hell have you been?"

He sounded almost angry, and I loved that, loved that he was frustrated that he had only just found me.

"Jin." His voice washed over me, low and seductive. "Please."

I knew what he was asking for.

"Please," he repeated, his voice cracking with the strain of waiting.

"Yes," I whispered, leaning my head forward, stretching my neck out for him, inviting him.

I heard his low, strangled moan a second before I felt first his hot breath on my skin and then a knife buried in the top of my spine. A shard of agony ripped through me, but I swallowed down my yell. I had been bitten playfully many times in my life, nipped and nibbled, but I had never been marked. Being marked was a world away from simply being bitten.

His long fangs thrust deep inside me, white-hot, razor-sharp skewers piercing, pushing though skin and muscle, tightening until the teeth met inside my body. The pain was violent, excruciating, at the same time filling me with throbbing heat. I felt myself sinking only to be held tight in his arms. My head, neck, and back felt like they were on fire, burning and consuming, receding only to build again and again, wave after wave of it drowning me. I was going to pass out, and I told him so even as my voice faltered and died in my throat. I was warm, warmer than I had ever been, and finally, after so long, I felt absolutely safe. When I tumbled into darkness, it didn't even matter.

Chapter Six

THERE HAD been yelling, I was sure of it, but when I opened my eyes, completely conscious, there was only silence. I had to get up and find Crane, but when I tried to move, I realized it was futile. My body felt like it weighed a thousand pounds; I couldn't even lift my head. Not that I wanted to—I was so tired, and the bed was soft and warm and smelled like clothes dried in the sun… and Logan. My body jerked with the knowledge that I was in the man's bed. From the faint rays of light coming into the bedroom from the outer room, I could see the sheets were pale, as was the down comforter. But there was no blood. I expected there to be blood. I had been losing blood, I was sure, but now there was nothing. Maybe I was so weak because I had lost too much, but where was it? It should have been all over everything, and yet there was only the warmth of the bed, the smell of my mate, and the soothing darkness. I closed my eyes to go back to sleep.

"What are you doing?" The yell came sharply from the outer room.

I sat bolt upright and realized my body was not as weak as I had thought. Who was shouting?

"Besides claiming my mate, you mean?" Logan's deep, resonant voice answered.

"Impossible."

"What is?"

"Logan, be reasonable. No matter what you feel, you cannot have a male mate."

The chuckle was deep but not amused, more cold and hard. "A semel and reah don't choose each other, Father; they simply are or are not mates. If they are, the reah accepts the semel and takes the mark. I knew the second I saw Jin that he was mine. He took my mark… he belongs to me. It's done."

"Logan, you—"

"Reahs are very rare, so rare, in fact, that of all the semels I have met in my life, not one has—"

"I know, but Logan, you must—"

"I wanted my mate. I always have. I never wanted a mating ceremony. I never wanted to settle. I agreed because I felt it was time, you felt it was time, the tribe felt it was time, but I always just had a feeling… and now I've been rewarded."

"Logan, you cannot take a—"

"Do you really presume to tell me that, as the semel of my tribe, that I cannot claim my reah because he's a man?"

"My son," he said, and I could hear the strain in his voice as he argued with Logan. "A male mate is—"

"A waste, my darling."

It was a woman's voice, and I had to see her. Surely she was the yareah, Simone, Christophe's sister. She had come to talk some sense into the semel of the tribe of Mafdet, her intended mate. I rose up off the bed, pleased that I still had everything on except my boots. I moved to peek through the crack of the door, lucky that it hadn't been completely closed. Once there, my eyes flicked to the woman, who slipped by Peter and Logan's brothers Koren and Russ and went to his son's side. Simone moved like she was boneless, like a snake, and her hands curled around Logan's forearm.

"Please," he sighed as he looked down at her. "Forgive me."

"There's nothing to forgive, because I won't release you from your oath."

"It doesn't matter," he told her. "A reah trumps a yareah, and you know it."

"I repeat," she insisted, her voice with a trill of edge to it. "I will not release you. You cannot have a male mate. It's a waste of you, of your seed, of your house. You can't throw your life away because of some stupid chemical pull on your body. You can't just—"

"I will do as I please."

"No."

"Watch me."

"Logan, you can't stand there and tell me that you're going to mate with a man! It's ridiculous!"

Her voice was luscious, deep and velvety, and she was flawless, creamy perfection. From her long blonde mane to her turquoise eyes, she was stunning. She and her brother could have been twins, ethereal beings descended from heaven. She was as captivatingly beautiful as he was. I watched her hand trail up Logan's arm to his shoulder, and higher, to the side of his neck, settling on his cheek.

"He has no tribe, Logan!" Peter shouted. "There is no alliance to be made! You have denied all the rules of ordination! This is not *maat*."

I watched Logan shake his head and brush Simone's hand away.

"No! He is trash! It is beneath you! You are to be mated with Simone! She is to be your yareah! The mating will unite your tribe with Christophe's, and you would think to throw her away to mate with an abomination!"

"He's a reah," Logan said tightly, closing in on his father. "He's not chosen or picked for me, he's not a yareah, he's a true reah, and that cannot be denied. You say it's not *maat*, but it is—it's the only thing that is. You are not serving me or my tribe if you try and have me deny him."

"Logan, you—"

"He's my reah, and I acknowledge him."

Simone laughed. "What would you even do with a male mate? You've never been with a man! Wherever would you get the idea that you would even enjoy—"

"I marked him, he's mine, and that is all you need to know."

I was going to be his first? I couldn't even imagine. I'd thought he was gay, the way he had accepted me so easily, but apparently there had been only women before me. How could he even want me?

"Logan, you—"

"He's my mate, born to be mine. He's all I want."

"No!" Peter yelled. "You put us in peril with this whim! By right, Christophe must make the covenant bond with Domin now on behalf of his sister. You will bring two large tribes together! Think of your family, your tribe! You cannot throw away your future for a worthless stray bastard! Logan Church, I did not raise you to act like this! You disgrace us all with this perversion! A semel must mate and breed! To lay with a male… to plant seed in an empty vessel… this is not your right!"

It hurt like a knife in my heart because they were the same words my father had hurled at me when he had driven me from my home—that I was a perversion.

"I am semel. I am the law… only I say what's right," Logan said softly, resolutely, returning my attention to him.

"Logan, what will your sylvan or your sheseru say?"

"They stand with me."

"I think you overestimate them, Logan. They won't want you to disgrace yourself any more than I do."

"Nothing I would ever do with my mate would be a disgrace."

The tone was icy with a thread of warning in it, and everyone knew that Peter Church had said too much. No semel ever allowed anyone to question them, and especially not about their bond with their reah. That was sacred.

"You would abandon me?" Simone gasped, drawing all the attention of the room.

Logan turned to look at her. "No. There is Koren; he will be your mate."

My eyes went to the brother whom he had so readily volunteered, saw his brows furrow in a scowl. There was no denying that the brothers Church were a beautiful lot, Logan with his gold eyes, Russ with the deep emerald, and Koren with the most gorgeous shade of olive I had ever seen, all with the same towering height, muscular frames, and chiseled features. And it had all been inherited from their father, Peter Church, a magnificent-looking man, as tall and strong as any of his sons, with hazel eyes that were now trained on Logan.

"I am not a reah," Simone said, bringing my attention back to her. "But I will only be yareah and so cannot, will not, mate with anyone who is not a semel. If not you, Logan, there is only Domin for me."

"You can mate with whoever you want, Simone. You want to be a yareah, but the truth is your choices are open. There is no law to say who you must take, because you have no birthright."

"Logan, I'm supposed to be your yareah."

"Because we agreed you would be, but you don't have to be."

Her eyes were pained. "I thought you loved me."

"Why?"

She flinched like he'd hit her. "I had no idea you were this cold."

"How can I be cold when I never told you I loved you, never said that our mating was anything but an arrangement that would be mutually beneficial? You would be the yareah of my tribe, the mate of the semel, and I would have children. If there was more, if I led you on or said anything different, please tell me."

There was a long silence as she deflated. It was obvious Logan had been brutally honest with her, and still she had changed it into a romance in her head.

"If you only want to mate with a semel and you don't want to leave home, then there's only Domin left. But there's a big world out there filled with other leaders and other tribes. Go find another semel if your heart is set on being a yareah."

"Logan." Her voice trembled. "We sealed our hands, and now you—"

He grabbed her hand and held it in both of his as he looked into her eyes. "You are not my mate, Simone. You never were, and this is the risk that any yareah who mates with a semel takes. If and when our reah crosses our path, there is no choice but to follow."

"So you would deny your reah for me if you could?"

"No," he said quickly, releasing her hand. "There is only my mate."

"Logan." She took a breath. "Have him if you must, but do it in secret. Let me be the one at your side for the tribe to see."

"My mate is the only one who will stand at my side."

She took another breath. "It's written in the law that if the mate of a semel is barren, then he may take a yareah to ensure the continuation of his bloodline. Your precious reah can't give you children, so you can still take me. You can have both of us."

"Logan, that would solve everything," his father said quickly. "Simone is being so gracious and selfless and trying to save the tribe for you."

"I know exactly where Simone's loyalties lie," he said, his eyes on his father. "And I will have no yareah. There will only be my reah. Anything else is sacrilege."

"Logan, be reasonable," Simone snapped, the frustration thick in her voice.

His scowl was dark as he turned to her. "Simone, we were going to have a ceremony to bring our tribes together. It seemed like a good idea for you to be my yareah because we get along, but I just found my reah," he said, lifting his gaze to all the men standing in the semicircle around him, at his father, at Koren, at Russ, at others I didn't know, and then back to her. "Do any of you understand? He saw Domin first; they spoke, but Jin rejected him. Then he saw Christophe, and he too was rejected. It's amazing, if you think about it. Jin, the only reah I have ever seen, rejected two other semels, but me… and I'm sure there have been many others that he's seen, but it was my mark that he took, only mine. He knows I'm his mate; I'm the only one in the world who is, and somehow, his path brought him here. It's a miracle, and all I want is to learn everything about him and have him stand beside me for the rest of my life."

"Logan! You cannot have a male mate! Your tribe will never accept him, and now is not the time for us to appear weak! Domin's tribe is like a wolf at the door! He attacked Koren, and his sheseru went after Delphine, and now, if you don't bond with Simone, then Domin surely will. With Christophe's tribe and his, we'll be overrun! It's your place to protect us, not leave us vulnerable while you take your mate!"

Logan shook his head.

"Logan, think about your mother and your sister, think about your brothers and me… think about your tribe. We need you strong; we need you rational. You are our semel. Do not lead us down the path to destruction because of your own selfish needs." Peter's voice cracked on the last word and he sucked in his breath. "Please, my son."

His father's agony sliced right through me. The fear, the frustration, the anger—it was all there in his barely controlled rage.

The silence after the tirade was thundering and consuming. There was no answer to Peter's anger. Logan had no choice but to send me away.

"A semel who finds his reah is semel-re, is he not?"

"Yes, but—"

Logan lifted his hand, and there was silence again. "I have found my reah, and so I am semel-re. I have sent Yuri and Mikhail to Domin and Christophe's tribes to bring them my news. I sent word to my friends and have received calls and e-mails back already. They all seem overjoyed for me. The sex of my mate, even though I told them, does not seem to matter to anyone but you."

"They lie, Logan. They fear for your sanity."

"I suggest we not tell them your thoughts."

"Listen to me!"

"No, you listen," Logan began, but he crossed the room fast and slammed the door shut hard in my face. He had no idea I was there. He just didn't want to wake me.

When I turned back toward the bed, I noticed another door, a second way out. I saw my boots at the same time. I didn't hesitate. Once downstairs in the kitchen, I pulled on my parka and got out my cell phone to call Crane. I had to find him and get out of there fast.

"Jin."

Turning, I was faced with a man I had never met.

"I'm Christophe Danvers's sheseru, Avery Cadim."

It made some sense that if Christophe were there for Logan's wedding feast that his sheseru would be as well, but what was the man doing in the kitchen?

"Christophe requests your presence. He needs to speak with you."

"Well, I—"

"We have taken the liberty of securing Mr. Adams. He is waiting for you out in the car."

Translation: they had Crane, and if I didn't go with him he could not be expected to keep my best friend safe.

"Okay." I took a breath.

He stepped aside so I could walk by him toward the door. I sized him up as I moved, and if he was the scariest man in Christophe's tribe, as the sheseru traditionally was, I wasn't really that worried. Compared to the size and strength of Yuri Kosa, Avery Cadim was downright scrawny.

When we reached the car, the door opened, and two men got out, holding Crane between them. His hands were tied behind him, and there was tape over his mouth. His eyes were blazing above the gag. I felt the fury rolling off him. My relief at seeing him unharmed made me tremble.

"Jin," Avery said, his hand going to my shoulder. "You get in the car without any resistance, and we will leave Mr. Adams here unharmed. We only needed him so that you would take our semel's invitation for you to visit seriously."

"Deal," I assured him.

I heard Crane's growl through his gag and saw his eyes suddenly widen a second before a hand rose in front of my face. I opened my mouth to say that I didn't need to be knocked out, I would go along willingly, before there was a horrible smell and blackness. Struggling to stay conscious didn't do a bit of good.

Chapter Seven

I TRIED to be scared, I really did, but the room was just trying way too hard to be shocking. It looked like some weird S&M fetish dungeon in a low-budget porno flick. From the walls with the shackles, handcuffs, and chains hanging from them to the bed with the metal headboard and frame covered in red satin, to the variety of leather whips on a stainless steel table, it was just cheesy. Hanging from shackles in the middle of the room, I should have been terrified. Mostly, I was annoyed. However long I had been unconscious was too long because the cuffs had bitten into my wrists by the time I woke up. I was cold, covered in goose bumps because my parka was on the table, and so was my shirt. All I still had on was my jeans and boots. It was cold in the "pleasure den," and I was freezing.

Turning around, I looked over the entire room, finally seeing the door to the left. Hopefully, it was open. I really didn't want to be stuck there until Christophe decided to grace me with his presence. Closing my eyes, I took a deep breath and shifted. I changed fast; I was a black panther and then a man again even before I had a chance to get tangled up in my clothes. Had I needed to move or fight, I would have had to strip down to my skin as I had the night I saved Delphine, but since I only needed to get loose and then instantly return to human, I didn't need to be naked.

After crossing the room to the table, I put on my T-shirt and sweater and grabbed my parka before turning back toward the door. It made sense that it was open when I reached it, because what were the chances I was going to get out of the shackles? No other panther I knew could have done it.

For most shape-shifters, changing from human to panther took long minutes, and if they hunted or fought or ran or did anything more strenuous than just lie around, they first had to eat, second, hydrate, and finally, rest. It sapped energy, and so because they didn't know me, Christophe and those in his inner circle had assumed I was the same. I was not only a reah but also able to shift faster than possibly anyone. The door was open because they had no idea who or what I was.

I was trying not to be smug as I slipped into the darkened hallway, because I had no idea where I was or how long it would take to get out or whom I was going to run into. From the muted dance music, I had a pretty good idea which way was out, but I moved slowly, cautiously, because I needed to be more careful and dial down the cocky.

Since my cell phone wasn't on me, I couldn't call Crane and let him know I was all right. That concerned me, because no doubt my best friend was having a seizure worrying about me. I had to get to him so he could see I was all right, and I wanted to get back to Logan.

Logan.

Just the man's name in my head filled me with excitement.

"Jin!"

The yell was loud and filled the long hallway. My absence having been discovered, I broke instantly into a run. Arms pumping, legs flying, I sprinted as fast as I could toward the sound of the pounding music. It was funny, but even when people chased you for fun and you knew logically nothing bad would happen even if they caught you, even then you ran like crazy and tried so hard not to get caught. When you were actually running from someone scary, the adrenaline was just wild.

I saw the door and the men in front of it, heard a sharp bang to my left, and bolted in that direction. The next door had only one man in front of it, and instead of slowing, I sped up. He was bigger than me, but my momentum was building the closer I got, and when I leaped at him, even though he got ahold of me, we went hurtling through the air together. Slamming to the floor atop the man who was lying prone over the broken door, I sprang to my feet, got them under me, and ran down the short hall. Careening around another corner, I found myself running by bathrooms before I was suddenly in a sea of people in the middle of a crowded dance club. The strobe lights, driving, throbbing music, and packed mass of bodies instantly filled me with calm. As I made my way slowly to the front of the club, I saw the men moving through the throng of people to reach me.

"Jin."

Turning, I found two of my co-workers, Darcy and Jeannie. Both women looked thrilled to see me, their faces and eyes lighting up like Christmas.

"Dance with me," Darcy demanded, biting her bottom lip.

I pressed myself up against her to a squeal of delight. Roving hands took my parka away before stripping my sweater off as well. She handed them to Jeannie, who pointed off the floor so I could see where she was disappearing to with my clothes. There was a whole big table of people I worked with, and when I waved, twelve people waved back. It was a relief.

In minutes, I had five of my girls with me, surrounding me, making sure no one they didn't know got near me. I realized that even though I hadn't been scared, my adrenaline had been pumping hard. It was a relief to be safe, and so I let myself go, surrendering to the music, letting it infuse me with joy. I got down to some serious dancing, showing off, letting the girls see how flexible my body was, how fluidly I could move, and how indecent a dance floor could be. The laughter, the hands all over me, the lipstick smears on my throat were all testament to how much they enjoyed my presence.

When I was pulled off the floor to the table, the guys there made room for me, getting up, letting me slide in, and pushing me to the back of the booth. I was passed a beer as the girls hung all over me, arms around my shoulders, hands on my thighs, crowding up beside me, making sure I couldn't move. I saw Christophe at the bar with three others, his sheseru, Avery, among them. When he crooked a finger at me, I flipped him off. As he crossed the floor to me, I asked one of the guys if I could borrow his phone. I sent Crane a text message that I was all right and I would meet him at our apartment whenever I could get a ride. I felt better just knowing that he knew I was fine. I didn't want him to worry.

The pat on my shoulder turned my eyes to Darcy, but she was looking up. Following her gaze, I found Christophe towering over the table.

"Jin."

The tall blond man looked decidedly pale. He had not expected me to get out of the room, and that was clear from the expression on his face.

"May I speak to you, please?"

"You wanna dance?" I asked.

He looked nervous suddenly, and I almost laughed. Big, scary werepanther tribe leader and there he was, scared to dance with a man in what was obviously his own club. What if people thought he was gay or something? It was hilarious.

"Jin!"

I did laugh then, because there beside him appeared his yareah. The man had not thought his mate was anywhere close by, as evidenced by both the surprise and terror that crossed his face. Getting up, I made everyone move so I could get out. When Talon Danvers flew drunkenly into my arms, I received her with a bear hug. She melted against me and was excited to meet everyone from work. I introduced her, and she smiled and waved before she tugged me after her back to the dance floor.

She was all over me as we danced together, and when we were joined by her attendants, three other female panthers, I was sure I was the envy of every straight man in the place. Talon Danvers was a stunning woman, with her onyx curls and eyes, caramel skin, and model-perfect body. Her friends were the same, all long legs, cascading hair, and feminine curves. That they could not seem to keep their hands off me was fun. I forgot about everything but writhing around with them, and by the time Avery stepped in front of me, I was all wrapped up in women.

"Christophe wants to see you."

"Tell my mate to go to hell," Talon said loudly, her lips on my throat.

I just shrugged within my undulating cocoon, but Avery grabbed hold of Talon's arm and yanked her up against him. He dragged her off the floor, and I lost track of them in the sea of people. Minutes later, when she reappeared at my side, holding my sweater and parka, she laced her fingers into mine and tugged me gently off the dance floor. I walked right out the front door on the arm of the yareah of the tribe of Pakhet. On the street, I turned to face her, and the fury on her face took me by surprise.

"Talon," I said her name gently. "Are you all right?"

"Is it true?"

"Is what true?"

"Are you really a reah?"

"Well, yes, but—"

"You won't take my life from me!" she screamed before taking a step back. "I don't care what Avery says; I'm not turning you over to him. What if he gives you to my mate?"

She was planning to hand me over to Christophe?

"I want you gone."

"But you don't have to—" I moved forward to touch her, but squealing tires startled me. Three cars pulled up beside the curb, and the men that poured out were moving fast. I turned to run, but there was a huge muscle-bound man suddenly barring my path.

"You're coming with us," he said coldly. "My yareah commands it."

That made no sense. Why would Talon want to hurt me? Why would her feelings suddenly go from warm to murderous? Why would she want me gone?

Then it hit me. Avery had told her what I was, but nothing more. It was a problem for her.

"Talon," I said quickly, pulling free of the man's grip to face her. "I'm not just a reah, I'm Logan Church's reah. He marked me."

"None of that mat—" the man began.

"What?" she yelled, slapping his hands away from me as well as everyone else's. "You're a mated reah?"

"Yes." I smiled at her. Even though Logan and I had made nothing official between us, I knew my confession would still save me from whatever end she had planned. The truth of the matter was that if I was mated, I was no threat to her at all. She could not, would not, have her mate or her lifestyle taken from her. She liked her money and the things her money bought. Only a reah could steal her semel from her… an unmated reah. If I belonged to another, there was no reason for her to hate me—or hurt me.

"Oh, Jin," she sighed, again swatting away the men who tried to put their hands on me. They were a nuisance to her, like buzzing flies. "Forgive me. It's Simone's life you're going to put into chaos, not mine."

I was terrified for a moment as I wondered how much she cared about the sister of her mate.

"And I couldn't give a shit."

Which answered my question. "Can I go now?"

"Of course," she told me, leading me down the street toward a limousine.

When we were almost to the car, a driver got out and walked around to the passenger door to open it.

"Bale, please take Jin back up the mountain and drop him at Logan Church's door. The semel of the tribe of Mafdet will be missing his reah."

The man's eyes flew open.

"I know," she smiled coyly. "A reah in the flesh. It's simply amazing."

I let her hug me good-bye even though I knew that if I had been unmarked, she would have killed me without a second thought. It was strange to be both coveted and feared at the exact same time.

I had the driver drop me at my friend Rick's place instead of taking me to Logan's or home. Since I was supposed to be watering his plants for him while he was out of town, it seemed like a good place to get some much needed sleep. Shedding my parka, boots, and sweater, I then made my rounds of the indoor plants, making sure everything was still alive. Central heat was a wonderful thing; there was no having to build a fire or waiting for a radiator to turn on, it was just toasty as soon as I cranked up the thermostat. It was heaven. I wanted to close my eyes, but letting

Crane worry about me was just plain evil. When I called his phone, I got him on the second ring.

"Hello?"

I cleared my throat. "Crane."

"Jin!" He caught his breath. "Where are you? Yuri's at our place, and you're not there, and—"

"I'm fine," I said, my eyes closing. "I'll see you in the morning."

"No, where are you?"

"I can't," I sighed deeply. "Tomorrow… I gotta rest, okay? You stay with Logan; you'll be safe there. Do you have my phone?"

"Yeah, it got dropped in the snow, but Jin, you—"

"Tomorrow," I repeated, feeling my body get heavy.

"Wait, please, you hafta talk to Logan, alright?"

I was barely conscious.

"Jin."

I grunted.

"Here," he said. There was rustling on the other end.

I did the deep exhale you do right before you drop off.

"Jin."

The man's voice slid through me, and as tired as I was, something inside tightened.

"Are you all right?"

"Yes." I smiled into the phone.

"I want to see you."

"I'll be asleep in seconds."

"Then I'll watch you."

"No, it's late… tomorrow."

"Jin—"

"I told her you marked me, so she didn't hurt me. Thank you. The mark saved my life."

"What are you talking about?"

"Talon Danvers," I told him, shivering.

"She was going to hurt you?"

"I think so. Unmated reahs scare yareahs."

"You're not unmated; you belong to me."

"We should talk about it. I'm not convinced that's the best thing for you."

"I am. You're my reah; therefore, you are the best thing for me."

"Okay," I breathed. I didn't want to argue with him.

"Did Christophe hurt you?"

"No, just hung me up in his S&M room."

There was a long silence where I almost fell asleep.

"Pardon me?"

I explained quickly about being shackled from the ceiling, giggling without meaning to. I had left serious and entered giddy, and there was no going back.

"He didn't do anything to you."

"Like what? Rape me? No, sir, he did not."

He took in a sharp breath. "I need to see you."

"You know, you worrying about me is real nice," I told him. "Maybe we could hang out tomorrow, if you wanted… if that'd be okay."

"Jin." His voice cracked. "I want to see you now… right now."

I was too tired even to move, but my cock certainly had other ideas. The longer the man talked to me, the harder I got. Just thinking about his mouth on me was making me squirm.

"Jin?"

"God," I groaned.

"What? Are you hurt?"

"No, I just… I wanna go to bed with you so bad."

"Do you?"

Oh, God, what had I done? I was stunned. I had just let the words fall out of me. Could I make no good decisions when it came to Logan Church? Was I completely incapable of rational thought where the man was concerned? The entire night had been a series of bad choices, one after another, culminating in sleep-deprived confessions. I needed to cut my losses. I hung up, turned off the light, and rolled over. My last thought was how the man had looked as he bent his head to kiss me.

Chapter Eight

THE MORNING had come and gone by the time my eyes finally drifted open. Used to checking my phone for the time, I looked around the living room until I saw the digital clock on Rick's DVD player. When I realized it was after three in the afternoon, I rose like Lazarus to stagger into the bathroom. I needed to get home. On the street fifteen minutes later behind my oversized sunglasses, I felt anonymous, and there was something very comforting about the feeling. The momentary thought crossed my mind that I could easily just slip town without anyone knowing. It was surprising, and telling, that I felt anxious with the whisper in my head of abandoning Logan. My heart hurt just thinking about not seeing the man.

In the cold air, the walk from Rick's place to mine left me frozen, but after a shower and a change of clothes, the world seemed nicer, gentler, and not as glaring. I didn't want to leave, but there was no food, and more importantly, no source of caffeine in my apartment. I had to go back out in search of coffee. I was surprised when I opened my front door to find Yuri Kosa.

"Oh, hey." I smiled up at him.

He just stared, his eyes all over me.

"You alright?"

"Jin," he said, slowly putting his hand on my shoulder. "Are you okay?"

"I'm fine, just starving," I said gently, patting his hand on my shoulder before I moved away, slipping by him toward the stairs. "You wanna eat with me?"

He caught me at the top step, turning me back around to face him. "Jin, I need to take you to Logan. We'll eat at his home."

"No, then his mother's gonna hafta cook," I said, lifting his hand off me and starting down the stairs. "First food, then the car ride."

His exasperated sigh let me know that I had won the argument.

Yuri wanted to know everything that had happened and listened very intently as I explained about Christophe's dungeon, the club, and the murderous intentions of his yareah. I was chuckling when I noticed his face.

"What's wrong?"

"You think that's funny? They kidnap you and chain you up and plan to kill you, but to you it's all fun and games."

"Lighten up." I yawned, pointing across the street to the diner. "If I got upset every time someone beat me, or chased me, or tried to rape me, I'd be crying in my cereal every morning. No one likes a whiner."

He grabbed my arm and spun me around to face him. "You are now the reah of the tribe of Mafdet. Anyone who touches you will answer first to Logan and then to me."

I suddenly had a gnawing ache in the pit of my stomach. "Did Logan do something to Christophe because of me?"

"Logan did something to Christophe because of what he did, not something you did."

"Oh God, what'd Logan do?" I was more annoyed than worried. I never wanted anyone punished in my name, like I was perfect.

Yuri's eyes were cold and hard. "Christophe didn't know that Logan marked you; your hair covers the mark, and because Logan has not… you don't smell like him, so for that, his life was spared. But make no mistake, for a semel to touch another semel's mate—you know the punishment for that, Jin."

"But I'm not his mate."

"All other cats, even semels and yareahs, must have mating ceremonies to seal the bond between them. But a semel finds his reah, and once the mark is given, they are a mated pair. You belong to Logan Church just as surely as the rest of us do."

"And so because Christophe touched me…."

"His choice was to meet Logan in the pit or accept whatever punishment Logan saw fit to give."

"Which did he choose?"

"The punishment, of course," he said, like I was crazy. "Have you ever seen Logan Church in his panther form?"

"No. When would I have?"

"Yeah, well, if you were Christophe, you wouldn't want to fight him either."

"So what did Logan do?"

"Not enough."

"Tell me."

"He assembled Christophe's tribe, and then he slapped him."

I scowled at Yuri.

"I know. The things he does… I just don't get it."

"He slapped him?"

"Yeah, he just… I mean, there he was. He just stood there and told Christophe to never touch anything of his again and backhanded him really hard like he was nothing. Like he was dirt."

"Christophe must have been humiliated."

"Who cares? Humiliation isn't going to hurt him."

But it would. In front of Christophe's entire tribe, Logan had slapped him and made him look weak. Christophe should have met Logan in the pit if he wanted to keep the respect of his people. Instead, by allowing Logan to hit him in front of them, Christophe had lost face. I wondered how he would ever regain their respect. A leader had to appear strong, powerful, and untouchable. Logan had stripped all of that from the semel of the tribe of Pakhet with a single blow.

"I would have killed him."

"And made Christophe a martyr instead of the pathetic excuse for a leader that he seems like now," I educated him. "Logan's brilliant."

He squinted at me. "Maybe that's why you're his mate; you get how his mind works."

I didn't want to debate that with him. "Let's eat."

Inside the diner, I ordered breakfast while Yuri had an enormous burger. He called Logan toward the end of our meal and explained that he was bringing me back. When he got off the phone, he looked miserable.

"What's wrong?"

"He's pissed at me for not calling him the second I found you."

"Why?"

"He wants to see you now."

"But he's not mad at you, not really."

"No, you just frustrate him to no end."

I couldn't help that.

THE CAR ride up the mountain was so calming that I almost fell asleep. Yuri didn't seem in the mood to talk, and I wasn't really either. When we rolled through the front gate of Logan's home, I felt my stomach twist. It was funny to want to be there and not there at the exact same time. I decided to stand outside on the porch instead of following Yuri inside. I just wasn't quite ready to face Logan Church.

"Jin."

Turning, I found my mate was suddenly there in the doorway.

"Hi." I smiled over at him.

I saw him swallow hard, saw how raw and red his eyes looked, how haggard and worn out he was. He was a mess.

"I'm sorry. I didn't mean to worry you."

His eyes raked over me from head to toe, taking me all in.

"I'm fine," I told him softly, holding out my arms. "Come see."

He moved so much faster than I thought he could, and when I was crushed to his chest, his arms wrapping me up, his face buried in my shoulder, I realized that just his presence soothed me. The man belonged to me, and there was no way around it.

"Look at me."

My head tilted back so I could see his face.

"Did anybody hurt you?"

I shook my head. "I already told you, no."

"Were you touched?"

"No, I—"

"What the hell?" he growled, noticing my wrists, grabbing each one tight. "The cuffs he used were silver?"

"He didn't purposely try and hurt me," I said gently. "The cuffs are just made of silver because he probably plays his bondage games with other panthers. If he doesn't use silver, what's the fun in it? If everyone can just break free, where's the game?"

"Jin—"

"He made a mistake, Logan," I told him, trying to soothe the pain and rage I saw in his eyes. The simmering fury was right there below the surface. I understood that he was holding it together for me. "He had no idea when he took me that you had already marked me. He would have never done such a thing had he known."

"That's crap, and we both know it. He wants my reah, and he can't have you. You're mine."

I lifted my hands to his face. "Yes."

He took a shuddering breath. "Why did you leave the room last night?"

I cleared my throat, taking a step back, away from him. "I woke up just in time to hear your dad. He seemed pretty upset."

"I see." He squinted at me, crossing his arms over his broad chest. "And so even after you let me mark you, your plan was to run from me."

"Did you hear your father? That was just the beginning. Your tribe's gonna react the exact same way when they find out I'm a man."

"And I care, why?"

I shook my head. "A semel's first duty is to his tribe."

"Is it?"

"You know, you can do the cool guy thing and answer me with questions all day, but it won't change anything. You can't have a male mate."

The way he took a deep breath, I thought for a second that he had resigned himself to my words, but when he grabbed hold of my arm, dragged me after him across the porch, I understood we were far from being done.

"Logan!"

He stopped fast and yanked me forward so I could see his face. "You either walk upstairs with me now or get carried up over my shoulder—which do you prefer?"

His voice was icy.

"I can walk," I assured him.

"Then do it."

I brushed by him, and even though I heard people call my name, even Crane, I didn't stop. I walked through the living room to the stairs that led to the second floor. I heard Logan right behind me and hurried. Walking down the long hallway to the end, I saw the double doors that led to his bedroom. I jogged toward them and opened one, slipping inside without closing it, crossing to the glass doors that opened out to the balcony instead. I turned to face him and found him locking the door after him.

"You want to talk—talk."

He took a settling breath. "You're driving me nuts."

It was not what I was expecting. "I am?"

"Yeah," he grunted. "You're my reah, not my yareah, not some mate I decided on. You were born to be mine, and instead of resigning yourself to that fact, you're fighting with me. What the hell? Where do you get off fighting with me?"

He was really irritated, and I found that completely endearing.

"And if you want to leave so bad, then go already," Logan said, drawing my attention back to him. "But don't go under any false pretenses. If you go, it's because you don't want to be here, not because I can't handle the fallout from my decision to love my mate."

Love his mate? His plan was to love me? "How can you talk about love when I've known you for less than a day? You can't possibly—"

"Because you love your mate, you idiot," he thundered, his voice filling the room. "That's what you do!"

I just stood there, staring at him. "Why didn't you tell me you're not gay?"

"I don't understand what that has to do with anything. You're a man, and you're my mate; therefore, from now on, I'm gay. Why are we even discussing this?" he asked irritably.

"You don't just become gay."

"Who says?"

"You just don't."

"Oh, 'you just don't.' Well, that's very logical."

"Logan—"

"Listen, I'm the same man I was yesterday morning when I woke up. The only thing that's changed from then to now is that now I have a mate."

"But you—"

"I never had a male lover before, that's true, but I've never had a mate before, either. All I can tell you is that when I look at you, my heart stops."

I refused to let his words take root. It was much too dangerous. "You were going to take Simone as your yareah."

"Which obviously means something to you," he said, the muscles in his jaw clenching.

"Yeah. It means that you're straight, and your plan was to take a female mate."

"You would have preferred that I was bisexual, because that would have been better for you. It would make sense that I could want you."

I nodded.

"Because as it is now, you don't get how I can really want you for my mate. Maybe I want to sleep with you to experiment, but there's no way I'll want to keep you."

It was like he was reading my mind.

"And if you let me have you, then you might lose your heart in the process."

I stood there and didn't break down, even though he had just gutted my soul.

"I assure you that when I take you to bed, you won't be the only one lost."

How could just his voice fill me with such a surge of feeling? Why was I having trouble breathing with just his eyes on me?

"You're all I will ever want."

He meant every word. I knew it inside, where everything was welling up and rising to the surface. The man could never lie to me; I would read that on him. He could hide nothing from me. I was his mate, after all.

"So, please, just stay with me."

"No one wants me around."

"I do." He exhaled slowly.

The way he was looking at me, I shuddered. I couldn't help it. "You should run away from me."

I got a slow, lazy smile that was very sexy. The man knew he was gorgeous and completely understood his effect on me. "I've never run from anything in my life."

I didn't doubt it. He was a rock.

"And I would never, ever run from my mate."

I could feel the heat radiating off his body as he stepped in front of me. "I don't want to complicate your life, and I'm not certain that you've thought this all—"

"Listen," he cut in, his fingers slipping around the side of my neck before they ran under my chin, tilting my head up so I had to look into his gorgeous amber eyes. "The decision's made. You're mine… you belong with me."

I shook my head. "But your family and your tribe are not gonna accept—"

"Anyone is free to leave my tribe at any time," he told me, his right hand sliding up to my cheek. It took everything I had not to lean into the caress. "Anyone who does not understand a semel wanting his reah is not someone I need anyway. Stupidity is not a trait I admire."

I took a shaky breath. "Yeah, but—"

"No," he said, his voice low, gravelly. "It's done. You belong to me."

"Logan, it's not that simple. I heard what your father said, and I know you have responsibilities to—"

"Last night when we found Crane outside and he told us that you had been taken, I couldn't even think, and that's never happened before. Always, I'm calm, rational, logical… it's a strength of mine. But everything was gone except rage. I have never been angry like that, and even now, I have a need to tear Christophe into pieces for daring to put his hands on you."

"It wasn't him who—"

"On his command, you were taken. All the responsibility falls to him."

I nodded.

"You are my mate. How dare he even speak to you without my permission?" Fury coiled within his voice like a snake. The man could explode into violence at any moment.

"I heard what you did," I said softly. "It's enough. Let it go."

I saw him take a quick breath, and the light that filled his eyes made my heart hurt, it swelled so fast. God, it was awful. I didn't just want him to do bad things to me, I liked him too. We could be friends. I could feel it. "So you think maybe you wanna date me?"

He rolled his eyes like I was just the most annoying thing in the world *ever* before he bent and kissed me. The kiss was deep and devouring, his fingers buried in my hair as he held my head so I couldn't pull away. As if I wanted to pull away. I just wanted to drown in him, to crawl inside his skin, into his heart, and live there for the rest of my life. When he smiled against my mouth, I sighed into his.

"My mate," he sighed as he lifted his lips from mine. The way he was looking at me, so possessively, made my mouth dry. "Listen, from now on, you go no…." He trailed off, inhaling deeply, breathing me in and trying to keep the command out of his tone. He was used to ordering people around, but he knew, instinctively, that it was not the way to approach me. "I need you to hear me."

I nodded.

"You are my mate. It is all there is, all that matters. I have my business to run, my tribe to lead, my family to support, and now I have my mate. My life is set. There is nothing more I want or need." His voice was low and deadly serious. "All right?"

I nodded quickly.

"I don't want to date you, or see you on the nights you don't work, or do any of the other million stupid things that I'm sure you have planned. I want you here with me all the time. I want you to take your place at my side in our tribe and sleep in our bed every night. You belong to me. You need to wrap your brain around it."

I tried hard not to tremble.

His smile was warm before he stepped away from me, walking back toward the door. "Now, I'm gonna go get you something to eat."

I didn't need to eat. "I just ate."

"Then something to drink. You look like you're gonna pass out."

I should have waited. He was giving me the time to adjust to him because he was an honorable man, a good man, a patient man. I should have taken things slow, but after two years of celibacy and the way his scent was driving me to claw through his clothes, I was teetering into frenzied need. I knew what I wanted, and to deny myself when the man belonged to me was just stupid. When I spoke his name, he froze where he was and turned to me.

"What?"

I cleared my throat. "Please mark me again."

He made a noise in the back of his throat before he rushed toward me, and I received him with open arms. I was wrapped up tight, and he crushed me to his chest as I lifted my head for his kiss.

"Are you sure?"

"Make me yours."

The strangled sound from deep in his chest rushed blood to my groin. I couldn't breathe.

I was spun around, pushed forward several feet, and then shoved face first into a wall, my legs kicked apart as his knee wedged between my thighs. His hands were all over me.

"I'm sorry… I wish it could be slow, but if I don't take you, show everyone that you're mine and bind you to me, then anyone that touches you… no way I could even stop myself from… so this is the only way, 'cause once you smell like me, no one will come near you."

My parka was yanked off me; my sweater was in pieces on the floor, the long-sleeved T-shirt beneath shredded as well, falling there to join it. My jeans were shucked roughly to my knees, my briefs following. I gasped as his hand wrapped around my hard, throbbing cock.

"It has to be like this. You have to submit."

Whatever he wanted. All my focus was on the hand fisted around my shaft, sliding over my skin. Throbs of pleasure were pulsing through my body as I squirmed against him.

"You're mine."

I was going to say something, anything, but there was the sound of crinkling foil, and anticipation drowned reason. My cock was leaking in his hand, and he was rubbing the slick, sticky precome over the head with his thumb. It felt amazing.

"I need the lube off the condom," he told me, his voice deep and seductive. "But I'm not going to use it. I'm not sick with anything. I'll show you… it's in my desk… later."

I trusted him. He was my mate.

"I need you to feel every inch of me inside you."

So hot—the man was so… fucking… hot.

"You're trembling," he growled before his mouth closed on the back of my neck, on the mark he had made the day before, sucking and licking at it, pressing my forehead against the wall. I was pinned there, held completely still, as he parted my thighs and impaled me in one swift, powerful forward thrust. The bite was forgotten; there was only the stinging heat as I gasped his name, my muscles tight and protesting for moments before they relaxed and engulfed him. He was so hard, the length filling me, the thickness stretching me, and his hand working me over, sending tremors of pleasure rolling through my frame.

"God, you're so fuckin' tight…."

I called his name as he eased out and then shoved back inside as hard as he had the first time. The thrusts were jarring as he drove into me over and over, chanting my name like a prayer.

"You feel so good," he growled, hand tangled in my hair, yanking my head back and twisting it sideways to find my mouth. It was intoxicating to be wanted, and his need and desire were there in his voice, in the way he clutched me and in the way his tongue slid over mine. He bit my collarbone and then sucked it, bathing the spot with his tongue, kissing up my throat, over my jaw, more nips and licking, the kisses possessive, consuming, as his hands kneaded and stroked my ass, my chest, down my abdomen to my thighs. He had me wrapped in his arms, and he was buried inside me deeper than I thought possible, so hard inside me. I was sure I could feel him in my stomach as he lifted me off my feet.

"Can you take it?" he asked, holding me so tight, his breath warm and moist in my ear as he pounded into me again and again.

"Yes," I cried out, feeling the sting of hot tears on my face. I was so close, aching with my need to come.

"Say my name. Say you're mine."

"I belong to you, Logan. I'm your mate, your reah."

He slid in and out of my now slippery heat, my ass milking his cock as he held me off my feet and drove deep inside, hitting my prostate. There was no way to hold back the moan that tore out of me.

"God, the way you take me in," he growled, his voice almost a snarl as he shifted his weight and leaned into me. I could feel his heart pounding in his chest against my back. "I have to taste… I…." He sucked in his breath, but I had heard the frustration and aching need in his voice.

I reached behind me for his hard, tight ass, my fingers gliding over hot skin, drawing his hips against me, trying to bring him deeper inside me. When instead he slipped from my body, I wanted to scream. I opened my mouth to beg him if I had to, but he twisted me around to face him, his hand instantly back on my shaft, stroking me.

I watched as he fell to his knees and took me into his mouth in one fluid motion. I didn't know anyone who could swallow cock like that, just open up his throat and take it, but I was sure I had never felt anything like it in my life. His mouth was so hot, so wet, his tongue stroking over every inch of my shaft, pushing into the slit, pressing against the underside as I pumped in and out of his mouth. I felt my balls draw up tight, my orgasm nearing, starting to roll through me, cresting like a wave.

He was a frenzy of motion, his fingers slipping into me from behind, pushing deep into my tight channel as he continued to deep-throat me, the suction unrelenting and strong. I screamed his name; my hands buried in his thick blond hair as I held his head and fucked his mouth. I tried to push him off me before I came, but his fingers dug into my thighs so I couldn't move. He wanted it all, and I watched him swallow and almost collapsed from my convulsing release before I was spun around and shoved back up against the wall.

"You're mine," he said, his voice so deep, so sexy, that I trembled just from the sound. I felt his hands spreading my ass cheeks, his cock pressed against my hole for a second before he eased deep into me. "I have to be inside you… I have to mark you… I want you… you're mine."

I was trembling hard as he pulled back before driving back in, deeper, drowning me in exquisite, necessary sensations, his tongue licking up the side of my throat only to bite down once more on the back of my neck.

"My mate, my mark," he growled into my hair, and it was by far the most possessive, wonderful thing I had ever heard. "No one else will ever be inside you," he promised, and the ferocity of the sound coupled by his teeth sinking into the back of my neck and the brutal push forward brought sizzling heat rushing through my body again. I screamed, and he yanked me back, his hand on my abdomen, feeling the muscles clench, my head falling on his shoulder as my legs buckled under me. Strong arms kept me from sliding down his body to the floor. He came with a roar, staggering against me, and buried his face in the side of my neck.

I felt ravaged and weightless, and it was heaven that he was there to hold and ground me so I wouldn't float away. We stood together, riding out the aftershocks of our orgasms, panting and trembling, his fingers digging into my skin, making sure I couldn't move.

"You feel that?"

I felt everything.

"You feel your body trying to hold me inside? You don't wanna let me go."

My muscles were clenching and unclenching around his cock, the spasms sending tendrils of pain and pleasure up and down my spine.

I caught my breath as he slid carefully, gently out of my body.

"Can you stand?"

I nodded.

He let me go slowly, licking a line up the side of my neck to behind my ear. "I need to clean you up."

I swallowed hard, my mouth dry.

"You look good."

My body jerked from the raw sound of his voice. The way he was looking at me, possessively, his eyes full of heat, I could barely stand it.

"I like you dripping with me."

I had come sliding down the inside of my thighs. Other men had wanted me out of sight and cleaned up as fast as I could do it. Logan Church, as I saw clearly, enjoyed seeing me ravaged.

"I want to take care of you. Don't move."

I stayed where I was, frozen, and he left and was back in seconds with a warm washcloth and another towel. When I was clean, he eased my briefs and jeans up my thighs to my hips. I got a kiss on my forehead before he returned everything to the bathroom.

"The shirt and sweater are goners," he said as he strode back into the room carrying a long-sleeved button-down shirt for me to put on. After I slid my arms into it, he wrapped it around me. "But I'm not sorry." I heard the amusement in his voice as I received a kiss on the back of my neck. It still ached but no longer felt as though a hot dagger had been driven into my flesh. I buttoned up my jeans and turned around. When I looked up, I noticed him watching me, his gold eyes glittering.

"What?" I smiled at him.

He shook his head before motioning me forward. "Kiss me."

I walked into his arms and wrapped mine around his neck, drawing him down. I slid my tongue over his bottom lip, and he opened for me, the sigh rising up out of him, his breath warm in my mouth. I let my tongue explore him as I claimed him. The noises he made deep in his throat, the way he kissed me back, ravenously, the way he pushed against me, clutching at me, all of it told me that he was right where he wanted to be. When he lifted his lips, pulling away just barely, his mouth hovering over mine, I felt him shiver hard.

"You should see your eyes."

I lifted up, slipping my tongue back into his mouth, and I tasted him again, savoring the feel of his trembling reaction to me. The need there in the low moan, his fingers digging into my back, the way he held me in his arms, molding me against his big, hard body—all of it spoke to his desire. When I could hear my heart pounding in my ears, I broke the kiss to take in some air.

"I can smell me all over you." His voice was hoarse, full of raw need.

"Is that a good thing?"

"Oh, fuck, yeah." His eyes were absolutely molten.

I took a step away from him since the air between us was thick and hot.

"I think now we should take a shower."

He was already acting like I belonged to him.

"C'mere," he said, closing the small distance between us and slanting his mouth down over mine. The kiss was possessive and hard, his hand fisted in my hair so I couldn't move.

The way he manhandled me, the way he kissed me, I had to be careful, or it could easily become all that mattered. When he pulled back, I just stared up into his eyes.

After several long, silent moments, he smiled slowly, the corner of his mouth curling seductively. "What?"

"Your eyes are really beautiful," I told him.

Instantly his hands were all over me. He bumped my chin up with his nose and kissed my throat before he bit it gently. "You are the beautiful one… my mate… your eyes… so gray… they get dark and smoky when you look at me." His voice was like honey.

My heart fluttered.

"We need to go to your place."

I felt like I was underwater.

"And get all your stuff."

"Wait." I tried to clear my head, which was hard when he was so close to me. "I can't just—I have a landlord and a job and…." Defending my life to him made me realize how insane I had been for thinking I could just walk away from the new family I had at work. My boss, my friends—running out on any of it was crazy. Why was my first instinct always to run?

"You're cute when you're flustered."

I needed to get my bearings, and he wasn't letting me.

"Let's go get your stuff," he repeated, not asking, telling. It was endearing and annoying at the exact same time.

"Listen, I just think we need to slow way down," I said, taking several breaths before I slipped around him, backing up away from him.

"Do you?" he said, following fast, allowing me no personal space. He touched my hair, brushing it back out of my face, running his fingers through the length of it to where it fell around my shoulders. "After what you just allowed, you want to slow down?"

How could I explain what had happened when I wasn't sure myself? It would be hard to tell him that I never did anything crazy or dangerous when it was all he knew of me. I was careful, never reckless except where this man was concerned. For my mate, I was wild.

"God, you're thinking so hard," he chuckled, bending to kiss my forehead, my eyes, my nose, and finally my mouth. When he sucked on my bottom lip, I lifted up into him and into the kiss. The sharp sound of someone barking out his name from the other room made me jerk in his arms. Instantly, my heart was in my throat.

"It's alright," he soothed as he went to the door and leaned out.

I waited, and when he stepped back in, he told me that he had to go downstairs. There were people he had to talk to.

"I should find Crane too," I told him.

"No, stay here, and I'll send him up here to you."

I nodded and crossed the room to sit on the bed. I was surprised when he walked over to me, bent, and kissed my nose.

"Don't leave the bedroom, baby."

"I am not your baby." I smiled up at him.

He smiled back, his eyes lingering on my face, before he turned and left the room.

Alone, I started to worry again. By the time there was a knock on the door, I almost shattered into a million pieces from the sound. When Crane slipped into the room, I could breathe again.

"Are you okay?" I asked him.

His eyes were huge as he stared at me.

"What?"

"Are you kidding?"

I squinted at him, unsure about what was wrong with him.

"Where should I start?"

I groaned loudly and leaned my head in my hands as he ranted at me. How dare I not tell him where I was? What the hell had I been thinking?

It was like an endless stream of sound, of yelling, and when he smacked my shoulder, I realized I had zoned out on him.

"Shit," I snapped, hitting him back. "Don't hit me."

"You're such an ass."

There was no argument there.

"When were you going to tell me about Logan Church?"

"Are you kidding?" I yelled, feeling like myself because I was looking at him. "You can't possibly think that any of this was planned."

"I dunno, was it?"

I just stared at him.

"Okay, fine, it wasn't," he said, taking a seat beside me on the bed, pulling off his sweater and then the T-shirt underneath.

"What're you doing?"

"That shirt is way too big for you," he said, passing me his T-shirt. "Wear this."

I discarded Logan's shirt and pulled on Crane's T-shirt. It was still warm from his body. "Thanks."

"So what? We're staying, right?"

"Right."

"So are we moving in here?"

"No… I dunno," I sighed.

"Well, we can't stay at our place because that guy Domin's skulking around. I'm thinkin' when he finds out that you're the big man's mate he'll really try screwing with you."

"Probably." I sighed again, lying back on the bed.

"So let's go get our shit and bring it back up here."

I rolled my head to the side, looking at him. "You're gonna stay here with me?"

"If your semel will allow it." He grinned at me.

"Shut up."

"You don't get it," he chuckled. "You're a mated reah now. You are the mate of a semel with a whole tribe behind you. That scary sheseru Logan's got, Yuri whatever his name is, he told me when I was on my way up here not to stay too long because Logan wants you to rest."

"What time is it, anyway?" I yawned, lifting my arm to look at my watch.

Crane took hold of my wrist to check the time himself. "It's a little after five."

"Then why am I tired?" I yawned.

"Oh, I dunno." He smirked at me. "God, you're an idiot."

I didn't even have the energy to yell at him. I just wanted to go to sleep beside Logan. I wanted him to wrap me up in his arms and hold me tight.

"Hello, can we focus? Do you want me to go get our shit or not?"

"Yes."

"Okay. I think Delphine has a car, lemme see if I can borrow it, and I'll go get our stuff and come back. It's just our two backpacks."

"Those are huge hiking packs, idiot," I said, dragging myself to my feet, looking around the warm, very masculine bedroom for my parka.

"There." He pointed.

Once I zipped myself up, I looked at him and realized he wasn't moving. "Are we going?"

"Are you sure you should?"

"What are you talking about?"

"Don't you have to ask first?"

"Have you lost your mind?"

His smile was huge. "Sorry. I forgot who I was talking to."

Chapter Nine

I DROVE home on autopilot and parked behind our building in the dark alley. Crane wanted to just grab our bags and leave, but I needed to shower and change. I smelled like sex. Walking toward the bathroom, I had to grab for the doorjamb as my legs went out from under me.

"What the hell?" Crane half shouted as he ran to my side, grabbing me and hauling me up against him, anchoring me against his bigger, more heavily muscled frame.

"It's… just been a really long couple of days."

"Are you gonna be all right in the shower?"

"Of course. Don't be an idiot."

He looked skeptical, but he let me go in alone.

I stood under the hot water until it ran cold. The bite Logan had given me still hurt when I washed it, and it bled again, but it stopped by the time I got out and staggered to my couch. I asked Crane what it looked like, and he said it looked like a bite from something big.

"That's really descriptive. Thanks."

"It looks bad, though; you must've bled a lot."

"I feel like I did, but I was trying to think… oh, that's right."

"What's right?"

"He drank it."

"What'd you say?"

I smiled at Crane, because he looked horrified. "When a semel marks his reah, he drinks the blood from the wound."

"Like a vampire."

"There's no such thing as vampires."

"I dunno about that, 'cause from the looks of it, Logan drank a lot of your blood."

"It wasn't that much. No more than I can heal."

"Then heal it already—shift."

But I was too tired; I yawned, instead. After a few moments, I realized he was smiling at me.

"What?"

"Just funny, you with a mark you swore you'd never take and never even want."

I flipped him off before I leaned back and closed my eyes.

I must have dozed, because the sharp knock on the front door startled me. I didn't even have to ask who it was; his scent was imprinted on my brain even in so short a time.

"Jin!"

I yawned as Crane went to the door.

"Open the goddamn door!"

I was surprised the roar didn't simply split the door in two.

"I'm coming," Crane yelled back as he opened it. He went mute when he was suddenly faced with the man. Logan's scowl was icy. "Sorry."

Logan stood there silently, hands shoved into the pockets of his lined peacoat. He was wearing a heavy sweater and jeans; he had showered and changed, but it had been done quickly, his clothes thrown on. He'd been in a hurry to reach me. His hair was still wet. Standing behind him, still but menacing, was Yuri.

"What?"

His eyes darkened to a deep, burnished gold, and his eyebrows furrowed as he walked into the apartment. "'What'? This is all you have to say to me?"

"We were coming right back. We just had to get our stuff."

Instantly his expression changed, like he was startled.

"Which is exactly what I said." Yuri rolled his eyes, brushing by Logan to Crane. "Get your crap, kid, we're going back. Mrs. Church already got your room ready."

He smiled at Yuri, shouldered his backpack, and told me he'd see me at home. He was explaining as they left how much he'd always hated the crappy little apartment. When Logan returned his attention to me, his scowl returned.

"You thought, what, that I ran off with Crane?"

"His smell was on our bed." His voice was low and ominous.

"Our bed?"

"Yes, our bed," he almost snarled, and I could tell he had been in a rage, as it still lingered in his tone, in the set of his broad shoulders, and in the dark, violent gaze.

I nodded. "So what?"

"You left my shirt."

"Because it's like wearing a tent." I chuckled, smiling at him, watching his eyes soften as he looked at me.

Several heartbeats ticked by before he spoke. "I was jealous."

"Don't ever be jealous of Crane. He's my friend—I've known him forever. We grew up together."

"There should never be a scent but yours or mine in our bed."

"Fair enough," I agreed, because that was more than reasonable. "Until there's children."

His jaw clenched, the muscles in his throat corded, and he nodded quickly. "Yes."

"You do want children someday, don't you?"

"Yes, do you?"

"I do," I told him.

We were silent for several breaths before he spoke.

"This is fast for you, I know."

"Yeah, it is, but I'm sure it's the same way for you."

"I just want to figure everything out, and we can do that slowly, but I can't allow you to be away from me while we do that."

"Meaning what?"

"Meaning that you can have whatever time you need to get comfortable with the idea of being my mate, but you will do it while you sleep in my bed."

I chuckled.

"What?"

"That makes no sense."

"You're my mate. You live with me. End of story." He coughed. "Now, where's your stuff."

I pointed to the backpack.

"That's it?"

"That's it."

He nodded before he walked over and picked it up, turning to walk straight out the front door without another word. I had changed into a sweater and had my laptop bag over my shoulder when he returned a couple of minutes later. I noticed that he was frowning.

"What?"

"How did you not see all those marks out there? It's a fuckin' mess."

He sounded jealous again, and I smiled in spite of myself.

"You got everything out of your bathroom?"

"Yep."

"Take a final walk around."

The man just couldn't keep himself from barking out orders. It was in his blood. "Okay." I smiled at him before I left the room. When I got back, he was standing at the window that opened out onto the fire escape. "You ready to go?"

There was no answer.

"Changed your mind? Don't want me after all?" I was terrified that maybe he had come to his senses. Already the idea of being without the man made my heart hurt.

When he turned I saw how furious he looked.

"What's wrong?" I asked, crossing the room to him.

In his hand, I saw the T-shirt I had been wearing the night Ben attacked me. It had bloodstains on it.

"Where'd you find that?"

"Here behind the armoire. What is this?"

I had thrown it at the trashcan, but apparently I had missed. "It's nothing," I said as I took it from him and pitched it in the garbage can. "Ex-boyfriend of a girl Crane dated broke in and attacked me, but it's all over now."

After a moment, he nodded, calming, and reached for me.

I went into his arms, and he held me tight, his face buried in my hair. "Don't worry about stuff that happened before you were around."

He let out a deep breath. "You know, I have always been the one who didn't fight. I'm known for it. I compromise and make concessions. I don't ever want to put anyone in danger."

"That's a good way to be."

"No, it's not, and just now, between Domin's marks on your door and that damn T-shirt, I get that. How things are now, it's not safe. You're not safe; my family's not safe; my tribe... because I'm not scary, everyone's in jeopardy."

"Respect is better than fear."

"Agreed, but without repercussions, respect is hollow."

"I don't understand," I breathed out, pulling free of his arms to look up into his face.

"This man who attacked you—why did he?"

"Because he thought I was Crane."

"Yes, but also, he thought he could attack Crane. Crane was weak, in his mind, and so he came after him."

"Not necessarily. He was just blinded by—"

"He thought Crane was weak. People who look weak are attacked. Domin thinks I'm weak because I want peace. When he attacks my people, I do not come after him with my tribe, instead, I challenge him to one-on-one combat in the pit that he never accepts."

"'Cause he knows he's gonna get his ass kicked."

"But meanwhile, my tribe fears his."

"Yeah, but you shouldn't just go picking a fight with him to—"

"I should go and see him, because now I am the same as the rest of the members of my tribe. I have something to lose."

I smiled up at him. "You're not gonna lose me."

"No," he said, and his voice was so ominous that I was surprised. "Come with me."

I locked the apartment and followed him down two flights to the alley.

"How come you have no stuff?"

"I have stuff," I teased. "What you just carried down, that's stuff. When I got here six months ago, everything I had fit in a regular-size backpack like the kind you use in high school."

He didn't seem pleased.

I was worried that I had somehow let Delphine's cute little Lexus get stolen when I didn't see it, but Logan told me Yuri had driven it home.

"But I have the keys."

He arched an eyebrow for me.

"I could have driven it back," I muttered. Obviously, the man had multiple sets of car keys for everything parked in his garage.

"No," he said, leading me to the limousine parked almost at the end of the alley. When he opened the door for me, I climbed inside before him.

"You want me to take the quick way home or the long one?" the driver asked from the front seat, making sure to make eye contact with me and smile.

"Take the long way so Jin can see our land."

"Got it," the reply came back before the darkened glass rose behind him, separating the front and back of the car.

"Our land?"

Logan turned to look at me. "Everything that belongs to me is yours as well—the house, the land, the business, the cars… everything."

"How can you just trust me so fast? What if I'm a bad person?"

His smile was wide. I amused the hell out of him, that was obvious. "You're my mate. You feel exactly as I do. You're the only person in the world I don't doubt, because you were made for me so that I could trust you with all that I have and with my heart."

I turned to look out the window so he wouldn't see me struggle not to break down. It was too much honesty to take in.

"Why did you leave without telling me?"

His voice, after long moments of silence, startled me.

I cleared my throat, turning to look at him. "I don't report to you."

"I think you do."

"I won't," I told him flatly. "I will come and go as I like. I won't stay home. I have a job. If you're looking for some traditional mate, you might want to rethink if you really want me."

We stared at each other for several minutes before he broke into a grin.

"Why're you smiling?"

"Because you're so transparent." He chuckled, smiling at me, his eyes glowing.

"What?"

"You're trying to run me off," he said, leaning over to kiss the side of my neck before he slipped off the seat and knelt in front of me, hands on my thighs as he slid me forward. "I plan to give you as much freedom as you need."

I watched him as he reached for me and pulled my hair out of the rubber band, moving it so it fell over my shoulder.

"This is beautiful. It should never be tied back."

"It's a pain," I assured him, even as I felt his fingers threading though it. My hair was longer than it had ever been, falling down over my shoulders, but not much further. "I was gonna chop it all off this weekend when I had—"

"No," he said softly. "I forbid it."

"You forbid it," I teased him, chuckling. "You think you can tell me what to do with my own hair, Mr. Church? What was it you just said about freedom?"

"I know what I said." He nodded, wrapping his hand in it, then watching it slide though his fingers. "I take it back. Your hair is mine, you're mine, and I'll tell you what you can and cannot do from now on."

"Is that right?" I asked, arching a brow for him.

His grin was huge, making his eyes glow. "Please, I beg you, do not cut your long, gorgeous beautiful black hair that I want to bury my face in while I sleep next to you."

When he said it like that…. "Okay," I barely got out.

His eyes ran all over me. "Jesus… my mate," he sighed, awe in his voice. "Tell me about your family, where you were born."

He was so eager to hear about me. "Can I ask you a question instead?"

"No," he said as he took off first his peacoat and then the sweater underneath, revealing smooth, golden skin, broad shoulders, washboard abs, and a sculpted muscular chest that should have been under glass in a museum somewhere. I tried to make sure I kept breathing. "I want my answers first."

"I'm from Chicago."

"And your family is still there?" he asked, staring into my eyes. "I can find them there?"

"Yes."

"Okay," he said, his big, strong hands on my belt.

I watched him work the buckle loose and then unsnap my fly and slide the zipper down. "Now can I ask my question?" I was so proud of my voice for sticking around.

"What?" he indulged, his hand slipping between the flaps of my jeans and under the waistband of my briefs.

"Was it safe, what we did earlier?"

He smiled at me. "I have a piece of paper at the house that will show you I'm clean. I'll grab it for you when we get back."

I felt bad for doubting him.

"It's okay that you asked me again," he said, the back of his fingers moving up and down my throat. "I shouldn't have rushed it. I should have gone slower, so you'd know it meant everything and that it wasn't just a quick fuck that I would forget."

My heart and soul, both wanted to fly out of my body and live in his. There was an urge, one I had never felt in my life, to surrender. "I was the one who rushed it." I smiled at him.

"Yeah, but I wanted perfection for you, and what I delivered was—"

"Amazing," I cut him off. "You were amazing. Don't kid yourself."

"I could be amazing again," he said hopefully.

My stomach rolled over, and my cock hardened in his hand.

"I really need to be back inside you."

Just like that, my body went up in flames.

"Reach into that side drawer there."

I leaned to my left and opened the small drawer built into the seat. The only thing in there was a bottle of lube. "I see you're ready for company."

"Look at it. It was put there for you."

The plastic seal was still around the neck of the bottle. "So, what, you stopped on the way to my place to pick up lube? Is that why you brought the limo—so you could fuck me again?"

"Yes," he said honestly, parting my thighs.

I had to smile. The man knew what he wanted.

"You take my breath away," he confessed, his voice a throaty whisper.

My eyes locked on his as he slowly stroked my shaft.

"I had no idea I could ever feel like this." He smiled suddenly. "Amazing."

I was barely listening, too consumed with my cock in his hand and the ripples of electricity that were slithering through my body.

"Can you see yourself when you look in the mirror? I know women that aren't as beautiful as you are."

I was listening, but more, I was feeling. His hand was sliding easily over my slick, leaking cock, and when his tongue licked over the head, I moaned loudly.

"Look what I can do to you."

I was shivering as he took me into his mouth, swallowing my shaft down his throat as he eased me forward so I was hanging off the seat. It felt so good, his mouth so hot, so wet, his tongue swirling over my sensitive skin as he sucked hard. My head fell back against the seat, my eyes closing as I drowned in the sensations. He knew what I wanted, needed: to be dominated without feeling powerless.

"Jin…," he breathed as I heard the rustling of plastic and then the snap of the bottle cap.

Two lubed fingers slid deep inside me, past the inner ring of muscle, and the pressure, combined with the hot suction on my cock, sent me hurtling into the sun. It was ecstasy, and I came in his mouth like he wanted, shuddering my release.

He drank me down, swallowing hard as he added another finger to the two in my ass, shoving deep and hard as I writhed against him.

"Look."

I couldn't get my eyes to open.

"Look." His voice was a sharp command.

I lifted my eyes slowly and realized he had hold of my wrist. But my hand was not mine; instead, there were long, dark claws where my nails should have been. My eyes lifted to his but stopped on his neck where the cuts were. He was bleeding. "Oh, my God, I'm so sorry," I gasped, jerking under him, trying to roll free.

But I was impaled suddenly on his fingers, and my back bowed as I almost swallowed my tongue. Everything he did to me felt so good, so amazing.

"Only with me, your mate, can you be free," he said softly, the smile wicked, and I felt the bite on the inside of my thigh. "And to me, seeing you like this, your fangs showing, your lips swollen, and your cat eyes… jet black… to know that I made you like this, my mate… you make me burn for you."

I felt his lips on my skin above my cock and then watched as he licked and sucked his way up my abdomen to my chest and finally my throat. His fingers moved deeper inside me, and I rose up off the seat to push my skin against his hot mouth. I saw his fangs for a second before they were buried in me. The pain was excruciating, but my attention went instantly to his withdrawing fingers. He put both hands on my hips and I was lifted, transferred from the cool leather to his lap.

His long, thick, dripping cock slid easily between my parted cheeks, reached my entrance, and pushed inside. I gasped because he was so big, so hard, stretching me instantly, painfully, tight.

"Did I hurt you?"

"Yes… and no." The sting was already easing, and I shifted against him, seating myself deeper so he'd know that the pain was of no consequence when balanced against the pleasure.

"I'm trying to be gentle."

"Gentle is not what I need," I whimpered, trying to get him to move. At twenty-four, my libido was boundless, and just his skin touching mine made me crazy. I had been ready to drop dead before I took a shower, but seeing the man, having his mouth on me, had woken me.

His growl was instant as he gripped my thighs, sliding his swollen rod in deeper as his fingers worked over my hardening cock.

I lifted up, feeling the slide of lube and every inch of receding pressure before his breathing faltered and caught as I sank slowly back down onto him, holding him tight within my clenching rings of muscle.

"I need to be buried in you."

"Please," I barely got out.

The second he pounded on the window separating us from the driver, the car slowed and stopped. He slipped back out of me, flung open the door, and yanked me from the car after him. It was pitch-dark outside, and there was no one on the road but us. The headlights of the car illuminated the trees on the opposite side of the street.

I was hurled up against the side of the car, gasping as my stomach and chest hit the cold steel, my hands flat on the glass, my face turned to try and see him in the cloaking darkness.

"Don't look at me," he snarled, and his voice was deeper, barely his, so low, almost guttural.

I turned my face to the darkness as his thighs touched mine, his hands grasping my ass, forcing my cheeks roughly apart, the head of his cock against my hole for a second before he buried himself inside me.

The pain was like a hammer, and then he pulled back only to slam into me again, this time deeper, harder.

I yelled, and he pumped into me fast, the pain becoming pleasure with every thrust. As my muscles relaxed and the heat built and built, I called his name. His arm came past me, and his hand, no longer human, plastered to the window, his claws clicking against the glass, sliding over it but finding no grip. He needed leverage, needed me at a different angle, lower so he could be buried in me like he wanted. Suddenly, his other hand gripped my throat, and I felt the long, sharp knives biting into my flesh. He was trying to be so gentle; I felt the restraint, the trembling of his body as he fought for control.

"Let me move," I whispered as he leaned my head back on his shoulder, the other, now cold from the glass, closing around my cock. There was something so primitive and scary about razor-sharp claws sliding over my shaft; he could maim me, kill me, but instead only wanted to fuck me. "Logan, let me move."

But he was lost, his body surging into mine, whimpering and growling, frustrated that he could not get deep enough inside me but unwilling to stop and pull out, refusing to leave the heat of my body. I flung myself sideways, trying to get back to the door, but he stopped me, slamming me forward against the car.

"Just stay inside me," I soothed, hearing the sharp whimper in my ear and knowing his need for release was desperate. "Follow me, move with me."

I inched toward the light, and he stayed inside me even as I fell forward into the car, into the warmth, my hands stopping me from hitting the leather seat, bracing my arms so I was bent over. His clawed hands dug into my hips as he thrust forward so hard he lifted me off my feet.

"Oh, God," I cried out, the sensation of him so deep inside me making me light-headed.

"Jin," he growled, and I felt the claws cut into my skin as he rammed in and out of me, setting a pounding rhythm that I was not strong enough to hold against.

My arms gave out, but he stopped me from collapsing with a hand at my waist, his other on the seat under me, all his weight and mine on his one arm. The muscles corded, and then, a second later, I saw that his skin was covered in golden fur. His face nuzzled my hair, and I heard the huff of hot breath before the knife was buried in my shoulder. Hot liquid ran down my chest and I realized instantly that I was looking at blood. My cock was so hard and swollen in his hand, and then he hit the spot deep inside me, and my orgasm roared through me. I screamed as semen splashed his hand and slipped down onto the seat. I went limp in his arms as he forced my face down, my ass in the air, my knees now under me. His long, slippery cock was gliding in and out of me again and again, and I knew I was going to pass out. I had never been used so hard, so long, and the fact was, he wanted to be deeper still.

"Stop," I said softly, my voice barely audible. I had a feeling, and I had to act on it. What he thought he wanted and what he needed were two different things. He thought he needed to tear me apart, but I knew better. He needed me to see him.

"No," he snarled, sounding like a beast instead of a man.

"Yes... stop."

His control, even as gone as he was, drowning in a frenzy of need, was absolute. I had told him to stop, so he froze, and I slid off his shaft and crumpled to the floor.

I rolled over on my back and looked up at him, at the half-man now towering over me. He was covered in golden fur, his face still his but bigger, wider, allowing for enormous sharp fangs and powerful jaws. His shoulders rose to a thick neck corded with muscle, but the rest was still Logan, just bigger, stronger, more heavily muscled, and even more powerful. His cock was unchanged, still human, still long and thick and cut and beautiful. It was amazing to watch his transformation, and I would have, would have studied him, but his eyes were full of pain and anger and need.

"Come here."

He shook his head.

We were beyond speech at that point, so I reached out my arms to receive him.

"I want you," I told him, staring into eyes now completely changed, having bled to all-gold. "Come here."

He was on me so fast, and I trembled in his arms as he licked a path up my throat to my jaw and finally to my lips. He inhaled my panting breath and gently bit my bottom lip before his tongue flicked inside my mouth, sliding in deep, as he came down on top of me, pinning me to the floor. His arms were wrapped tight around my back as he continued to claim my mouth. Never had I been so desired, so needed, wanted, and craved. And even more, I was safe. This man would never hurt me, and I was certain of it for reasons I didn't understand but accepted nonetheless.

His tongue was tangled with mine as he lifted my legs over his shoulders, rose to his knees, and guided his shaft to my entrance.

"Fuck me," I breathed as he slid inside me.

We both froze for a heartbeat of time before he eased out only to push in again as far as he could go, the powerful forward thrust and his hips at just the right angle to fill my world with pulsating, devouring bliss.

I yelled his name, demanding he not stop… ever. I reached up to hold the face of the animal he was, saw the heavy-lidded, lust-filled eyes, and heard the satisfied growl as he plunged down into me.

I wanted to make him promise to never let me go, but I swallowed it down instead. My tongue felt thick in my mouth, my body heavy and liquid as his claws again dug into my hips, pulling me tight to his groin, his shaft buried so deep in my body. His teeth were on my collarbone, biting, licking, and sucking as he marked me. I would be black and blue in the morning.

"Jin," he said slowly, lifting his head to look down at me, his voice deep and husky, so sexy and so his.

I could only stare, the man having returned completely to human form.

"How did you know?"

"Know what?"

His lips curled into a sensual, lazy grin as his fingers dug into my thighs, the animal not completely gone. "That I needed you to accept me as both man and beast?"

"I just… I know you."

He nodded. "I have never changed this way for anyone but you. Only you shatter my control, and only you can repair it. You are my strength now, and this is your piece to carry for the rest of your life. You are responsible for me, to me. Do you understand?"

My voice was gone; I didn't even try to talk.

"Never, ever leave me."

My eyes flitted away. I couldn't maintain his stare. He was so much stronger than me, inside and out.

He thrust deep inside me, and my back bowed. I had forgotten for a moment that he was still buried inside me, but he had reminded me, hard.

"Mine, forever."

I absorbed his words, the gravity of what he was saying, the threat as well as the promise.

"God, will you look at me? Don't take your eyes off me."

When I lifted my gaze to his, he bent and ground his hot mouth down over mine, his tongue slipping between my lips, kissing me deep and thorough, showing me whom I belonged to. No one had ever wanted me the way he did.

"Mine," he growled into my hair, rubbing his face in it.

I had so much inside to say, but the feel of him filling me at the same time he stared down into my eyes, never looking away, his gaze unwavering, was too much. I yelled myself hoarse. My name came out as a roar as he found his shattering release. He was careful not to crush me when he collapsed.

WE RODE in silence, both of us with our clothes back on, me sprawled in his lap as the car ascended the mountain road up toward his home. I was horrified that the driver knew I was having sex in the back of the car, but Logan proclaimed it natural and that a semel never apologized for claiming his mate wherever and whenever he wanted. Before I could give him a piece of my mind, he pulled me into his lap and wrapped me in his arms.

"Look outside."

I turned my head to the left, and the window lowered.

A gust of cold air blew against my face, but it was the view that made me catch my breath. There was a small lake framed by giant pines on the opposite shore, and the reflected moonlight made it seem as though a million tiny diamonds glittered across the frozen surface, winking at the sky. To my right, there was a sheer wall of ice that had been blasted smooth by the wind. It shone like frosted glass and seemed dusted with iridescent powder. The scene was like a postcard, and as we came to a stop, there was only the still night air and yawning silence. I didn't want to talk, afraid that I would splinter the world with just the sound of my voice. It was a perfect moment.

The window was still down, but there was no way for me to be cold, not with Logan giving me his heat, his big, hard body like a furnace.

"As far as you can see, it's all mine. Not my family's, mine. They all live down in Reno except for Koren and Delphine, but me, I live up here on the land we hunt on. I have the glassworks, and attached to it is a showroom where I—"

"Show off your art?" I asked, turning in his lap to look at his face.

"No," he chuckled. "I'm not an artist, love; we make glassware. We used to just do bar glasses and drinking glasses, beer mugs, all that kinda stuff, but now we're starting to make fancy stemware like champagne flutes and goblets and—"

"Jewelry?"

"What?"

"Beads?"

"I'm sorry?" he chuckled, his hand back in my hair, twirling it around his fingers.

"Do you make glass beads for earrings and necklaces or glass rings, like they make in Italy? Do you do any of that?"

"I… no." He was staring blankly at my face.

"Is something wrong?"

"No, but what you just said was brilliant."

"What'd I say?"

"Making jewelry is a really great idea."

"Sure. Women will dig it, and they've gotta be your core demographic, right?"

He squinted at me. "Lemme guess—college degree in marketing?"

I grinned. "Yeah. What you need is a web site."

He nodded. "I'll let you take care of that for me."

I just smiled.

"So tell me everything about you, starting now."

I shook my head. "No. I refuse to have our first real conversation while I'm sitting in your lap. If you want me to get dressed, have coffee in your kitchen, be all serious, I say okay. But I'm not baring my soul in the back of your car."

"Okay," he said, his hands sliding over my shoulder blades, down the length of my spine to the curve of my lower back. "You feel so good."

"So do you," I said, my hands flat on his smooth, sculpted chest, my fingers moving over the warm, golden skin, down the flat, cut stomach, and lower, to his unbuckled belt.

"Tell me something," he said, and when my eyes flicked to his, I realized that they were heavy-lidded, narrowed in half. "Did it hurt—before… did I hurt you?"

"No," I assured him, my hand over his heart. "I swear."

He nodded, reaching out to brush the hair out of my eyes. "I am so crazy about your face."

"Well, I'm kinda fond of yours, myself."

There was a deep sigh before I saw a shadow cross his beautiful chiseled features. "Tell me about the guy who attacked you."

I pulled back, staring into his eyes. "It was Crane's situation, not mine. I got involved because the guy came for him and found me instead."

"He wasn't a cat, was he?"

"No."

"Then why was there blood?"

"He surprised me while I was asleep. As soon as I was actually awake, I got him off me." He nodded. "But I'm okay; you can see I am."

He grabbed me suddenly, wrapping me in his arms, holding me tight, a hand buried in my hair, the other across my back, hugging me to him. I felt the shudder run through his huge frame.

"Everything's fine," I said into the side of his throat, kissing the warm skin. "And besides… I have you to protect me, now."

"Yes, you do," he promised.

I felt the tears well up in my eyes.

"You have a soft heart," he said as he kissed me deep and slow, and it was as sensual and hot as it had been rough and demanding earlier. I had to be so careful, or I could fall so very hard.

"I have a question for you," I said as I eased back, my eyes on his.

"Ask me anything."

"If I'm the first guy you've ever been with, how did you know what to do?"

His hand went to my cheek, caressing it. "I did what I would want done to me."

"With your mouth," I clarified.

The smile was evil. "Yes."

"And the rest?"

"I wanted to be inside you, so I was."

"Well, I've never known a straight man that gave a better blowjob."

He chuckled. "Well, I'm not straight anymore."

"No, I guess not," I sighed, my body getting heavy, my eyes barely able to stay open.

"There's no 'guess,'" he said, tucking me against his chest and stroking my hair. "My mate is a man, and therefore I can be no other than gay."

He was amazing, plain and simple.

"I will protect you from now on—and your annoying friend, as well."

He was right, Crane was annoying, but that Logan included him without question made me happier than I could express.

"Rest, baby, I have you."

I was going to mention to him again that I was not his baby, but between his fingers massaging my scalp, the heat from his body, and the steady rise and fall of the road, I didn't feel like arguing with him.

Chapter Ten

LOGAN AND I stayed up well into the early hours of Sunday morning before I finally passed out in his arms. The last thing I remembered was soft kisses along my throat. When I rolled out of bed after ten, Logan was gone, so after I showered and changed, I went to find him. Downstairs, in the kitchen, I was surprised by the number of people standing around, talking, plates of food in their hands. I realized the house was probably filled with people there for the mating ceremony the following day, and my stomach clenched. Everyone was expecting him to take Simone as his mate, and there I was in the mix. I would have gone back upstairs if someone hadn't called my name. When I turned, Eva Church was suddenly beside me.

"Good morning, Jin."

I tried to smile.

"What's wrong?"

Was she kidding?

"Sweetheart?"

I gestured around. "All these people are here to see Logan take Simone as his yareah, and I just feel like…." I trailed off, suddenly wanting to scream. Didn't everyone know that the man belonged to me?

"Jin," Eva chuckled, taking my hand and holding it tight. "Honey, look at me."

My eyes flicked back to her face, and I noticed how she was looking at me, like she was proud. What in the world was going on?

"Jin, dear, no one is under the impression that Logan is still taking Simone as his yareah. He made an announcement. Everyone knows that you're his mate."

I was confused. "But then what are all these people doing here, if they didn't come for a mating ceremony? I don't get it."

"Sweetheart, everyone's here to see you."

"Me?" I was stunned.

"Yes. I had no idea… I never knew, I mean, I knew reahs were special and rare, but I had no clue whatsoever that… I wasn't raised to understand. I didn't know that you…." She trailed off, her eyes welling up, softening. "Goodness, Jin, I'm rambling, but I didn't know that a semel finding his reah was just this side of a miracle. I didn't know that there was a special title, that the semel became semel-re, and that's it just about the biggest deal ever."

I took a deep breath.

"Darling, I had no idea." I smiled at her as she stared back. After several moments, she took a breath. "Well, you must be starving," she said as she smiled, giving my hand a final squeeze before she let it go. "I've been cooking all morning. Let me make you a plate, all right?"

"Sure," I agreed.

I took the plate she offered me when she was done piling it with food. She was used to making portions for her huge sons. She would have to learn moderation with me.

I took my breakfast and a huge mug of coffee and walked first through the hole in the crowd that was made for me and then to the couch by the fireplace. Before I could start to eat, there was a throat clearing.

I looked up into the face of Logan's father.

"We haven't met formally."

"But I know who you are," I said, rising to face the man. "I'd offer you my hand, but I know you wouldn't accept it."

Peter shook his head. "I would, though. I would like to."

Was I dreaming?

He offered me his hand. "I'm Peter Church, Logan's father, and you're his reah."

"I am." I nodded, taking the older man's hand and shaking it. "It's a pleasure, sir."

"Oh, Jin." He smiled warmly. "The pleasure is all mine. I can't even tell you."

It was? Since when?

"May I speak to you, please?" he asked as he finally let go of my hand.

I gestured to the loveseat across from me before I sank back down.

"Jin," he said as he sat, leaning forward, hands clasped. "You must forgive me. You see, I never found my reah, and so even though I knew of them, I'd never seen one myself. I thought that a reah was really the same as a yareah. I had no idea it was any different at all. I mean, how could it really be? Taking a mate or finding one, big deal."

"But all this," I said, gesturing around at the milling crowd, "all these people, this has changed your mind?"

"Yes."

"So you'll accept me because of this," I said, trying to keep the chill of out my voice.

"No, not just because of this," he said softly. "I know now that your very presence is a blessing. I didn't understand that yesterday."

In his eyes, I saw only sincerity. The difference from the day before was like night and day.

"Can you forgive my blindness?"

"Yes." I nodded before I started to eat. If I were stuffing food in my mouth, maybe he wouldn't notice that I was close to tears. I had never been emotional, but since Logan had come into my life, I was a wreck.

"I was scared that Logan would lose our tribe, but this morning, people started showing up."

I tried to act like I was listening, but he couldn't know the words weren't really important, only the way he was looking at me. The father of my mate was excited, and he radiated warmth and acceptance. I could barely hold my fork because my hands were shaking.

"Jin? Are you all right?"

I nodded, taking a sip of my coffee to wash down the lump in my throat.

"This must all be fairly overwhelming."

He had no idea. No matter how hard I tried not to get excited, I could feel it welling up inside me. I blamed Logan. In a matter of days, the man had managed to tear down walls that had taken years to construct. I was so close to having a family again, and I was scared to let it happen and scared that it wouldn't.

"You were banished from your tribe for being a reah, or for being gay?"

I cleared my throat, but still my voice came out hoarse and cracking. "Both."

"I can only imagine. There you were at fifteen or sixteen, changing for the first time, only to discover that you're a reah. Your father had to have been terrified."

I shook my head. "He was horrified."

He nodded. "I'm so sorry."

No one could know the extent of the ambush. In a matter of minutes, my father had gone from being the person I admired most in the world—my teacher, my friend, my hero, my protector—to the man who tried to kill me, all in the course of one afternoon when I was sixteen. I had already changed several times without telling anyone. My parents had both been waiting for the day I could first shift into a panther, but when I had finally done it and become a werepanther instead, taking the form that was half-man, half-beast, I knew I was a reah. It made sense, because even though I loved girls, I had never had the urge to make love to girls. I accepted being a reah, and at the next hunt, before we began, in front of my father and my semel and the entire tribe, I announced that I was a reah, gladly accepted being gay, and shifted for them into werepanther form so there could be no mistake.

I had anticipated confusion and shock, not outrage and anger and my father calling for my death. I was vile and filthy. My mother called me an abomination and ran away, my brother turned his back on me, claiming I was dead, refusing to speak to me ever again, and while I was staring after them, the tears streaming down my face, my father attacked me from behind, putting me in a choke hold and hurling me to the ground. Then the beating began. I lifted my head only once, to look for Crane because I could hear him screaming. It took three men to hold him down. I wasn't able to see him for long, as my semel had delivered the first kick to my face.

There were pieces I remembered and time that I lost. I was ordered to shift back to full human, but I was afraid that in that form, I would die, so I remained in a ball while they did their worst. I went in and out of consciousness. I woke up once, and my father, whom I loved, was cutting off my hair with a knife. When they saw I was awake, they beat me until I passed out. The second time I woke up, my sheseru, Crane's father, was yelling at the men gathered around me. He would bury me alive, he roared, before he let anyone rape me. He told them that if they violated me, they would then be no better than me, a perversion. I understood that he had saved me from that horror even as he proceeded to break my arm in two places with a baseball bat. I had never known pain like that.

I woke finally on the side of the road, naked, bleeding, gravel embedded in my skin, pieces of it torn off from where I had been dragged, Crane told me later, behind a car. When I heard the running footsteps, I thought I was done, but when my eyes lifted, I found Crane. He wasn't sure where to touch me, but he picked me up, getting blood all over his clothes, and carried me to his car. He hid me with friends who didn't understand why I wasn't in a hospital but, being young, didn't question him. Crane was the oldest of our group; he was eighteen, the rest of us younger, and so he was deferred to, his popularity working in our favor so that everyone kept quiet. We knew a lot of rich kids with rich parents who were always away. It was easy to hide out in pool houses and cabanas and spare rooms. It took me a month to heal all the damage.

Crane and I were exiled, considered dead, and could never return to the tribe, but because the tribe could not have questions asked by outside authorities, Child Protective Services, our principal, our teachers, or the police, an apartment was rented for us downtown, close to our school. But that was all that was done. We had to pay to keep the heat on, pay for our food, our clothes, and college, if that were where we were headed. It was hard for us at sixteen and eighteen to work full-time and go to school, but we looked trustworthy, so I was given the graveyard shift at a copy shop and Crane took a job as a security guard. We both graduated with athletic scholarships; I could swim like a fish and Crane was an amazing defensive lineman. We left for Arizona as soon as we could. I had decided as I flew away from Chicago that never again would I concern myself with any part of being a werepanther. But now, because of Logan Church, everything had changed.

In a matter of days, Crane and I had gone from belonging nowhere to belonging to a tribe again. It was too good to be true, and the moment I let myself be happy, I was terrified that something would go horribly wrong. I never let my guard down, I had never trusted any panther after that day when I was sixteen, and I never breathed another word about being a reah to anyone. When Crane and I accidentally came into contact with other panthers, we parted company quickly before they sensed anything out of the ordinary. I had been careful, scary careful, Crane told me often, until I had smiled at Yuri Kosa. It was the first time in eight years that I had willingly revealed what I was.

"Jin."

I came out of the fog of my memories to see the face of Logan's father.

"I'm sorry that you heard my harsh words about you to Logan. If I could take them back, I would, but I cannot. I will only ask that you give me a second chance."

I nodded because I was afraid to speak.

"Everyone makes mistakes."

"Yes," I barely got out.

"And now look."

I watched Peter, saw the delight there as he gestured around the room, saw Logan crossing the floor to me, smiling wide. I realized that just seeing the man made my heart swell.

"Morning," he said as he took a seat beside me, leaning in to kiss my forehead. "Can you believe it?"

I squinted at him, and he turned to look at Peter. "You didn't tell him?"

"I was getting to it. I wanted to apologize first."

"No, you don't have to," I told him.

"Yes, he does," Logan said flatly, his voice lowering to almost a growl. "You were afraid to stay with me because of what my father said. He will make amends."

"Jin." Peter rose and then knelt in front of me. "When everyone heard that Logan had found his mate, meaning his reah… suddenly they all wanted to join our tribe. Twenty people came before any of us were even awake this morning. I got up and found them all on the porch freezing." He smiled at me. "And then more and more people came, all of them just waiting around to see you, meet you." He took a breath, staring at me. "I forgot that a semel who can find his reah is considered semel-re, and that *any* panther would choose to be a follower of his."

I didn't trust that it was going to be this easy. Things were never easy for me.

"Baby, look at me," Logan ordered.

I turned to look into the honey-colored eyes of my mate.

"Because of you, our tribe will be bigger than either Christophe's or Domin's, even if they unite. Everyone wants to be in a tribe with a semel and a reah."

"Why?"

"A semel able to find his mate is a blessed man, and so is his tribe. A semel with a reah is the kind of man people want to follow."

I nodded.

"So now I only have to meet Domin in the pit, and everything will be finished."

It took me a second. "What'd you say?"

He took my hand, leaned forward to look into my eyes. "He finally accepted my challenge."

Even though I was frightened for him, I knew Logan could beat him. In that second, I was prepared to be supportive.

"He had a stipulation, though."

My heart stopped. "What stipulation?"

"He asked me for the sons of something." He shrugged. "It's not important. The only thing that matters is that he accepted. I'll beat him, and then everything will be perfect."

I could barely breathe.

"He promised me, in front of witnesses, that if I win, that he will release those in his tribe that want to join mine, and he will pledge to never again attack any member of my family or my tribe. Everyone will be safe."

He looked so pleased, completely ignorant of his own peril, his concern, as always, with others before himself.

"Isn't that amazing?"

I absorbed his words, and I knew that it was too late to safeguard myself from loving the man. The thought of losing him hurt worse than anything I could imagine. He was my mate, my other half, the only person I would ever, *could* ever share the bond I felt in my heart. And he had just allowed himself to be killed because he had not spoken to me before he agreed to a deal with devil. He had no idea the advantage he had given Domin Thorne.

"Logan." I breathed out his name. "Why didn't you talk to me first?"

"Jin, I—"

"You should have consulted me." My brain was whirling, trying to remember, as fast as I could, every law I had ever read and everything my father had ever taught me.

"No," he said flatly, brows furrowing. "I shouldn't have. I will always do what I feel is in the best interest of the tribe, and those decisions do not concern you."

"Everything about this tribe concerns me."

"Jin—"

"Especially anything you decide personally."

"Baby—"

"You have no idea what you've done," I said, feeling like there was cold wind blowing through me. "You've changed my path just as surely as you've changed your own."

Instantly there was concern in his eyes. "What are you talking about?"

"Do you know what the four Sons of Horus means?"

"That's what it was." He smiled at me.

"Do you know what it means?" I snapped.

His smile faltered and then fell away as he looked at me. "I didn't even know what it... no, I—"

"You agreed to let Domin Thorne bring four others with him into the pit. You won't be facing just Domin; it will be him and probably his sheseru and sylvan and another two of his khatyu."

Logan absorbed what I'd told him. "Okay."

"Okay?" I half yelled. "That's all you have to say?"

"He won't win."

"He can't lose," I corrected.

Logan grabbed my hand and held it tight in his, his smile meant to be reassuring. "Baby, I'll win, I promise."

But he couldn't. Against one, maybe even two, my mate would prevail, but one against five… he would be outnumbered, out-muscled; there would be too many sets of teeth and claws, too many ways for him to be cornered, pinned down, maneuvered around. He would be slaughtered.

"And if he wins?"

"He won't."

"If he does," I repeated, yelling this time, standing up, looking down at him.

You could hear a pin drop in the room.

"He won't win!" he roared back, standing up in one fluid moment to tower over me. "Don't you have any faith at all?"

"I have faith," I told him, and I heard my voice shake. "When it's fair."

"Jin." He took a shallow breath, reaching for my hand. "Let's go talk about—"

"By law, if he wins, he can cut out your heart," I said, taking a step away from him.

"Yes, but—"

"He can hold you down and use his claws and dig it out of your chest." The words were more for me than for him; hearing them spoken, they had weight and significance. Aloud, I understood the moment for what it was: life and death. My mate could be butchered alive if and when he lost to invincible odds. I couldn't even breathe.

Logan grabbed my arms and yanked me up against him. "He won't win. If I die, we'll be parted, and I can't allow that."

The words were confident, meant to express his feelings for me, but he was still talking like there would only be him and

Domin in the pit; he didn't comprehend his peril. I did, though; I understood that the fight would be blood sport and nothing more, the torture and slaughter of my mate that I would never, could never, allow.

I shoved him off me, taking several steps back. "When is the challenge?"

"Tonight. What's—"

"If it's tonight, where's his sheseru?"

"He's here."

"And Yuri's with Domin?"

"Yes." He was squinting at me. "Everything's being done according to—"

"Where's his sheseru?"

He looked over his shoulder and yelled, "Markel!"

A man cut across the room to us. He was tall, lean, his face angular and carved. He was dressed all in black. He looked like something animated, a lovely work of manga, something that couldn't possibly have existed in nature, too fragile and perfect.

"Reah," he breathed, his dark cobalt blue eyes swallowing me. "I have so wanted to meet you. I have never seen one like you before."

"We met," I realized. "The night you were hunting Delphine, we met."

His eyes widened even as he sneered at me. "If I'd known you were a reah, I would have taken you myself and only afterward presented you to my semel once you were tamed."

Tamed? He was talking about rape.

"You forget yourself," Logan barked.

He scoffed. "I meant no disrespect to you, Logan. It's just the truth. I didn't get close enough to him, or I would have known."

"No," I spat back. "You ran like a dog. You make me sick!" I roared at him, and he flinched when I charged him.

Logan's arm across my chest stopped me from reaching him.

"He's so passionate, semel." He smirked at Logan. "You must enjoy that."

I felt Logan's heartbeat against my back, felt how steady it was. It calmed me enough that I could get out the words that needed to be spoken. "I call for the Law of Bast."

Markel's head snapped up, and his eyes were huge as he stared at me.

I repeated it in ancient Greek for him as I had been taught.

"No." He shook his head.

"We both know it's not your choice."

"What?" Logan asked, turning me around in his arms. "What is the Law of Bast? What is that?"

But my focus was on Markel. I had my head turned away from Logan so I could see him. "You must accept… Domin would have to accept."

"But, reah, do you know what—"

"Say it!" I railed. There was no delaying the inevitable. It was his place to agree.

"I accept the Law of Bast on behalf of my semel, Domin Thorne," he breathed, his eyes fixed on me. "Who will stand as aset?"

"Simone."

He nodded slowly. His expression that had been so confident and full of contempt only moments before, was now saddened, the smirk erased from his face, replaced by a look of confusion. "Why?"

"Because Domin can't have his heart. It's mine."

"But, reah, surely—"

"Get out!" I roared. "Send Yuri back safely, or you and your semel are subject to the punishment of the law."

"I know the law! Don't presume to lecture me on the law!"

I was shaking with fury, and so was he.

"The winnowing happens when you are still alive, reah! I will take the flesh myself."

I spit at him, and he lunged at me. Logan caught him by the throat and held him off the ground.

"You forget yourself, Markel," he warned him, his voice icy. "This is my mate, my reah. You can be butchered for this transgression."

He went pale because it was true. Anyone who threatened the mate of the leader of the tribe was considered to have forfeited his or her life.

"Get out of my house," I snarled, letting him see my fangs as Logan released him. "Deliver my challenge to Domin and return my sheseru!"

He turned and ran for the door, others I didn't know were with him following.

"Look at me," Logan yelled, shaking me.

I lifted my gaze to his.

"What is the Law of Bast? What have you done?"

I twisted free of his hands, stepped back and faced him. "Your first concern is your tribe. Mine is you. You've never had a reah, so you don't know, but I am your protector."

He took a step forward, and I took one back.

"What the fuck is going on?" Logan shouted, grabbing my arm, yanking me back to him. "What have you done?"

"I am your protector."

"Why do you keep saying that?" he snapped. "Yuri, my sheseru, he is my protector."

"He's your enforcer," I corrected. "Only I, your mate, your reah—I'm the only protector you have, Logan Church."

His brows furrowed. "What is the Law of Bast?"

I took a deep breath. "The Law of Bast says that I will fight in your stead."

His eyes got huge; he was stunned, and I used that second to pull free and take several steps away from him. There were others around us, Mikhail, Peter, Koren, and Russ. I saw Crane crossing the room to me.

"I won't allow it."

"You have no say," I told him.

"My word is law!" he yelled, trying to grab me.

I moved out of his reach.

"Except in regards to your reah," Peter said, his voice soft, almost sad. "Jin's voice is equal to yours."

"What are you talking about? Only my word has—"

"The commands of the reah equal that of the semel in all matters but tribal law," Mikhail told him. "You know this."

"This is law!" he roared.

"It's not," Peter assured him. "It's an individual challenge."

"We haven't had our mating ceremony," Logan yelled. "He's not my reah yet."

"He bears your mark," Koren reminded him. "In the eyes of the tribe, by the laws and customs of all tribes, he is your reah."

"I need to get out of here," I breathed, heading for the doorway.

"Jin!" I heard Logan roar after me. "Don't you dare walk away from me!"

"I'm not allowed to see you anymore," I said, taking hold of Mikhail's arm as I passed him. "You need to keep him away from me."

"What?" His face drained of color. "Are you crazy?"

"No," Peter yelled from behind me. "Hold your semel at bay, Mikhail. It's the law."

Mikhail looked like a cornered animal.

I tried to soothe him with my voice. "I have to be sequestered before my trial," I said softly as I moved by him. "It is your duty to keep me safe, to keep my path to the pit clear. I'm going back to my room. Keep your semel safely away from me."

He was ashen, shaking. "Keep my semel from you, from his mate?"

"It's the law," I said solemnly, looking at Logan over my shoulder as he was almost to me.

"I don't under—"

"Your semel accepted a challenge from a man that knows more about our laws than he does, and now he has been spared because I, in turn, know more than Domin. I will deliver your semel, and you need only to do your duty and keep him away from me. The next time he sees me will be in the pit."

His face looked like I'd struck him.

"I'm sorry," I whispered as I moved by him. "You have no choice."

"Jin." Mikhail's voice cracked. "You cannot do this."

"*He* did it by acting rashly." Everything was blurring suddenly, and I had to get out of the room before I broke down in front of everyone. I would not shame Logan with such a display of weakness. "Keep him away from me."

"Jin!" Logan bellowed my name.

Before he could reach me, Mikhail and four other men had him. He screamed for me, but I left the room without a backward glance. It wouldn't do either of us any good.

I WAS on the covered balcony outside Logan's bedroom, sitting quietly with Crane on the chaise beside me. I was watching the snow fall when Peter found me. It was silent before he got there except for the howl of the wind.

"Logan wants to see you."

"I can't. It's the law," I told him, not tearing my eyes away from the blinding whiteness, the mountains, trees, and ground all being relentlessly covered.

He sighed deeply. "I never had him learn all the laws. He had no idea about the Law of Bast."

"Or the Sons of Horus," I reminded him.

"No."

I nodded.

"It's my failing, Jin, not his."

"The failure was in his rashness," I insisted. "Had he consulted his mate, I would have explained the danger to him, and he would have turned down committing suicide. As it was, he didn't think about me at all."

"He thought about his tribe."

"And in so doing, would have gotten himself killed."

"He's the semel, Jin. He's never going to think of you first."

"A true semel thinks of his tribe through his reah, consults his reah as he would his sheseru or sylvan, and speaks his heart to his mate at all times."

"How would you know?"

"I feel it."

There was no argument for that, because he didn't know. The man had never found his reah. "He should have come to me first before agreeing to anything."

"This union of yours is a day old, Jin. He needs time to change his thinking."

"Unfortunately, he's not going to get it."

Peter went silent for several long moments before he spoke again. "Tell me, is your father a sylvan?"

"Yes."

"So he taught you all the laws."

"Yes."

"I should call your father, Jin, just in case…"

He didn't want to say in case I died, but we both knew I certainly would. "Do as you like," I told him.

"Tell me where he is."

"Logan knows. Ask him," I said, turning to look at Crane. He was tired, and worrying about me wasn't helping. He had basically passed out.

"He doesn't look concerned," Peter rendered his judgment.

"Looks can be deceiving."

We were silent again before we were interrupted by Koren, who came striding out onto the balcony. He walked just like his brother and his father, like he was king, like everything he was looking at belonged to him, put there specifically for his pleasure.

"Is there something you want?"

"Yeah," he said, crouching down beside the chaise I was stretched out on. "I wanted to tell you that I never had a problem with you, just in case you thought I did."

"No…?"

"No," he assured me. "You're my brother's reah, and that's all I care about. Period."

I stared into the olive green eyes of my mate's younger brother. Logan was born first, then Koren, and finally Russ. I would have enjoyed learning about my mate's siblings if I had been given more time.

"I just wanted you to know that."

"Thank you."

"You're welcome." He nodded, his eyes soft as he looked at me. "Yuri is back."

"And he's fine?"

"He is. Would you like to see him?"

"Yes."

"Simone is here," Peter chimed in quickly. "You named her aset, so you should see her if you feel up to it."

"I will see her."

"I'll go get them both," Koren offered, bolting from the room. It was uncomfortable, being around someone who was going to die. I would have run too.

I thought Peter had gone with his son, but when he cleared his throat, I realized he was still there. I turned my head so I could see him.

"Please forgive me, Jin. I had no idea the kind of man you were."

I shrugged. "It doesn't matter."

"Don't talk like you're dead," he commanded.

My eyes flicked to his. "And why not?"

His jaw clenched, and I saw the pain in his eyes. I looked back to my serene view and forgot about him. Minutes later, Yuri joined me. He looked terrible, his eyes consumed with worry.

"Why are you acting like this?" I asked. "You would rather lose me than your semel. Don't deny it."

"I don't want to lose either of you. We've only just been blessed with you, my reah."

I smiled at him. "Since when did I become your reah?"

"When you took the mark of my semel and became his mate. From that second, you became the reah of my tribe. I am as pledged to you as I am to him."

I stared into his eyes and saw that the pain was real. Losing me was going to be hard for him, even more so because he would have to watch and do nothing. He would stand there, frozen, knowing that he could save me at any time but was forbidden from doing so.

"I don't know if I can bear it."

"You will bear it because Logan's going to need you." I squinted at him. "I expect you and Markel to uphold the law. Call Christophe and have him send his sheseru, Avery, as well, see if he himself will come and bring his sylvan. I know he hates Logan right now, so seeing him lose his reah might appeal to him."

"Jin, don't—"

"The more people there, the better. I don't want Domin going after Logan when I'm dead."

The muscles in his jaw were working, his eyes red-rimmed as he held himself together. "Please don't speak as though you're—"

"Enough with the crap," I said irritably. "There's going to be five of them in the pit with me. I can't hope to win; I can only hope that, by my sacrifice, I can keep Logan safe."

He looked away from me.

"If I don't die during the fight, they'll perform a winnowing, Markel already told me."

His head snapped back around, and his eyes were terrified as he stared at me.

"If they do it in front of Logan, you'll have restrain him."

Yuri sat there absolutely still but for his blinking eyes. "They'll skin you alive."

"They'll cut first, or maybe use a whip," I answered as coolly as I could, working hard not to let any emotion creep in. "I don't know, but that part and after… when they finally cut my throat… I need you to be the sheseru that no one should ever have to be and keep your semel restrained. It may be days before you'll be able to release him. Do you understand?"

He nodded.

"Domin will have my life, and he is to be either paid or given land. I don't remember how much. It's in the ode of Sekhmet, but I'm not sure where."

"I know where it is."

"Good. So you'll pay him, and then your tribe and his will live without any more hostility. He and Logan's feud will be done."

"You honestly believe that Logan won't kill Domin?"

"Yes, I do, because you won't let him. It's your place, yours and Mikhail's, to never let him near Domin again for as long as either of them lives."

Tears slid down his cheeks.

"This is *maat*. You know it is. Logan can't kill Domin, and it's the only way he'll ever stop tormenting Logan's tribe. I can't watch Domin kill Logan, and without your semel, the tribe is dead."

"Yes."

"So this is all I know to do to save the man I love."

"You love him?"

I had said it out loud. "Shit."

"Have you said it to Logan?"

I looked away from him.

"Jin?"

"Go away. I'm tired."

"Jin, I—"

"Go away, Yuri."

"I just… I don't want you to—"

"Jin!"

We both turned to Simone as she charged out onto the balcony. She fell to her knees in front of me, grabbing my hands in hers, her face lifted to mine as if she were praying.

"What the hell's going on?" Crane growled from the other chaise, Simone's voice having woken him.

"What you took, you have replaced. Bless you, reah!"

"Are you all right?" I asked her.

"I don't know what I am or how to feel. To be chosen as aset is a great honor, but the reason for it is barbaric, and… I want you to live."

I sat up and made room for her beside me on the chaise. "I truly never meant to cause you any pain. That was never my intention."

"I know that." Her voice cracked as tears filled her eyes. "And I know you didn't steal him from me. You're his mate, his true-mate, and I was a choice he made. It's not the same."

"But now everything's different."

She nodded, the tears making speech difficult.

"Listen," I said gently. "When I fall, he's yours, and I expect you to protect him as I would until you die."

The tears were rolling down her cheeks.

"If I live or die, your place is high. You are aset, the throne, and you cannot be taken by another who is not a semel. Do you understand? An aset has the same station as a reah."

"I know. I know the law." She trembled, her hands clutching mine, her voice dropping to a whisper. "Forgive me for what I said yesterday. Please, reah, I'm so sorry."

"You were worried about your place and what people would say," I soothed her, smiling. "And besides… you didn't want to lose him since he's really hot and all."

She gasped her hand over her mouth.

I smiled slowly, and she suddenly had her hands on my face. "I'm your servant, now, before anyone else, before my brother, before Logan… there's only you, Jin. You've made me aset by your sacrifice, and I can never repay the honor."

I grabbed her, and we hugged tight.

"I promise you that I didn't want him like this, and if I had known yesterday what your heart was like…." She pulled back to look into my face. "I would have just stepped aside without a word. Why didn't we talk yesterday?"

I smiled at her. "We could've been friends."

She grabbed me tight, her face buried in my shoulder. "We're friends now."

I gave her a last hug before I stood and walked to the edge of the balcony to allow Simone and Peter to leave. Seconds later, Crane joined me, standing still and silent.

"I want you to stay here, even after, okay?"

"I don't think I can," he said slowly. "This will be the place you died, Jin, and I'll be reminded of that fact every single day."

"But it's also the place I was happiest," I countered. "Think about that instead."

He took a deep breath. "Everything will be different after."

"You won't." I forced a smile. "You'll be the same."

"I won't," he said flatly. "I'll be different after I watch you die. We all will."

We didn't talk after that, and I was glad. I needed the quiet to prepare myself. It wasn't every day you died.

Chapter Eleven

I STEPPED out of the bathroom after taking a shower, and there, in my room, was an enormous panther. He was larger than any other I had ever seen, like he could have hunted mammoths. Powerfully muscled, sleek and strong with the dimming light from the sunset bathing my room in gold, my mate was glorious. In any form he took, the man was breathtaking.

He had come from the balcony, and so I rushed across the room to close the open door. When I turned around, for a moment I found that just looking at him was mesmerizing. Then he took a step toward me. Instantly, I took one back.

"You hafta go," I told him. "You're not supposed to see me before the trial."

Instead of moving, he crouched down, settling himself on the floor, showing me that he was no threat. As I watched him, he lifted his head, stretching his neck, an invitation for me to move closer. It was so hard to stay away, but I did it, intuitively knowing that touching him would only be torture for me.

"Please go," I begged him, taking a step back toward the bathroom.

He lifted his head and inhaled deeply, the purr loud and deep as it came out of him.

"How did you get in here?" I asked, even though I knew.

They had left him alone for only seconds, all the people keeping vigil around him. He had been waiting, watching, knowing that there would come a moment when everyone was occupied, family, friends, all eyes off of him, and in that flicker of time, he had made his escape and come to me.

"Logan," I said, taking another step back. "Please go."

He purred instead, and a wall of heat slammed into me as his pheromones filled the room. I grabbed for the bookcase to steady myself. I was desperate to submit. To be dominated was chemically, emotionally, and physically ingrained in me, and to fight against the onslaught of seeing him and smelling him was almost too much to bear. I needed him to go away.

He came toward me, his eyes never leaving mine, and because my legs could no longer hold me, I slid down the side of the bookcase to the floor. I could hear my heart beating like a rabbit's as he advanced on me, but I didn't move, frozen where I was, waiting.

He stretched out beside me, and my hands sank into the thick golden fur, savoring the feel of the silky texture. I was unable to keep from running my chin over the top of his head. The rough tongue that licked behind my ear, down the side of my neck, to my shoulder, made me shiver. When he lowered his massive head, rubbing his chin over my groin through the towel wrapped around me, I let out a hoarse moan, my fingers clutching at his fur. Just that much contact made me hard.

He moved fast, fluidly, his body like water running through my hands as he forced me down on my back, huge paws on either side of my head. I looked up into hungry eyes and felt my heart flutter in my chest. He bumped my chin with his nose, and I leaned my head back, exposing my throat. The flick of his tongue sent shivers spilling over my skin, causing deep trembling. When his weight settled over me, lightly, not pinning me to the floor, pushing my thighs apart, I arched up against him, my hot skin needing more.

"Reah." The word came out as a snarl.

My eyes, which I hadn't realized I'd closed, popped open as I looked up into his leering face, transformed that fast from beast to werepanther. His clawed hands shredded the towel as I tried to squirm away; my hips were grabbed and lifted as he yanked me forward, bending and engulfing my cock in searing, liquid heat. His name tore out of my throat.

He sucked hard, and his tongue swirled over my shaft, so strong, rough over my sensitive skin, making me writhe under him. Everything was wet and slippery, his saliva sliding down into my crease from his ongoing attention. I froze for a second when his fangs accidentally touched me, piercing just slightly, but the electrifying pain was easily overcome by the frenzied needs of my body.

"Please, Logan," I begged, all duty drowned in my need for my mate. "Fuck me."

My shaft was released as his arms slid under my bent legs, his claws digging first into my hips and then my ass as he spread my cheeks and sank slowly into me. My body spasmed as the sensations rolled through, and I caught my breath when he slid almost all the way out only to glide right back in seconds later. When his fingers closed tightly around my hard, throbbing cock, I moaned loudly. I had never had a lover who wanted me as much as Logan did, never had one who wanted to hear my cries of pleasure, and never, ever had I been made love to instead of just being fucked. The tears were unexpected, but reasonable.

"Beautiful." His voice was full of gravel. "So beautiful."

I felt the change in his rhythm from slow, sensual stroking to hard pounding that rammed into me, pushing me forward across the floor until my hands hit the bed frame, and I braced myself against it. He roared then, as he was able to bury himself inside me, drive deeper with every thrust, his face twisted into a grimace of pain before his head was thrown back in pleasure.

His massive body was covered in fine, golden fur but changing in front of my eyes. In seconds, I had a man plunging in and out of me, his eyes clouded with desire and passion and pain as he bent to kiss me.

His lips touched mine as his hand fisted my cock, sliding easily over it, pumping hard and fast. The kiss was fierce and possessive, his tongue sucking on mine as he moaned into my mouth. I couldn't ever remember wanting anyone as much as I wanted this man.

"My mate," he growled possessively as he tore his mouth from mine, shifting his angle to stroke even deeper inside me.

My ass was filled; his hot tongue tangled with mine, and his hand was like a slippery vise on my shaft. The convulsing, mind-blowing orgasm started at the base of my spine and surged up through me, exploding out of my cock, splashing across his hand and abdomen. I felt hot come burst inside me as Logan drilled me into the floor so hard that I had no air to yell with. My body was boneless, weightless, as unrelenting tremors swept through me. I couldn't move. I just lay there as he slid from my body, rolling me over on my stomach. When he brushed my hair aside, exposing the back of my neck, I trembled with anticipation.

"Do you belong to me?"

"Yes."

"You think you're so strong, but I'm stronger."

"Yes," I whimpered, writhing under him.

"Yes, what?"

"Yes, my semel."

"I will never allow anyone to hurt you," he promised before he bit me.

It felt incredible, and the very last tremor of my orgasm tore through me.

"You're mine."

"Oh, God, yes," I promised.

I felt his smile before I was released, rolled back over, and then lifted into his arms. He carried me around the side of the bed and then fell down with me, quickly pinning me under him so I couldn't move. His hands were gentle as he brushed my hair back from my face, looking at me with more love and tenderness than I ever thought possible.

"I thought you had no faith in me, and at first I was furious, but then I understood."

I stared up into his amber eyes, and the pain in my chest was almost overwhelming.

"You would do anything to protect me, even sacrifice your own life."

"Logan, you—"

But my words were swallowed by his kiss. It wasn't gentle, instead rough as his mouth ground down over mine. His fangs cut my lips, and the copper taste of blood was on the tip of my tongue. He lifted up to look down at me, and his smile was very satisfied, very smug. "You look completely ravaged; the blood on you is very hot."

I could only stare up into his eyes.

"Christ, the things I wanna do to you.... You'll be lucky to make it out of my bedroom... ever."

The noise in the back of my throat could not be helped.

"Baby, sweet baby," he groaned. "You think you're big, and strong, and powerful, but if you could see yourself just once as you really are... your face... so fragile and so beautiful."

"Logan—"

"I've never had a lover like you... whatever I do, you take and scream for more."

"Logan," I soothed. "Please don't interfere with—"

"You were made for me in every way. I'm so proud to be your mate. Just looking at you makes me happy. You're more important to me than...." He took a breath, visibly upset. "How the hell do you get off even thinking of asking me to live a *second* longer than you? It's insane."

"No, Logan, I—"

The kiss was deep, and wet, and hard, lasting longer than the air in my lungs. I was panting when I pushed him off me, his eyes glinting with the very last traces of sunlight.

"I cannot, will not, live without you. Reahs may protect their semels, but it goes both ways."

"Please lis—"

He kissed me breathless, and I was gasping for air, panting beneath him when he finally lifted his lips from mine, the deep, masculine chuckle that rumbled in his chest not to be missed. "I can do this all night if you don't listen to me."

I waited as I caught my breath.

"Okay." He grinned lazily. "Here's the thing, I get now that I've got not only a mate who is sexy as hell, but also one who's much too smart for his own good."

I was afraid to say a word.

He waited a minute, checking to see if I was going to push my luck again. When I was silent, he gave me a devilish smile that made his eyes twinkle before he flipped on the hurricane lamp on the nightstand. "I will not allow Domin or anyone else to ever touch you, let alone hurt you. Nothing Yuri could do, outside of killing me, would keep me from your side."

He was blurring as hot tears filled my eyes.

"And as far as anyone…." He took a deep breath through his nose, and I saw him struggling for control, trying to hold his smile for me. "I read the law, and I asked Yuri about winnowing…." He cleared his throat, suddenly clutching me so tight I gasped. "Never, and that's my final word to you. I will not allow you to step a foot into that pit."

I shook my head. "I can't allow you in, either."

"I know." He nodded, and suddenly his mouth closed on my throat, and I felt his fangs pierce my skin. There was no time to be surprised; he was on me so fast, and my struggling was in vain. I felt like I was drowning, but there was no panic, only lulling heat filling my body. I was heavy and hot at the same time. I could not keep my eyes open. I felt like I was looking down a dark tunnel that got smaller and smaller until there was only darkness.

Chapter Twelve

I WAS freezing and exhausted down to my bones. Everything hurt, and I wanted to sleep, but I struggled to open my eyes and regain consciousness. I needed to wake up so I could kill my mate. How dare Logan bleed me to try and make me too weak to move! I was supposed to be protecting him and saving him, but instead, he had humiliated me in front of his tribe, made my sacrifice inconsequential, and betrayed the trust between us. I hated him, and he would pay. I rolled over onto my stomach and shifted.

I stretched every muscle in my body and stood up in my human form before I shifted back to panther again. Every time I changed, my body was forced to go through the metamorphosis that caused muscles to stretch and reform and new blood to pump furiously through my veins. With every shift, I got stronger, and had Logan ever once seen me turn, he would have known that his trick, the bleeding, would not work. But he didn't know anything about me, not really, and in that second, I was glad I had never confessed my love for him aloud. To have spoken the words and to then suffer his betrayal would have been too much.

I staggered to the glass door that led outside to the balcony, opened it, and stood there a moment gathering my strength before I bolted forward. By the time I was up and balanced on the stone railing, I was a black panther. From the balcony, I leaped across the space between the house and the enormous oak tree that grew beside it, and from there, I ran down the trunk to the ground. It took only seconds. Instantly, I raised my head and inhaled. The smell of my mate was there faintly on the wind; I just needed to trace it.

I ran in every direction until I found the scent, first just a trace, and then, as I started to run, I could almost taste him. He was closer than I had imagined. Wherever the pit of the tribe of Mafdet was, it was on Logan's land. Even in the driving wind and the falling snow, I could find it. I stopped suddenly, shifting one last time before I took off again. I felt better, almost completely restored, and by the time I found Logan, I would be ready to fight him for the right to face Domin and the others. As I ran toward the woods, I took in the warring scents of fear, panic, and blood. The pit was very close.

The amphitheater was built into the side of the mountain so that it was a wall of enormous stones on one side and smooth marble on the other. There was one way in, at the top, so that if you were one of those fighting for your life, to get in you had to take the stairs down past everyone to the floor. I hid in the shadows near the entrance; everything else was lit by hundreds of kerosene lanterns. The way the shadows fell, the way the flames flickered in the huge bonfire in the center of the floor, the howling wind, the snow just dusting the ground—it seemed primitive and almost haunted.

The growling and snarling made my teeth grind as I saw Logan cut around the edge of the fire and turn to face the four others. In that instant, I realized the challenge had already begun, and I had been out longer than I thought. What I had presumed to be an hour had actually been more like two or three, and as I looked at Logan, I saw the toll the fighting was taking on him. His fur was soaked with blood, his walk was stilted, broken, and he could not lift his head any higher than his shoulder. As the panthers advanced on Logan in a pack, I saw Domin was close to my mate's size, and the four other golden panthers at his side were just as big as he was. It was only a matter of time before they killed Logan; there were just too many.

I saw Domin's snarl pull his lips back from his teeth, saw the long sharp fangs dripping with blood at the same time I finally understood the cause of Logan's limp. His right shoulder was shredded, and all his weight was being carried on his left front leg. In that second, my anger evaporated; only protecting my mate mattered. I flew down the stairs, came up behind Domin and landed on his back, slamming him down to the floor, my fangs buried in the back of his neck, my claws beside my mouth. His cries of pain made the others stop and turn. All of them lifted out of their attack positions, standing there staring at me on top of their semel as I held him pinned to the floor. I tightened my jaws and Domin moaned painfully, loud and long.

Logan was shaking with fatigue; there was no telling how long he had been holding off all five, counting Domin, alone, but he didn't collapse. He held his ground, his eyes locked on me. Domin shifted under me, and I looked away from my mate, my adversary trying to upset my balance by shrinking and changing his body mass quickly. I slipped into my werepanther form with him and twisted around and under him, the claws of one hand still buried in the back of his neck, the other driving up into his chest. He staggered forward and collapsed on top of me. Had I been in the pit alone, I would have never taken him by surprise, but the others were concentrating on Logan and so could not offer him any help or advantage. I lifted my head and sank my teeth into his throat, tasting his blood on my tongue.

When Logan roared, it caught me by surprise.

There were more, streaming into the pit, and had I thought about it even for a moment, from what I knew of Domin's tribe, I should have known that because they were rabble instead of family, they would take this opportunity to kill Logan. He fought valiantly, but there were just too many. He was still standing, even though he only had three good legs, but with the addition of five more panthers, nine in all ripping at him with claws and fangs, he finally went down, buried under a mountain of fur. No one from the tribe of Mafdet came to help; they knew Logan wouldn't want any of them to die for him.

I had no such reservations. Shifting back to panther form, I kicked with my back legs and hurled Domin off me so hard that he hit the rock wall with enough force to shake pebbles loose. He was unconscious when he hit the ground. Turning, I ran for Logan. I hit the mass of muscle and bone that covered my mate and tore into it, biting, clawing, pulling, and yanking, trying to free him. But I was inconsequential, only one trying to move so many huge predators. I could not hope to make an impact. But whereas they were in the frenzy of bloodlust, I was clearheaded. When the fire flickered in the corner of my eyes, I knew instantly what I had to do.

I used my powerful back legs and leaped as high up into the bonfire as I could. There were screams and shouting, and I was certain that everyone thought I was killing myself because I believed Logan was dead. The sacrifice was normal and expected for the reah, the semel strong enough to live without their mate, the reah not. While it was romantic, very *Romeo and Juliet*, my focus was on life, not death.

The heat was blistering, the air stifling, and the smoke was trying to choke and suffocate me, but I was clearheaded; I knew how to keep myself alive. Once I was at the top of the burning mountain of wood, I shifted and then shifted again and then again, over and over, ceaselessly, without a break in rhythm. Man, werepanther, panther, from one to the other fast enough so that the fire couldn't catch me, couldn't burn through one body before there was another in its place. I ran on top of the flaming mound, my legs under me singed and then changed, and it hurt, and yet, it didn't, the piercing, devouring pain like electrical shocks, there and gone almost before my brain could register it.

My vision blurred and my skin felt liquid as it formed and reformed like quicksilver, my body becoming energy, losing the memory of being mass, of being solid. Time became a continuous stream as I felt myself lifting, floating, becoming less a creature of the earth and more like one of the air. Only the chant of Logan's name tethered me, my love keeping me from succumbing to the drop into oblivion. There came a wave of overwhelming body-numbing exhaustion at the same moment I felt the first faint wavering of the inferno roaring around me. Slowly, first in flying embers and twigs, then in an avalanche of roaring, consuming flames, everything began to drop out from under me. The mountain finally teetered, tumbled, and fell.

My leap to safety was long, and I stretched my entire body out as the panthers attacking Logan were covered under a deluge of burning, falling wood. The screams were immediate; in the face of their fur burning off, Logan's attackers shifted back into men. People streamed from everywhere to pull them out as Logan came charging out of the flames. His fur was singed, his right shoulder showed exposed bone and muscle, and there were bloody paw prints where he had stepped, but he was whole, and he was still in panther form. That he was able to maintain his beast and not shift was a testament to his strength, and with Domin unconscious and the rest of Domin's khatyu, his fighters, screaming in agony, it was Logan's clear victory. He was the undisputed champion, and it was there for anyone to see. He looked at me, but I nodded toward Domin, and he limped over to him.

I ran to the first man who was being held down as he screamed. The burns were all over his body, dark and cracking, seeping with blood, but I bumped him with my paw and put my face over his. I shifted to human and then back to panther. I did it twice more before he stopped screaming and tried. He shifted slowly, and when he was a panther, he was badly burned, but when he went back to human form, the burns were better, not blackened and charred, instead red and blistering. His eyes were less wild, less crazed with pain, and he nodded ever so slightly. The cry went up for the others to shift. They had no idea, and I was astounded. Shape-shifters relied on their bodies to heal damage, but they never thought to help it along. The more we shifted, the quicker we revived. While most could not shift as fast as I, any morphing at all would help with their healing.

As I turned away, there were whispers and murmurs, something about a reah, but I didn't hear what it was. I was tired, and moved to the side as Logan's tribe filled the floor of the pit. He was in human form, covered in a long, padded silk robe that Mikhail and Yuri had draped over him; Peter was kneeling at his feet as he tied it at Logan's waist. It made him look like a king, the midnight blue robe worn only by the semel of the tribe. He strode over to Domin, who was now down on one knee, naked and shivering in the cold, as he had returned to human form. Logan stopped in front of him, and Domin raised his eyes.

"My heart is yours. Take it quickly."

Instead, Logan gestured with a tip of his head, and Peter brought him another robe, deep red, quilted. After Logan took it, he settled it around Domin's shoulders. "The tribe of Menhit is gone. Your tribe will forever run with mine; you are now maahes, prince of the tribe of Mafdet, and you will be my emissary to others, my voice, my persuader, and my counselor for peace. Blood has been spilled; let there now be kinship between us."

Dark brown eyes locked on gold ones. Logan just stared at him, and after a few moments, I saw the tears run down Domin's cheeks.

"Will you take your place at my side?"

If Domin did, he would no longer lead his own tribe. He would no longer be a semel; his sheseru and sylvan would be mere tribe members. Only Mikhail and Yuri would carry those titles. But as I looked at his sheseru, Markel, and the man I knew to be Domin's sylvan, and the others, all looking at him with astonishment on their faces, I knew that everyone wanted peace. They looked broken, struggling to hold back tears in red-rimmed eyes, their trembling bodies streaked with blood, and soot, and burns. Everyone was tired, everyone was in pain, and everyone wanted solace. The feud had gone on so long, Logan's father having fought with Domin's, but now it could be over if Domin could only swallow his pride. There was silence as we held our collective breath.

Part of me hoped that Domin would spit at Logan's feet, tell him to go to hell, and thereby seal his own fate. The tribe would fall on him, and he would be dead in seconds. I wanted him to suffer as Logan had, but at the same time, I could imagine nothing worse than losing his birthright and his tribe. He would forever be Logan's servant if he accepted his new role and nothing more.

Domin nodded after long moments and leaned his cheek against the back of Logan's hand. It was a sign of his complete submission.

"Take us in, semel. We are one tribe. I will be your emissary, speak on your behalf, and be your loyal maahes."

There were instant cheers and applause, whistling and yelling as Logan turned his hand over and Domin pressed his cheek into his palm. Both he and his tribe belonged to Logan, and he would protect them all. It was done; the feud was finally over in a way no one could ever have expected. In that instant of joy, I rushed up the steps to get away. Even over the cacophony of voices, I heard his. He was roaring my name. I looked back down at the floor of the pit and Logan was looking up at me, clutching his wounded arm. Having shifted only once, he had to have been in excruciating pain, but he only winced when someone touched him, instead gesturing for me to come to him. I looked at him long and hard and then lifted my head to the wind.

"No! Reah!"

My head snapped back toward the floor of the pit.

Peter held out his arms to me.

"You are a blessing, reah! Don't leave us!"

"You saved your mate," a woman called up to me, "but then helped those that tried to kill him. You are a gift, reah! Stay!"

"Jin!" Mikhail cried out. "You are a mated reah! You cannot leave your tribe!"

"Jin!" Eva had her arms out to me, begging me with her eyes. "Come here, darling. Let me be your mother now."

My heart hurt.

"Jin!" Koren yelled up to me. "Stay with us. We need you."

He was letting everyone know how he felt about me. It was very humbling, the faith and trust.

"Jin, goddamn it!" Crane roared up at me, trying to make his way through the crowd and then up to me. There were so many people, though; he would never make it in time to stop me. "You better not move!"

"Jin!" Domin's voice broke, and I saw the tears. "Please… our tribe… please, my reah."

I couldn't look at him. He had been so proud, and now he was so shattered. It was hard to see.

"Jin."

My head turned, and Delphine was there beside me. I hadn't even seen her.

"Please don't go, Jin," she said quickly, forcing a smile even as she looked as though she were going to cry. "Logan won't ever be the same if you leave. You might as well have let them kill him if you're just going to run away."

"He lied to me and made my sacrifice meaningless. He was supposed to let me protect him."

"Oh, honey, how could he have? He's the semel, after all; he's the leader, and you're his mate. You've been alone, and you've had no one to lean on for so long that you don't remember what it's like to be loved and protected and cherished."

"No, I—"

"What he did was stupid, thoughtless, but it was all he could think of. He had one moment to surprise you, and that was all. He was sick afterwards; he was terrified of your reaction, but all he knew was that he had to keep you safe. The thought of you in the pit was the worst thing he could ever imagine. Do you understand? The thought of losing you, just you—there was nothing worse than that for him."

I turned to look down at him and saw he was slowly climbing the stairs to reach me. I had no idea what to do, but whatever it was would not be done in front of so many people.

"No, Jin!" I heard Delphine cry before I was down the other side of the ravine, looking up at people only inches tall from where I was. I took a breath and then turned and ran. No one could catch me, and that knowledge soothed me.

Back at the house, I packed and took Delphine's car. I didn't worry about Crane; he was safe with Logan, and so I pushed him from my mind. My only thought as I ran was of my mate. Nothing made sense. How could he love me and then betray me? How could I have been so ready to trust him and then, in a single moment, have that trust so completely shattered? It was like my family all over again. I needed to think, and I needed time to do that. I hoped I would be given that time.

Chapter Thirteen

WHEN Raymond Torres built Paragon at the beginning of the nineties, he included in the design a small hundred-square-foot studio apartment behind the bar of the lounge. The original purpose was for him to have a convenient place to take willing women he picked up in the course of the night. It needed to have a bathroom and a bed, but unfortunately, once the shower stall and toilet were put in, there was only room for a twin bed. There were no windows; it was a cramped, small space. It felt more like a prison cell than anything else; romantic and cool it was not, much more like someplace a stalker would stash his prey. Sitting behind the bar, the sounds of clinking glasses, loud and drunken conversations, and water going off and on came through the paper-thin walls all night long. It was the last place anyone would want to rest and the last place anyone would ever look for someone who needed it.

I locked myself into the room that no one but Ray and I had a key for. It was clean even though it was cramped, and I shed my parka and shoes before I turned off the light and collapsed on the bed in the darkness. The shifting had taken all my energy, and only adrenaline had carried me from the pit back to the house and eventually to the restaurant. I had called Ray when I was in the parking lot because I couldn't get out of the car. He had reached me in seconds, and while he helped me inside, I asked him if he could do me just one more favor.

One favor turned into three, but my boss didn't seem to care. I needed a place to sleep, I needed to eat immediately, and I needed someone to drive Delphine's car back. An hour later, two of the waiters returned the Lexus to the road in front of Logan's home. I didn't want anyone to see it parked in front of the restaurant, not that anyone would be looking for me for a while. If I was weary, Logan had to be exhausted. He was probably passed out in his bed. The thought was not comforting, because half of me wanted nothing else than to be lying beside him, wrapped in his arms. It was the other half that was the problem, the half that kept reminding me I had been betrayed before. Too tired to think anymore, when Ray had insisted I sleep upstairs, I didn't fight him. I sank into oblivion, and I didn't even hear a sound.

I WOKE up the following evening, having slept for over sixteen hours, ravenous. I had made sure to eat before I initially went to bed because it was dangerous not to. After any shifting, panthers needed to refuel and hydrate, so I had eaten a steak and drank what felt like a gallon of water. I was still too tired to walk, but when I called Ray, he brought me up a hamburger and fries, a glass of milk, and more water. I told him that being served by the boss man was nice. He made sure to tell me that he simply didn't want anyone but the two of us knowing about the room. He didn't give a crap about me; he was just protecting his secret. But the affection in his eyes, the way he tousled my hair, gave him away. As we sat and talked, I knew he wanted to ask what was going on, but it was nice that he didn't. He left a half an hour later, and I fell back to sleep in seconds.

The following day, I was up by five in the afternoon, again ravenous, but finally able to get up out of bed and shower. Once I was changed, I went downstairs to the huge bustling kitchen of the restaurant. I waited for the jeers but realized that technically, I hadn't even missed a day, since I had been given extra time off for working two weeks straight. I was back when I was supposed to be, and that was funny somehow. In the middle of life-and-death battles, I had returned to work on time.

In the kitchen, Ramon had me sit on the counter while he fed me. Breakfast for dinner had always been my favorite, and after an enormous omelet, a pound of ham, toast, and a half a gallon of apple juice, I felt better. He watched me chug down more water, and when I got up and thanked him, he asked me where it had all gone. He always made a point of telling me that someday, my metabolism would change, and because of my eating habits, I'd end up weighing a thousand pounds. I told him not to worry about it.

I came out of the kitchen in time for Ray to ask me if I was working or not. Since the alternative was going back upstairs to my jail cell to stare at the ceiling, I opted for working. When Mike showed up an hour later, he asked me where my shadow was, and I answered honestly. I had no idea where Crane Adams was.

The nice thing about being busy was the way time passed. I was running, and that was good for me because there was no time to think. At the end of the night, as I was cleaning up, I heard my name yelled across the room. I didn't look up; I just continued wiping down tables until Crane reached me.

"What the fuck are you doing here?"

I just looked at him.

"Jesus Christ, Jin, Logan is losing his mind, and you're working?"

I moved to walk around him, but he stepped in front of me, blocking my path.

"Jin, your semel needs you!"

Shoving him sideways, I crossed to the bar. He was right behind me.

"What are you going to do? Run again?"

I didn't answer him. I was too angry. In a matter of days, his loyalty had completely shifted from me to Logan.

"I'm gonna need to tell him where you are."

"I doubt he doesn't know," I told him, not even looking at him anymore.

"If he knew, he'd be here."

"No," I said softly. "He's giving me time to think."

"He's a mess, Jin. Look at me."

I lifted my head and saw the muscles in his jaw flexing, the furrowed brows, and the hands fisted at his sides. "He hasn't slept yet, he won't shift and heal his wounds, he won't eat.... You need to come back to the house or it won't matter that he won—there won't be anything left of him."

I stared because I had never seen him so serious and earnest in my life.

"Please, Jin, even if you're not gonna stay... make him eat and sleep. We both know that no one would ever force you to stay against your will."

I cleared my throat. "Logan Church is a strong man and a leader first. He's probably eating now. Go home and see, Crane."

"Jin—"

"Go away, Crane."

Since I didn't look up, I never saw his expression, but I heard the door slam shut when he left.

An hour later, I was on the road, walking toward the diner for coffee and a piece of pie, when a car rolled up beside me. It slowed but didn't stop, and when the driver's side window came down, I was looking at Mikhail.

"Hey," he said softly.

"Crane's got a big mouth."

"Yes," he agreed with no argument.

I shoved my hands down into the pockets of my parka. It was cold outside, and even with the parka and my knit cap and my scarf, I was still frozen, my breath visible when I spoke. "Logan's a semel first before anything else. He knows his duty. He'll take care of himself."

"But see, there's the thing. He did his duty, and he saved his tribe and his reah, and he even saved Domin," he said. "But he didn't save himself."

"How did he save me, exactly?"

"You'd be dead if you had gone into the pit with five panthers."

I stopped walking and turned to face him. He slammed on the brakes and got out of the car faster than I would have thought such a big man could. "I was prepared to protect him!"

"You would have been killed, plain and simple," he yelled back, poking me hard in the collarbone to drive home his point. "Logan was never gonna let those jackals have his mate, and you goddamn well know it! And now you're punishing him for saving your life the only fuckin' way he knew how!"

"I saved him, not the other way around!"

"He saved you!"

"So I did nothing."

He grabbed the lapel of my parka and yanked me close. "You saved his life, and by law, since you had already taken on the challenge, you were the only one of us who could have gotten into the pit with him and not caused him to forfeit."

"Until the others cheated," I reminded him.

"Yes," he sighed. "It could have been an all-out war at that point, but we all knew that Logan would rather die than have any more of us in the pit with you two."

"I know."

He let me go, and I took a step back from him.

"Jin, you were amazing," he said, the awe clear in his voice. "You… I've never seen another cat like you. I have never seen anyone shift like that in my life. I had no idea that could even be done, but still… Logan sacrificed himself because he went into the pit first without you to face five panthers because he would not allow them near his mate. Do you get that?"

"Of course, but that's not the issue."

"It's all the issue there should be."

"No, it's not."

"Jin, I know that without you, I would have a dead semel today; I get that. But what you need to understand is that if he doesn't sleep soon, if he doesn't eat and let his body feed on something other than itself, if he doesn't stop bleeding… he will be just as dead."

I stared at Mikhail. "I don't want to stay there."

"Okay."

"Promise me."

"You are my reah," he said urgently. "No one can make you do anything against your will."

I checked the dark sapphire blue eyes, and he held my gaze.

"You don't understand that your place is highest."

I nodded my head toward the car. "Let's go."

There were a lot of people at the house when I arrived. Yuri, who had met us at the front door, walked ahead of me, and Mikhail walked behind me so that no one could stop my progress to the stairs. When Koren called my name, I hurried, and Logan's advisors intercepted him. If they hadn't all hated me before, they most certainly did now, for what I was putting Logan through. I didn't feel like getting yelled at. I just wanted to see Logan myself and make sure the situation wasn't as dire as everyone was painting it.

He was in bed, propped up, and I saw the wounds he had sustained during the fight had not healed. The sheets on the bed were stained with dried blood, his skin had lost its normal gold color, having changed to gray, and his breathing was labored. The fire in the room was not big enough to keep him warm, as evidenced by the fact that his lips were blue. I realized instantly it had less to do with me and more to do with no one taking care of him. I couldn't imagine whose word had kept his mother from his side. I walked back out of the room and yelled downstairs for her. Minutes later, she appeared at the doorway where I was standing.

Her face was contorted with pain. "Jin?"

"You make the food; I'll put it in him."

She stared into my eyes, and I could not, for the life of me, read her expression.

"Okay?"

She grabbed my face, and the smile was huge. "I love you, you know."

I was startled; it was not the reaction I was expecting.

"Oh, Jin." Her eyelids fluttered rapidly in an attempt to keep from crying. "I just adore you."

I kissed her forehead, asked her to send up Koren and Russ, and stayed where I was. Seconds after she left me, Logan's two brothers appeared, but they didn't rush forward. My eyes slid over them, and I saw the anger on their faces.

"You don't have to like me," I growled at Koren. "We just need to get him bathed and get the fire a lot—"

"You're not looking at me," Koren snapped, and when my eyes flicked back to his face, I saw that he was trying hard not to break down. "I am so thankful for your presence, reah. He is the semel of our tribe, and so with you gone, there was no one here to contradict his shouting or his ranting. He ordered us out of his room… all we could do was wait for him to call us back."

I nodded.

"Jin."

My eyes moved from one brother to the other.

"I need you to listen." Russ's voice broke as he reached for me but stopped himself from touching me. "We are all so thankful that you're here. After what he did to you… that you would still come… thank you, reah."

I looked back and forth between the two men.

"You have no idea what your being here means," Koren assured me.

I nodded. "I'll run the bath."

Once the enormous tub was filled with warm water, I called for the two men to carry Logan in. Having stripped him out of the ceremonial robe, which he had been wearing since the fight in the pit two nights previously, they brought him into the bathroom. I started to worry when he didn't wake up even when he was immersed in water, but as I slid my fingers through his hair, I saw him shiver. I moved to turn the hot water back on, but a hand slid around my wrist to stop me. Turning my head, I saw his beautiful honey-colored eyes.

"My mate," he sighed, and I saw him swallow hard. "You have to for—"

"Can I wash your hair?" I cut him off gently.

Tears rolled from his eyes as he nodded.

"Russ, grab me a pitcher," I directed his brother. "Koren, help me sit him up."

"I can move," he said hoarsely. "You don't need Koren."

I nodded, and we were suddenly alone. "Take my hand."

He reached for me, and when my skin slid over his, I saw him shiver again.

"You're cold."

"It's just you," he said, his eyes all over me. "I always tremble when you touch me."

"No, you don't." I smiled.

"I do." He exhaled slowly. "I'm just normally good at hiding it."

I took a breath. "Lean forward."

He did as I asked, and as I washed his hair, using the pitcher Russ brought me to rinse it, I saw the water change from clear to pink.

"I'm gonna drain this out and turn on the shower at the same time. There's too much blood in the water. I don't want it to get back on your skin."

"Whatever. I don't care," he whispered. "Just keep your hands on me. Please don't leave."

"Can you stand?"

"I can do whatever you want."

But standing proved to be more difficult than he thought it would be, and I ended up under the water in my jeans, T-shirt, and hiking boots to keep him from falling. It was funny; I always thought of myself as big, but with Logan standing over me, a full head taller than I was, I felt suddenly small and fragile.

"Jesus, you look good wet," he growled, and it was deep and sexy, his left hand wrapping in my hair as he tilted my head back, exposing my throat. "You are so beautiful… my mate, my reah."

But he had the body to die for, not me.

I felt his mouth on my skin before I even realized he had bent toward me. The kisses trailing over my collarbone were featherlight. "We need to get you back to bed."

"Whatever you want," he said hoarsely, his hands on my shoulders. "Just stay here."

I didn't respond, just helped him out of the tub.

Wrapped in towels, Logan was able to move back to the freshly made bed mostly under his own power. The room had warmed, and the food sitting on the tray beside the bed smelled amazing. Looking at it, though, there wasn't nearly enough protein. I asked Koren, who was stoking the fire, to go downstairs and bring me back some meat. He told me to give him my clothes and he would get them dried. When I started peeling off my shirt, I heard Logan say my name. I was surprised when I turned to look at him to see how dark his eyes had become. He looked exhausted, completely wrung out, except for his eyes. They were molten with anger.

"You will change in the bathroom and bring your clothes to him. There is a towel there, and you will cover yourself. No one but me sees your bare skin, reah. That is the law."

I knew he was right, even though it was ridiculous. Being a mated reah carried a long list of do's and don'ts. Most were observed so the semel didn't feel the need to rip anyone who got too close to his mate to pieces. I realized that was the reason Koren and Russ had not touched me earlier; the reah was supposed to invite others to touch them, and the semel agreed or not. As I saw the way Logan looked at his own brother, I understood the reason for the rules. The semel could be rational and logical about all things but his mate. Reason fled in the face of the bond.

I darted back into the bathroom, changed, and came back out wrapped only in a towel.

"I'm not a woman," I told Logan, "so a lot of those antiquated rules won't pertain to me. I don't need to be completely covered in front of everyone but my mate, and besides, I was naked in front of your entire tribe just the night before last."

He made a noise in the back of his throat, clearly frustrated, and when he opened his mouth to speak, his fangs had lowered, top and bottom.

Koren took that second of silence to bolt from the room, and we were left alone. I watched Logan struggle for control of his weakened body. His hands fisted in the sheets, the muscles in his jaw and neck corded and clenched, and he closed his eyes.

"Stop fighting it, you idiot," I snapped. "Just shift already."

"But I don't know how long I can—"

"Shift!"

"I want to talk to you."

"You will do as I say."

"No! You will do what I say and not leave me!"

"You did this to yourself because you're an ass!"

“I must speak to you!” he yelled, but it came out as more of a snarl, as he had shifted in the middle of speaking to me. It was fast, not the blink of the eye that mine was, but still impressive.

“There you are.” I smiled, my anger having fled instantly. I knew the reason, and it was petty. He couldn’t talk to me in his panther form. He could only listen, and it was a relief. “How could you be so careless, Logan? This was dangerous.”

He turned his enormous head to look at me, and I grabbed the plate of meat and held out the first piece of venison to him.

“You came up here to just sit for a minute alone without any noise or anyone talking at you, with orders not to be disturbed, and you fell asleep.”

He finished the first piece, and I fed him the second and third before putting the plate on the bed. It was gone in seconds, easily two pounds of meat. I got up and went to the door and called down for a bowl; seconds later, Russ was there with one I’d asked Koren to fetch earlier.

“I’m gonna give him tap water now, but you need to bring a lot of bottles up here for when he wakes up later.”

He nodded but didn’t leave.

“What’s wrong?”

“Will he be all right?”

I cracked the door. “See for yourself.”

“Oh,” Russ breathed. “He shifted. Thank God.”

“He’ll be fine,” I said gently before I looked back at Logan. I was surprised to see him crouch down, flatten his ears against his head, and bare his teeth. “Go. Hurry up with the water.”

“Amazing,” Russ breathed out, mesmerized by the sight of his brother in his beast form snarling at him.

“You should go,” I said softly, urgently.

“Look at him. He has no idea who I am. In that form, as tired as he is, as fatigued, all I am is a threat. You’re the only one he recognizes whether he’s a man or an animal. All he knows right now is that you belong to him, and I’m standing too close.”

“Yeah, so go already,” I said, shoving him out the door before closing it behind him. “Whole family of idiots except for your mother,” I muttered, walking by the bed.

Logan waited for me, frozen, and when I came back with the bowl, now full of tap water, he tilted his head at me.

"Russ's bringing you bottled water from downstairs for later, but for now you need to drink all this." When he didn't move, I yelled. "You're an animal. Drink the goddamn water!"

He bent and drank from the metal bowl. When it was drained, I got up and filled it again. As I watched him lap up the water for the second time, I realized how close to death he had been. When I flicked him on the nose, he pulled back, growling.

"You fell asleep without eating or drinking. What were you thinking? We're all taught the same thing after the first time we ever change… you make sure your blood sugar is level, you take in a ton of protein, and you hydrate. If you screw around, you run the risk of coma and death. If nothing else, it's like the worst hangover ever. You know all that, and still you sat in here like an idiot and almost got yourself killed. It's a testament to how strong you are that you were still coherent when I got over here."

He tried to put his head in my lap, but I pushed him away.

"By the time you realized you were in trouble, you were too weak to do anything about it," I scolded him. "And everyone thinks you were upset about me, and so it was some broken-hearted reaction to me being gone, but that's bullshit, and we both know it. You fucked up and now, how it looks to everyone, I'm the cause of all the crap that keeps happening to you."

He leaned toward me, but I flicked him on the nose again. When he snarled, I smacked him.

"Drink the water," I commanded.

My order was followed instantly.

After several minutes of watching him drink and eat, I got up to add more logs to the fire and then turned off all the other lights. I wanted him to sleep.

"Can you shift halfway?"

In answer, he became a werepanther, falling back on the bed heavily.

"Good," I said as I sat down beside him, pulling the comforter up around his shoulders. When I tried to lean back, he took my hand and put it over his heart, pressing it down tight.

"Reah," he barely got out in his gravel-filled voice, more growl and purr than anything else. "Here, reah."

I lived in his heart, and mine felt like it was breaking.

"You need to sleep," I told him, looking into eyes that had bled gold, no white there at all, just enormous golden pools. "Please sleep."

He shook his head, easing my hand slowly across his chest, my arm with it. He wanted me to lie down with him.

"I'll stay until you fall asleep."

His growl was loud as he yanked me down, my head knocking against his chest as one clawed hand cupped my ass and the other wrapped around my wrist. I wasn't going anywhere.

I lifted my head, and my lips brushed under his chin as I spoke. "Go to sleep."

The hand on my ass had other ideas. Logan worked the towel up until the razor-sharp claws slipped over my bare skin. I heard his whimper of need, but I knew also that he wasn't going to just sleep; he was going to pass out. And if his body had release, he would slip away even faster. In his werepanther form, he was much more susceptible to his carnal appetite. All I needed to do was tempt it, arouse it, and satisfy it.

Kissing his chin made him purr with contentment, and when I licked down his throat, he leaned his head back so I could reach more. He let me go so I could rise over him and kiss down the side of his neck to his collarbone. I watched his hands claw through the sheets as my mouth closed on his right nipple. I licked and bit before I moved to the other, slowly, sensually, taking my time to make him writhe under me. Moving lower down the flat, cut stomach, I ran my tongue through the deep groove in his abdomen as my hand closed on his rock-hard shaft. When I pulled back, his eyes were glazed, he was panting, and his body could not remain still under me as I stroked him.

The whimpers and whines increased as his body arched up off the bed, needing more from me but unable to give voice to the request. When I leaned forward, grazing my tongue over the swollen head, his cry was hoarse. He tried to buck up into me, bury himself in my throat without success. He wasn't strong enough to move anymore, exhausted beyond reason; he could only writhe beneath me. I swallowed him down, sucking and licking over every inch of his long, thick cock, into the slit, around the crown, down the prominent vein that ran along the side, and back up underneath with teasing pressure and just a ghost of fangs.

He was so beautiful, head back, eyes closed as he squirmed under me, moaning loudly, his cock like hot, swollen steel in my mouth. He was lost in the exquisite sensations pulsing through his body, and I was the reason for his rapture. It was amazing because he was so strong, so full of heat and power, and yet I was the one he was begging, I was the one making him burn. He relinquished all his control to me.

"Tell me what you want," I asked, laving his rod, nuzzling his balls, making everything slick and wet and hot.

All he got out was the word "hard," but I understood. He wanted his dick sucked hard, and it was not a request, but a command from a semel to his mate. I could do nothing but fulfill his desire. I swallowed his shaft down my throat, my face buried in his groin. The ragged moan was torn from his chest.

I knew it felt good, knew I gave a phenomenal blowjob, having been told countless times, and yet it was different with him because he belonged to me. As I deep-throated him, making the suction strong and fast, the head of his cock bumping against the back of my throat, I felt him swell even larger in my mouth, heard my name roared as he came, and my hair was gripped painfully so I couldn't move, couldn't pull away. I swallowed hard as a small spray of hot semen coated my throat. As dehydrated as he was, it made sense that there wasn't more. He pressed me against him as his body shuddered with his climax.

I held him in my mouth until he went limp and let go of me. As I leaned back, wiping my mouth, I saw him struggling to hold on to consciousness. As exhausted as he was, when I smiled at him, I saw a shudder ripple through his frame before the light left his eyes. He passed out, returning instantly to human form, a man again, one utterly spent. Rising gently up from the bed, I stood over him, stroking his hair as there was a soft knock on the door.

"Come in."

Koren slipped into the room, my clothes in his arms. I took them and thanked him before I darted into the bathroom. Standing back over Logan minutes later, I noted the steady rise and fall of his chest. He was sleeping soundly and would be for quite some time. It comforted me to know he was going to be all right.

Once downstairs, I waited for Mikhail in the alcove beside the stairs.

"Jin."

I turned my head and saw Peter Church.

"Jin, your boots are still wet. They won't be dry for hours; why don't you stay until they are?"

"No." I shook my head, backing toward the door. "I need to go."

"Why?"

"I have a lot to think about. I just came to make sure he was okay."

"The second he wakes up, he'll come for you."

I scoffed. "The second he wakes up, he has a newly formed tribe to deal with. Where is Domin, by the way?"

"Koren's been watching him; he's still sleeping. I'm surprised you're not."

I shrugged. "I heal fast."

"And shift fast, and run fast. I've never seen anything like you."

"After a male reah, how much weirder can it get?" I smiled at him as Mikhail walked up beside me. I turned to go, but Peter's hand on my shoulder stopped me.

"Come home soon, Jin. Logan's not the only one that needs you."

It was a nice thing to say. "Do me a favor."

"Anything," he said sincerely.

"Will you watch over Crane?"

He nodded. "Of course. He's on his way up from the guest house to see you; maybe you want to stay and speak to him, eat something.... Eva's dying to feed you."

The man was trying so hard to stall me. I smiled at him and put a hand on his shoulder. "No, just have her feed him, and you keep him safe."

"I will, Jin. I'll take good care of him."

"Thank you, sir," I said softly, walking out the door Mikhail held open for me. Treading through the snow with Logan's sylvan beside me was peaceful until he started talking.

"He's right. We all need you, and we all want you with us. Now that we know what we can have, a mated semel and reah, it's hard that you're not here. I feel it like I'm hollow inside and a cold wind is gusting through me."

I turned slowly to look at him, arching an eyebrow.

He flipped me off and then smiled wide.

"Little too poetic, ain't it, sylvan?"

He let out a deep breath. "You make a joke of the love I feel, and I want to tell you to go to hell, but when you smile, I can't resist you. Just seeing you brings me joy. It must be overwhelming for Logan."

I kept silent.

"He must be in thrall to you."

"I don't know about that."

"He loves you. Isn't that enough?"

I wasn't sure if it was.

Chapter Fourteen

FRIDAY NIGHT at work, and I was trying, as usual, not to think about Logan Church. A whole seven days had come and gone without a word. While it was good—I had moved into a new studio apartment since Crane was no longer my roommate, accepted the general manager position, and hired five new waiters—I still could not get my mate out of my head. I told myself that when things calmed down for both Logan and me, work for me, the tribe for him, that we could get together and talk. I told myself that every night when I went home to an empty bed.

I was coming out of the kitchen, in the process of my usual rounds of checking on everyone, headed toward the bar, when I was intercepted by one of my new servers.

"Hey boss," Tanya Greeley smiled. "Two really hot guys at the host stand are asking for you."

I looked around and saw Domin, a toothpick hanging from his lip, and Koren, standing there scowling beside him, arms crossed, waiting. I jogged across the restaurant and was greeted with a hug by both men. It was surprising, more so from Domin, the change in him pronounced, warmth having replaced malice, his smile engaging, his eyes glittering. Standing there, all six foot two of him, thick, wavy brown hair, chocolate brown eyes, smiling lazily at me, he had never looked better.

"Hey," he said, and I was struck by the ease radiating off the man. "We miss you, reah."

"What are you guys doing here?" I asked, leading them back outside to the wraparound porch in front of the building.

"We just thought we'd say good-bye on our way out of town," Koren answered, his hand on my shoulder, squeezing gently. "How are you?"

He looked so much like his brother that, for a moment, I stared. And while Koren Church was a stunning man, the oldest of the Church men was the one who had me spellbound. Only Logan's eyes burned me up.

"Jin?"

"Sorry. What were you saying?"

"I asked how you were."

"I'm fine." I coughed. "Where are you going?"

"New York. We're going to meet with a friend of Logan's, a semel," Koren told me, studying my face with his olive gaze. The scrutiny was nice, like he was worried.

"What do you need to speak to another semel for?"

"Simone," Domin yawned, giving me an eye roll to drive home his point of boredom. "She needs a mate, and since you made her aset, the only mate she can have now is a semel."

I looked at Koren as he dropped his hand off me. "But why're you traveling with the maahes? The law doesn't call for him to be escorted when he makes covenant bonds with other tribes."

"Because I don't trust him," Koren assured me, his tone matter-of-fact. "God only knows what he'll promise to get what he wants."

I looked at Domin.

He gave me a wicked grin. "He doesn't trust me. He thinks I'm just biding my time to fuck Logan over."

"Are you?"

He waggled his eyebrows at me. "Wouldn't you like to know?"

"See?" Koren pointed at him. "That's why I don't trust him."

But when I looked back at Domin, I saw the slow curl of his lip at the corner of his mouth, took in the heavy-lidded eyes and his deep sigh. He was screwing with Koren and having a good time doing it. He was Logan's man now and would not betray that trust. But for some reason, he wanted Koren to think he would.

"So because this guy's actually a coyote and not a cat, I'm not letting him out of my sight."

My eyes flicked back to Domin. "Coyote?"

"Trickster." He grinned at me, arching an eyebrow.

"Oh," I nodded. "So what's your intention?"

His eyes glinted. "My intention is to show my friend here a really good time, get him to loosen up, and, you know, see if Ethan Locke, the semel of the tribe of Tefnut, wants an aset for a mate. We'll see if we can convince him to visit and meet her."

"Sounds like a good plan," I said, squinting at Domin, watching him turn his head and watch Koren. And I wondered why, if Domin had attacked Koren as Koren had told everyone he had, why he was now choosing to travel with the man. And why did Koren take care of Domin after the challenge in the pit? It didn't make any sense, and neither did the way Koren was looking at him. He looked more anxious than mad. Domin made him nervous, and I wondered why.

"Let's go," Koren snapped at the same time his phone rang.

"You better get that," Domin teased.

Koren made a sound of pure exasperation as he turned away from us to answer.

"Hey."

I looked back at Domin.

"Look."

He pointed into the trees beside the restaurant, and I saw the flash of iridescent eyes in the darkness before the long line of an enormous panther moved and then sank back out of view.

"Jin, Logan's right there, waiting. He can't do what he needs to do until you return. He can't think, he won't eat, and you need to fix that, fix him, before the tribe falls apart. He has to be strong, or he'll lose everything."

"Domin, I—"

"And so will the rest of us."

I didn't know what to say.

"Stop fuckin' around and worrying about your wounded pride and realize that he made a mistake because this thing with you was like a minute old. He needs you. Go to him."

I shook my head. “It’s only been a week. I dunno if—”

“If you were a woman, he’d have dragged you back already. He would have done the caveman thing, been all strong and silent, and everything would be all fixed up. But you’re a guy, so he has no clue.”

I watched him pace just beyond the tree line. “I went up there and made sure he was all right and he is. He doesn’t actually need me.”

“You’re an idiot, you know that? Everybody knows that mated semels and reahs go nuts if they try and stay apart. Why are you being such a hardass about this?”

“Dom—”

“It’s a physical bond just as well as an emotional one. It will take its toll on you in so many ways if you don’t go to your mate.”

“I’ll live,” I said flippantly, not believing for a second that I should or could or would want to.

“But he won’t, and that’s the point. We all serve him, not the other way around.”

I nodded, smiling at him. “Well, you’ve certainly taken your new role as speaker for the semel to heart.”

He shrugged. “I realize now that what I really want is very simple.”

“What’s that?”

“I just want a mate I love, a place of my own, and to not be afraid all the time.”

Who knew Domin Thorne and I wanted the exact same things?

“And I’ve known for a while who I want to fill the mate seat,” he said, his head turning to Koren, who was ignoring both of us as he talked on his phone. “I never wanted to be a semel, to lead… you have to care about others first, and I don’t.”

I studied his profile as he gazed at Koren.

“My father died when I was ten, and I was left with no one. I knew he hated Peter Church, and so it was all I had. The feud kept the tribe focused. If we were fighting, we didn’t have to focus on anything else. Now, with Logan, they all see what they were missing. They know what a real semel is." He turned back to look at me. "Not one of my cats will give him a moment of trouble. All they all want is to belong."

I nodded. I knew what it was to want to belong.

"And knowing that their semel has a reah.... Do you understand how blessed everyone feels?"

"Not really."

"Because you still don't get how amazing you are."

"Dom—"

He put up his hand to stop me. "Jin, not only are you a reah, but you have power that I have never seen. The speed is phenomenal, and you don't lose any of your humanity in your panther form. Logan, me, everyone I know—we're animals when we change into a cat, but you... you're still you, and I have never even heard of that."

I had no idea what I was supposed to say.

He took a quick breath. "You need to understand that as sure as I'm standing here, that if I could have, I would have killed Logan a week ago in the pit."

"Why are—"

"And now I would not," he said simply. "I am content to be Logan Church's maahes, to be his ambassador and do all that I can to serve him."

"I believe you."

"Good."

"So why are you screwing with Koren and tormenting him with doubt?"

"Because if Koren doesn't trust me, he won't let me out of his sight," he smiled wickedly.

This was what I had suspected his motivation was. "You could just be honest."

"What's the fun in that?"

"What does Koren want?"

"I don't think Koren knows." He sighed. "Yet."

"Can I ask you a question?"

He turned back to look at me.

"When you tortured him… did you?"

His smile was wicked. "It was a certain kind of torture."

I could only guess what had gone on. "You know you owe Logan for giving you a real home."

"Yes, I do," he agreed, his smile suddenly gentle and warm. "But he had no idea that he wasn't just getting me."

"What are you talking about?"

"Well, you know the custom is for the sylvan and sheseru to live with their semel until they're mated and have homes of their own."

"Yeah, I know."

"Well, so where do you think my sheseru, Markel, and my sylvan, Ivan, have to live now?"

I grunted. "With Logan?"

"Yep. They have nowhere else to go. And you named Simone aset, so she has to live there too. Crane got booted out of the guesthouse 'cause Logan's folks took it over, and Russ moved back to be close to the rest of his family." His smile was wicked and wide. "It's a mess. Crane's got a room on one side of Delphine, and Markel's on the other."

"Markel was hunting Delphine. God knows what he would've done to her that night if Crane and I hadn't interfered."

"Yeah, I know, but he apologized."

"He apologized?" I was stunned. "That's it?"

"Sure. He said he was sorry like a million times. He even broke down all weepy and whiny like a girl, and of course, when he did that, she comforted him. Blah, blah, blah. It was fucked up, but he got what he wanted."

"What'd he want?"

"Her to forgive him, which she did." He shrugged. "Now they're pals. Him and your boy Crane too. It's like we're all just one big happy family, all eleven of us. Twelve, once you get there."

"What's with the sarcasm?"

"'Cause once Crane and Markel discover that they've both got it bad for Delphine, it's gonna be a mess. You need to be home before that so you can mediate that shit."

I sighed deeply. Family problems sounded like heaven.

"And Peter walking around giving Logan advice on how to run his home ain't gonna fly much longer either. Logan's ready to explode."

"Wait. I thought you said Logan's folks were in the guesthouse?"

"They sleep there." He made a face. "But they live in Logan's house."

"How is he taking having everyone around?"

"None of it would get to him if you were there, but right now… he's brooding and angry and foul. We all hate him 'cause he's bein' a dick. But you can't blame the guy; he needs his mate. Would you please just go to him? He's losing his mind without you."

"Can we go, please?" Koren barked at him, rejoining us, having finished with the conversation he was having on the phone.

"Sure."

He yanked Domin forward but turned fast and poked a finger into my chest. "Don't be an ass. Just take the night off and go to your mate. You belong up at that house with the rest of us. If we gotta suffer, you do too."

"Has Domin moved in as well?"

The question confused him, and it was written all over his face. "'Course, why?"

I shrugged. "No reason. Just asking."

Koren nodded before telling me one more time to go to Logan and pulling Domin along after him toward the car.

"You don't hafta grab me!" I heard Domin's deep, throaty laughter. "You just say the word, and I'll follow you anywhere."

"Shut the hell up!" Koren snapped back, but he didn't let Domin go.

I watched them until all I could see of the car was taillights in the distance. Turning to look at the tree line, I saw Logan pacing back and forth. He would either wait around or not, but I couldn't leave. I ducked back inside to finish my shift.

At two in the morning, after I closed up, having sent everyone else home, I stripped out of my clothes and slipped around the side of the restaurant, already in my panther form. I crossed the street and ran for the trees. I saw him immediately. He was ten yards from me but stopped, frozen, staring. When he took a step forward, I took one back. Instantly, he dropped to the ground, not moving. I did the same. After long minutes, he lifted his head in silent invitation, tipping it so I'd know that he wanted me to follow. I rose, and he was on his feet fast, diving forward into the deeper brush.

It was a beautiful night for a run, and as I followed him, I felt the thrill of speed surging through my body. I was so lost in the wind on my face, the feel of the cold snow crunching under my paws, and the smells of the forest that when he was suddenly beside me, nipping at my shoulder, I was startled. I veered hard left and went up the side of a small hill. When I reached the top and saw the cave, I understood this was where he wanted me. I had been herded to his lair.

The cave was deep, and we twisted through the tunnels until we reached the end, where there was a small fire in a pit and a mound of animal pelts, prey animals taken during past hunts. It was warm, dry, and cozy. This was his secret place, the place only he and his mate would ever see or know about. As I wheeled around to face him, I saw him walking slowly toward me on two legs, having shifted back to his human form before entering the cave. Logan was beautiful, absolutely mouth-watering, and just seeing him, all that gorgeous gold skin over his muscular frame, made my resolve falter. He simply annihilated me.

"I'm sorry," he said softly, walking to the furs and kneeling down slowly. "All I wanted to do was protect you. I had no idea you were such a capable fighter or that you could do all the things you can do. I will never again underestimate you, and if you tell me you want to stand beside me, whenever, wherever, I promise I won't second-guess you."

I just stared at him.

"That's not to say that I will ever allow you to be harmed, because I can't. I'm not strong enough to take anything happening to you."

I moved a step closer.

"You saved me, and by doing that, you saved us all. I'm semel-re because of you. People will come to us, and there will be challenges, and now that everyone knows… there's never going to be a dull moment, I can tell. But, Jin… I know you need time to think, but I can't even rest without you, and I need to rest. I need my mate." His eyes pleaded with me. "Come home."

I knew he needed me. I needed him, too, but there was more to be said.

He cleared his throat. "You know, I have never seen anyone shift as fast as you, and neither has my father. He's actually awed with your power, and frankly, so am I. It was really something."

I kept waiting.

"My mate is amazing."

"Amazing" was nice to hear.

"Baby," he said warmly, "I need you. You know all the laws, who I should trust and who I shouldn't. You're so smart, and kind, and so… so beautiful."

I crouched down, silent.

"Here, kitty-kitty." His smile twisted, became lazy and sexy. "C'mere."

Hell no. He had to explain himself.

"Aww, c'mon," he chuckled. "You're killing me."

I tipped my head like I wasn't sure what he was talking about.

His laughter filled the space around us. "Shit."

Being in love with this man was fun. If he kept his sense of humor and trusted me, and if I could stop being afraid and have faith in him, we actually had a chance.

"Okay, how 'bout this: thank you, baby, for saving my life."

He was getting warmer.

"And I'm so sorry for what I did." His voice dropped down deep into his chest, and the smile fell out of his eyes. He wanted me to hear him; he wanted me to know his words carried weight and substance. "Please forgive me. I had no idea what else to do. If I knew then what I do now, I would have never done it. I know you were just starting to trust me, and I screwed up. I'm so sorry, baby. It will never happen again. I swear on my life."

I waited.

"I've never had a mate before. I didn't know that when I found you that I would feel like this." His eyes stayed locked on mine. "It's been overwhelming. I didn't know that feeling vulnerable could make me feel strong at the same time."

I knew what he meant. It was so hard to let someone close to you because that gave them the power to annihilate you, if they chose. It was terrifying and exhilarating all at the same time.

"And I know I hurt you because I didn't trust you to know what you were doing, but I was so scared. I have never been that scared in my life. And maybe if it was just you in the pit, the others would have just given up. Domin told me he would have never hurt you, not a reah, and Markel and Ivan said the same thing, that hurting a reah was not something anyone would ever or could ever do." He smiled suddenly. "'Cause, you know, reahs are kinda rare."

I felt the warmth of his voice slide over me. I had fallen so hard, so fast for this beautiful man with his big heart.

"So if I had just let it alone, stayed out of your fight, then there probably would have never even been one." He sighed deeply. "But I certainly didn't know that, and neither did you. We were both counting on fighting, and you did what you did to protect me, and I did the same. You are my mate, my love. I could never let anyone hurt you."

I watched him, saw the soft glow of the fire flicker on his skin, the flames reflected in the amber chips in his eyes, his hands clenching and unclenching with his need to put them on me. He was a study in restraint.

"Please, baby, please let me show you how trustworthy I can be."

And I wanted to, needed to, but I was so scared.

"I'm scared too," he said like he was reading my mind. "But you gotta just jump in and hope for the best and have faith that the love you feel, the other person feels right back."

I trembled with my need to go to him.

"Jin," he said sharply. "Trust me. Have faith in me. I love you. I want you."

I waited, hesitating, everything I had been thinking for the past week swirling through my head.

"Jin." He smiled, his eyes sliding over me. "Please come here. Let me put my hands on you. Let me have you."

I lifted up, then forward, my ass in the air, tail swishing from side to side as I rubbed my chin on my paws, releasing my pheromones into the air.

"I never saw you in your panther form before that night." He groaned. "You're gorgeous."

I watched as he shifted back into his beast. When he started slowly toward me, I leaped back before he could touch me, but not far enough to escape his long reach. I was batted sideways and hurled down into the furs. Instantly, he was on me, and the heat rolling off his huge body killed my flight reflex. His mouth was on my neck, holding me down, and I felt the shudder of need tear through him.

A heavy paw replaced his mouth, and then it moved further and further down my back. I didn't move, and when he bit my back leg, I lifted up, my ass again in the air. The long, slow lick over my hole caused a spasm to rip through me. He chuckled, and between that and the hand that wrapped around my cock, I knew he had shifted to his werepanther form. I did the same, and when his long tongue licked up between my cheeks, I jerked under him. Claws thrust into my skin to still me as his long werepanther tongue slid inside my channel, probing, the roughness adding to the pleasure as he swirled deeper and deeper inside. The hand around my shaft pumped in rhythm to the thrusting tongue, and I let my head fall back on my shoulders.

"Shift for me," he growled, withdrawing suddenly, throwing me down on my back.

I looked up, and there, again, was my beautiful man.

"Jin," he said, bending toward me, spreading my legs to take me into his mouth.

I watched him swallow down my cock, and I couldn't resist touching his hair, watching my dark, clawed hand slide through the blond waves, him so very human and me so very not.

He lifted his eyes to me. "I wanna touch your skin; I want to taste it. Shift now."

I did, and he moved fast, pinning me under him, lifting my legs over his shoulders, wiping saliva and the slick precome leaking from his cock over the bulbous head before he buried himself in me in one hard, brutal thrust. The burn was overwhelming, and I cried out even as the sizzling heat started to subside.

"My mate," he growled, curving his body over mine, seating me deeper against his groin as he captured my lips and kissed me hard.

"Logan," I moaned into his mouth as he began slowly pushing in and out of me.

He yanked my head back, and his mouth was on my exposed throat, licking, biting, and sucking so hard I knew he was going to leave marks. "You," he snarled, and I knew he was hovering somewhere between man and beast, "may never leave me again. I forbid it. I won't warn you a second time."

He had defended his tribe but had been denied the right of claiming his mate afterward. His betrayal of me had been great, but mine was worse. My place was at his side; even when he was stupid or foolish, it was where I belonged.

"Forgive me, my semel," I begged, and I felt my words tear through him, my submission making him moan with fresh need.

"You belong to me."

"Yes."

He pulled my hips closer to him and pounded down into me, so hard, so possessively, his huge, slippery cock smoothly gliding in and out of me so deep that I swore I could feel him in my heart. I knew that was where he wanted to be.

"Look at me."

I lifted my eyes, and the silhouette of the man took my breath away as I watched the play of muscles in his shoulders, chest, and abdomen, admiring his beauty, the long lines showing his strength and power. His eyes swallowed me, and I felt light-headed.

"Never leave again," he said, impaling me so hard, so fast, that I thought for a moment that he had split me in half before I felt the first throb of my orgasm rising deep inside me. "Swear it."

"I swear."

"You will be punished if you run again."

It was a promise, not a threat, and when I reached up to pull him down for a kiss, he thrust forward, burying himself to the hilt inside my body.

"Logan!" I screamed instead of "stop." The angle was too much, the sensations overwhelming, crossing over from pleasure to pain, back and forth so fast that I was lost, drowned, unable to think or reason, only feel. His mouth was on mine, the kiss slow and sensual, demanding and thorough. His tongue missed nothing.

"I claim you, body and soul!" he roared, and that was the animal in him, possessive, dominant, staking his claim as he licked his palm slick and then fisted my hard, throbbing cock. He jerked me off as he slammed in and out of me, and as turned on as I was, it took only seconds for my back to bow as I rose up under him and yelled his name through my blinding orgasm.

My muscles clenched around him, my body tensing up, and in seconds, my name filled the small space as he cried it out, filling me before he collapsed on top of me.

It was useless trying to push him off.

He moved with a grunt, a smile plastered on his face. "You're mine."

I tried to drag in oxygen.

He rolled up onto his side, propping his head on his elbow as he looked down at me.

"God, you're beautiful," I told him.

"No, I'm looking at beautiful."

But I was right. The man was all chiseled perfection—the sculpted chest, the hard pecs, the deep groove that ran down his abdomen—everything was taut and cut and hard. I reached out and touched him, relishing the feel of his hot, silky skin under my palm, feeling how his muscles clenched. "You like me touching you."

"Yes, I do," he said, leaning down to kiss my throat. "I like everything you do to me and all the ways you react to me. Sometimes I want to eat you, and other times, I just want to hold you next to my heart."

I lifted up and eased him down under me, my mouth slanting over his, kissing him deeply, my tongue tangling with his. I watched his eyes close and felt the shudder ripple through his body, amazed at what my touch could cause. I moved slowly and covered my sweet man with light kisses on every square inch of his body, and he yawned and stretched languidly, obviously content. When he had had enough, he rolled over on top of me, pinning me under him, and I lifted my legs and wrapped them around him so he could settle between my thighs. It was gentle this time, our eyes locked together, all the heat translating into sensual movement, my lover seductive instead of fierce, our bodies melting into one.

Chapter Fifteen

THE FOLLOWING night, Logan showed up early to pick me up from the restaurant. I took him inside and introduced him to everyone I worked with. As it turned out, my boss was the one most excited to meet him.

"Logan," Ray said, shaking his hand hard. "You're a godsend. Now that Jin has a new partner and a great job, why would he ever leave?"

"I dunno," Logan smiled smugly, his hand sliding through my hair before he drew me forward, anchoring me to his side. "Why would he?"

"You see?" Ray said, slapping my free shoulder. "Change is a good thing."

How could I argue?

"Let's go home," Logan growled at me, playfully pushing me toward the front door. "I need to put you in bed."

We drove to my new apartment, which I had thankfully only taken on a month-to-month basis, and I was going to show him around before he stopped me.

"Just grab your stuff," he growled. "I hate this place. I just wanna go."

He hated anywhere I was that wasn't his home. He wanted my clothes, my books, and my laptop in his house and put away.

"You know, now that I have a good job, I'll probably start buying a ton of clothes and shoes and all kinds of crap."

"Whatever you want," he said, watching me as I walked around picking things up.

Once we were driving away, I warned Logan that we had a lot to talk about when we got home, so I hoped he had no other plans.

"Talk about what?" he complained. "We talked last night."

He had no idea about anything. Ours would be a very tricky blending of lifestyles and priorities, and there was his new tribe and everything else to consider. It was going to be a mess.

"I love you," I sighed, unable to keep the smile from my face, leaning back and looking at him through heavy-lidded eyes. "I really do."

"I know," he grunted, very pleased with himself. "You can't live without me. I'm like cheese."

It took a second to process his comment. "I'm sorry, cheese?"

"Sure. Air's overrated. Try living without cheese."

The man was insane, which, it turned out, was just perfect for me.

AT HOME, I was busy putting away more of my things when Logan came into the room with a plate of sandwiches and two glasses of milk.

"What is this?"

"Late-night snack."

"Well, thank you." I smiled over my shoulder at him as he sprawled out on the bed.

"Uh," he started and stopped.

"What?"

He visibly winced as he looked up at me.

"What's wrong with you?"

"Okay, so what would you say if I told you that your father was in town?"

I stopped breathing.

"Oh, you should see your eyes," he said, getting off the bed and crossing the room to me. His hands were warm on my arms. "You okay?"

"My father's here?"

"Technically, he's in Reno."

I just stared up into his face.

"My dad called him, remember? He told him all about your plan to fight for me in the pit, and that was the last the man heard."

"He thought I was dead."

"No." He shook his head. "I'm sure he just wanted to see you."

"He came to take my body home."

"He did not," he snapped.

"I hate him."

"You don't hate anybody. It's not in you."

I sighed heavily, drew away from him, and walked to the bed. I started picking at the meat inside the sandwich.

"Move the tray before the milk spills."

I did as I was asked and put the tray on the nightstand.

"I figured your dad would look like you."

I shook my head. "No, I look like my mom. My brother, Kei, looks like my dad, except his hair is black like mine, not light brown."

"Are his eyes gray too?"

"No, they're blue just like my father's."

"Your mother is what, Japanese?"

I nodded.

"How did they meet?"

"They met when he was in the Navy and stationed in Tokyo."

"She must have named both you and your brother, huh? Jin and Kei aren't exactly names you hear every day."

"I think you do if you live in Japan."

"That's what I mean."

I let out a deep breath.

"Are you hungry?"

I shrugged.

"You want something else?"

"No," I said, suddenly very interested in the pattern on the comforter.

"Listen. He invited us to have breakfast with him tomorrow morning. He really wants to talk to you and catch up."

"He's just disappointed I'm not dead," I said, getting up off the bed, feeling caged suddenly.

"Jin," he warned.

I shut up.

"Look at me."

I lifted my head, and my eyes found him.

"I'd like to talk to him. He was really interested in me."

"Oh, I bet." I started to pace. "You're the man that mated with the abomination. I'm sure he thinks you're on some mission from God."

He laughed hard, and I couldn't contain my smile. The man just melted me.

"Do you want me to invite him up here or do you want to go to the hotel and see him?"

"Is he alone?"

"No. His semel is with him."

"Gabriel Pike is here?"

He squinted at me. "No, I think he said his name is Archer."

"Archer Pike? Are you sure? Archer is Gabriel's brother."

"I'm sure I heard right. He said his name was Archer and that he was the semel of your old tribe. He came with your father."

"Interesting. I wonder what happened to Gabriel," I said, looking at Logan.

"Maybe he stepped down?"

"Why would anyone do that?"

"I have no idea." He yawned. "The reasons that people do anything are beyond me. Like why would anyone run from their mate?"

I rolled my eyes. "Are we talking about this again?"

"I will never let you leave me again."

I groaned. "I don't want to leave you."

"But you can't, even if you did."

"Why are we talking about this?"

He went silent for a moment. "You know, I still can't believe that you came up here and took care of me even after everything."

"I love you. Why wouldn't I?" When he didn't say anything back for several heartbeats, I looked over at him. He was staring at me. "What?"

"I just like it." He cleared his throat. "You telling me you love me."

I walked over to the bed and bent toward him. He lifted his head to receive the kiss and was smiling at me when I pulled back.

"I love you, too, Jin."

We were silent, watching each other, before his expression darkened. "Listen, maybe it's too much, too soon. I can tell your father to leave, and we can visit Chicago instead."

I shook my head. "No, invite them back up to the house tomorrow. That way, if it gets weird, I can just come up here."

He nodded, looking at me.

"I can, right? They couldn't follow me up here?"

"To violate a semel's home is a trespass, and you know that. You're mine. Without my permission, no one can see you."

"Really." I snorted out a quick laugh, baiting him. "No one?"

"Jin—"

"Not your mom," I threw out.

He growled back in his throat.

"Or say, one of your brothers."

"God, you're annoying."

"Or Yuri or Mikhail or—"

"Are you done?"

I chuckled and he threw up his hands in defeat. Ordering me around was never going to happen, and the sooner he realized, the better off he was going to be.

"Are you through taunting me?"

I didn't answer him, instead walking to the window and looking out at the falling snow. I was so happy for the first time in so long, and now my father, my family, had to come and spoil it. And what if, when Logan spent more time with my father, heard his rant, what if he started to question his decision about me? What if the new semel convinced Logan he was making a mistake? What if he got Logan to see me as an obstacle instead of as the permanent person in his life? What if everything I finally had just went away?

I wanted to belong, and now I did, but how solid was my new life, really?

"What are you thinking about so hard?"

"Nothing." I shook my head.

"Liar," he judged.

I was silent.

"It was really nice of him to come all this way and see if you were okay."

I dragged in a deep breath. "It wasn't nice. He wants something. He doesn't give a shit about me, I assure you."

"That's crap. It was nice of him. Say it was nice."

"No."

"Come on, say it. It was nice."

I turned and looked at him over my shoulder. "No."

"C'mon," he said, getting up, moving toward me.

"No," I repeated sharply. "What's with you?"

"You're being a brat. Say it's nice."

"No."

"Say it."

"No," I snapped.

He lunged for me, and I moved to dodge him.

"Quit, Logan. I don't feel like playing with you."

He reached for me again, and I crossed the room quickly, putting the bed between us.

"I said stop," I half sputtered, my tone exasperated, and I saw his eyes darken to a deep burnished gold. "So stop. I'm not in the mood. Don't be a dick."

He nodded right before he dove across the bed for me.

"Logan!" I yelled, trying really hard not to smile. "I said stop!"

He climbed off the bed, and when I moved toward the door to put more space between us, he followed me. I was being stalked, and I put out my hand, pointing at him.

"When I say stop, you stop! You never listen to me."

"No." He smiled suddenly, stilling, his eyes so soft, so warm that my heart hurt just looking at him. "I always listen to you, and watch you, and notice every little thing about you. So I know that what you need right now is for me to show you that you're mine. I need you to understand that you belong to me, and that I have the power, not you."

"Logan—"

But his hand went up to quiet me. "I need you to understand that I'm strong enough for you to lean on, because you haven't had that in a very long time. You need to depend on me, trust my love, and know that it's not going to break or change. I need you to surrender so you'll know that I can protect you from anything."

Instinctively, Logan knew what I needed, like he could read my mind. And maybe he could. He was my mate after all.

"So now… you better run," the sultry voice teased as he advanced slowly.

But did I want to? Why would anyone run away from a walking, talking wet dream come to life?

"Or you could just let me have you," he suggested.

But that was much too easy. So when he dashed toward me, I ran into the sitting room that was attached to our bedroom, putting the small loveseat between the two of us. His eyes were narrowed in half, and the smile was wicked… I was more than willing to let the man do whatever he wanted to me. And even though we were playing, there was an undercurrent of emotion there that had my jaw clenching and hot tears welling up in my eyes. What would have happened to me if I had never found this man who understood me and how my very twisted brain worked? I bit my bottom lip to keep it from trembling.

"C'mere," he said, bracing his legs apart, ready to dart whichever way I decided to run.

"No, you c'mere," I countered, gesturing him close.

He put his hand on his chest. "Me come to you? You're ordering me around now?"

"What is that?" I caught my breath, pointing toward the door.

In the second that he looked I bolted for the door, but he was faster in human form and drove me into the wall, shoving me up against it, pinning me there. He manhandled me, which I loved, and I couldn't stifle the soft moan of pleasure as his knee pushed between my legs. He held my wrists above my head, and his chest pressed into my back. I shivered under him, and I heard a very satisfied male chuckle as he kissed the side of my neck.

"I could get away if I wanted," I boasted, my voice barely there.

"If you wanted," he said seductively, his voice low and husky against the whorl of my ear, biting the lobe very gently. "Maybe."

My breath caught as I melted in his grasp.

"Listen to me. I am not like anybody who's ever had you before. I will never let you go. Do you understand?" His voice was low as he gently bit the back of my neck, swirling his tongue over the spot before he sucked hard.

I nodded, loving this dominant side of him, the side that could hold me down if he wanted, while all the time I knew he was not the kind of man who would ever hold me against my will. The heart of the man had dominion over his power.

"All those guys who fucked you, all those guys who ran from you when they found out what you were, your parents, your old semel, and your brother… none of those people are me. I own you, body and soul. You get it?"

"I get it."

"And you will trust me to love and protect you always."

"Yes."

"Good, I'm glad that's settled."

The man picked the damndest times to drive home his point.

"Now, you'll feel my love," he promised before he bit me again, sucking with greater force. "'Cause you need to understand that nothing and no one is ever going to change the way I feel about you. You're my mate, you idiot."

I trembled in his arms, pliant, while he unsnapped my dress pants and reached down the front. My head was thrown back on my shoulders, my back arched, and he kissed my throat as he pulled down my briefs and spread my legs apart.

"Say my name."

"Logan."

"Who owns you?"

"You do."

I was shoved forward over the back of the loveseat, and his tongue, impossibly long, impossibly strong, slid into my crease. I gasped because the sensation was overwhelming. It was amazing that before me, Logan Church had been straight, because the man loved all the same things I did, and apparently me being a man was of no consideration at all.

"You're perfect for me. Your lean, hard body fits mine like a glove."

He could definitely read my mind. When he had me panting and begging for him to be inside me, he spun me around to face him, swallowing my cock down his throat at the same time as his fingers slid between my ass cheeks. It was torture; his talented fingers were swirling inside me, and my throbbing shaft was buried in his hot, wet mouth. I was on sensory overload, and the tears were suddenly there, rolling down my cheeks. All of it was too much—his love, his desire, the faith he demanded from me, and the submission he required.

"What do you want?"

"Oh, please," I moaned, "just fuck me, mark me… make everything go away."

"Already marked you, but…." I was suddenly backed over the loveseat. I heard the lid of the lube snapping open and vaguely wondered where he had stashed it. "I would love to be inside that hot, tight little ass of yours."

I nearly came right there, but the sensation of him buried inside me did that a second later, as he hit my prostate on the first try. No other man but my mate could bring me to orgasm with just the promise of sex. He was too hot for his own good.

"I think I'm gonna make you come until you pass out," he said as I collapsed in his arms, sliding slowly in and out of me.

Good God.

"Let's try."

I couldn't. There was no way I could have another orgasm so soon.

"My sweet baby," he groaned into the side of my neck.

Just the man's voice brought on fresh need, and seconds later, I was trembling again as he pushed inside me as deeply as he could, the hoarse moans tearing out of him as he held my hips. He felt so good, so hard, and the hand slick with lube sliding over my shaft had killed my power of speech.

"You will never worry again."

I would, but I didn't want to argue with him. "No," I lied.

"You are my love."

"Yes," I agreed as he thrust into me so hard that he lifted me off my feet. I screamed out his name over and over.

"Is there anything hotter than you yelling my name?"

I couldn't answer. I was reduced to panting as he bit down hard into my shoulder.

"The answer is 'yes,' because you squirming around on the end of my dick trying to get me in deeper to fuck you harder... that's gonna kill me," he said before hugging me so hard I could feel his heart beating as we both came.

Later, when I came out of the shower, he was dressed in sweats and a T-shirt, sitting on the edge of the bed putting on a pair of crew socks.

"You did that on purpose."

He looked up from pulling on the last sock. "What's that?"

"You know."

"I have no idea what you're talking about."

I nodded. "You know, sometimes I just can't get close enough to you. I wanna climb inside your skin and live there."

He smiled at me. "I love you, too, Jin."

"I'm sorry I put you through so much shit."

"Yeah, saving my life, that was rough."

"You know what I mean."

"We're okay, baby. Everything's okay."

"Is it?"

"Yes."

I nodded.

"Seems to me," he said softly, "that you're still filled with fear instead of me."

"No, I—"

"You're so scared of being abandoned that you can't even see me."

"I see you."

"Not really," he said, getting up and walking over to me, grabbing the back of my wet hair before bending and kissing me hard and deep. "You still think I could stop loving you."

"No." I shook my head, swallowing hard. "I don't."

"Then stop worrying," he pressed. "Okay?"

"Okay."

"Look at me."

"I am."

"Are you?"

"Logan, I'm not blind. I can—"

"Look into my eyes."

I searched them as he put his hands on my face, bent, and kissed me, running his tongue over the inside of my mouth, not missing anything, sucking hard and devouring my lips. I could kiss him for hours, stopping only for breath, soft sighs, and whimpers.

"Logan," I got out, my hands on his forearms, holding on.

"You smell good," he growled into my mouth, his lips not lifting off mine, kissing me again, deeper, his hands pulling the towel away so I was naked in front of him. "You're so beautiful."

"Logan, you can't want—"

"I want you all the time, baby," he told me, shoving me down on the bed, crouching between my legs, one hand on my cock, the other on my thigh, making sure I couldn't move.

I threw my arm across my eyes, but he barked at me to look at him.

"Logan," I said shakily, writhing under him.

"Watch my mouth on you, Jin. You know you love to watch me."

As I stared down into his eyes, I saw his pupils dilate, his lips open, and my cock slide into his mouth. How in the world was I so lucky as to have a man who looked like some Norse god come to life with a heart that beat just for me?

"Logan." My voice cracked on his name.

He ran a hand over the muscles in my abdomen before tracing the delicate skin in his mouth with his very talented tongue. My back bowed, rising up off the bed as he swallowed me down.

"Oh God," I moaned. "Please, Logan."

"Please, Logan, what?"

The only thing I could voice was his name over and over in endless litany, but from his smile and the way he kissed me, I knew he understood the desire I couldn't voice.

My cock slid from his mouth as he rose and moved to the nightstand. Fishing the lube from the drawer, he unsnapped his jeans and sat down on the bed, coating the long, hard shaft jutting from his groin until it gleamed in the light. When he was done, his head turned to me.

"Come here."

I was trembling as I crawled to him.

"Ride me."

It was an invitation, not an order, and that, combined with the heat in his eyes, took my breath away. As I straddled his hips, I felt his hands cup my ass, and I slowly lowered myself over him.

"You are so tight and hot," he groaned, one hand taking hold of my stiff cock, stroking me as I lifted up only to sink down again, impaling myself on the hard, thick length of him.

I closed my eyes. I felt too good, and staring into his eyes was too much. When I came seconds later, my release made my whole body shake.

"Look at me."

My eyes drifted open, and I was surprised when he wrapped his arms around me, holding me so tight, his face buried in my shoulder as warm come flooded my channel.

"Wrap your legs around me. Hold me tight."

And I did. I held him with my arms, my legs, the clenching muscles in my ass. I held him tight to my heart with everything I had, and he pressed me to his and didn't let me go.

Chapter Sixteen

EVEN AFTER so long, I had a vision in my mind of how my meeting with my father would go. And while logically it made no sense, I still, somewhere deep inside, hoped for an outcome that would return his love to me. It was a basic human need, to want the love of your parents. That morning I realized that even with all the time that had passed, it was still ingrained in me to want it. Crane didn't understand it at all.

Sitting on the counter while I did the dishes, he was drying plates as I lifted them from the soapy water and then rinsed them.

"You…." Crane trailed off, and when I realized he wasn't going to say any more, I turned to look at him.

"What?"

"Just… I don't want to see you get hurt again, is all. I mean, I know that no one's going to beat you, but I don't even want you to care about him being here."

It was impossible for me not to care. Even with all my forced bravado, telling Logan the man had only made the trip out to claim my dead body… I hoped it wasn't true, had prayed it wasn't true.

"Hey."

Lost in my thoughts, I was surprised to look up at Crane and find him peering out the window instead of at me.

"They're here."

"Who's here?"

"Your dad."

But it was too early. It was two hours before the time he had set with Logan on the phone that morning. "Are you sure?"

"Uh, yeah," he said like I was stupid, glaring down at me, "I know what your dad looks like. I grew up with him just like you."

"I didn't mean that you—"

"I'm gonna go say hello," he announced, cutting me off, slipping off the counter to the floor. He balled up the dish towel and beaned me with it, striding toward the swinging door. "I wanna talk to him before he talks to you."

I rolled my eyes, rinsing more plates. "I think it's hilarious that you of all people are gonna try and lecture my father, and even more funny that you think Logan will let you."

"What?" Crane stopped at the door, turning to look at me.

"You've been walking around with me for so long that you've forgotten all the rules of hospitality," I told him. "Neither of us is getting near my father until Logan calls us."

"I don't—"

"He's a sylvan traveling with his semel, being received in the home of another semel," I explained to my clueless friend. "There are rules that have to be observed, and you and I are still hours away from seeing him face-to-face."

"But I thought that's what you wanted?"

"I do, but I would never dishonor Logan by barging in there before he called me."

Crane's smile was sly. "Well, now, haven't we been whipped into shape?"

I flipped him off. "It's not like that. Logan doesn't get to tell me what to do. You of all people know—"

"I know, I know," Crane groaned. "Sorry."

I gestured with a soapy hand for him to come back to me. "It's just that me disagreeing with Logan, fighting with him… only you, his family, people who live in this house… you're the only ones who get to see that. In public, in front of the tribe, they only get to see me observing my place as reah and honoring my semel."

He nodded, and I noticed the trembling smile, the clenching of his jaw, and how he had to quickly rub his eyes.

"Jesus. What?" I smiled at him, my friend with the soft heart.

"Nothin', just you bein' a reah… I knew you'd be a good one. I just never figured you'd get the chance."

We stood in silence staring at each other.

"Excuse me."

Both Crane and I turned to the door where a man I had never seen in my life was standing. I felt my brows furrow.

"Hi." He smiled, slipping into the room, hand extended forward. "I'm—"

I cut him off sharply. "You need to go back to the group. You're violating a lot of rules of—"

"Danny?" My father poked his head into the room, apparently looking for the man standing in front of me.

It was hard to wrap my brain around the fact that I was suddenly seeing my father after so long. The moment was surreal.

"Dad," I said before I even thought the word in my head, just his name tumbling naturally out of me.

"Jinnai," my father said, using my full Japanese first name.

"Hello, sir."

"I'm glad you're not dead."

What was the correct response to that?

"Thank you, sir," I said, washing off my hands, flipping the water off and then wiping them dry, all of it taking forever to accomplish. I felt like I was moving through caramel as I walked across the room to him. It felt like a dream, like the movement in dreams, how you should be able to run but never can. He put his hands behind his back, his signal to me that we would not shake. I shoved my own down into the pockets of my threadbare jeans.

He squinted at me. "Does your semel make you wear your hair that long?"

I took deep breaths. "No."

"Is he sterile?"

I immediately knew where this was going. "No."

"So he's capable of having children, then?"

After eight years, close to nine, of no contact with the man, and these were the first words he was going to speak to me? In front of a stranger, no less? "I assume so, yes."

"But this man, this supposed semel, he's willing to give up everything for you?"

"He's not giving up anything."

"He's giving up his bloodline... his future. I would call that everything."

I stared at him and he stared back.

"Jin."

With much effort I dragged my eyes from my father back to Crane. He was pointing at the stranger in our midst.

"Who's the kid?"

As I returned my eyes to the man who had first entered the kitchen, I reassessed my first impression and had to agree with my friend's observation. He was a boy, not a man, and if we were stretching it, maybe sixteen. "I don't know you," I said flatly.

He coughed to cover the nervousness I could feel rolling off him. "I'm your cousin, Danny. I've been living with your family for—"

"Never mind," I said softly, feeling a sharp pain in my heart. Instantly I knew I was looking at my replacement. My father had needed a new me, and had one. "Are you learning all the tribal customs and laws?"

He looked confused. "Uh... yes, I am."

I nodded, taking a quick breath before I looked back at my father.

"We need to get back," he announced. "I just came looking for Danny because he wandered off. He doesn't know all the rules of visitation yet."

But my father would have told him, educated him, made sure the boy didn't embarrass him. That meant my dad had ulterior motives. "Yes," I agreed quickly, turning and walking away from him, back to the sink. "You better go before you're missed."

"Good morning," a voice called out as the door that led from the kitchen to the driveway opened and Peter Church came through it. "Jin, I—oh." He was surprised to find anyone there besides me, and while he smiled when he saw Crane, his furrowed brows let me know that my father and my cousin were a concern.

"Good morning," I greeted my mate's father, drawing his attention to me.

"Jin," he said slowly, moving further into the room, putting a bag of green apples down on the counter. "These are for you and

Eva to make the pies later. I'm sorry, who are these people?" He sounded irritated.

All of a sudden, I was really glad to see him. I let out a breath and felt like me again. "This is my father and my cousin Danny from Chicago."

Peter nodded slowly and then stepped closer to me, moving so that my vision filled with him, shielding me from the others. "Jin, you know them being in here is considered a grave insult to your semel. They should not be in your presence without—"

"No, I know," I stopped him. "My dad just followed Danny in here. They were just leaving."

"Good," he said, turning around to look over at my father. "This is extremely inappropriate behavior, sir, but as our reah is your son, I'm sure my son, our semel, will overlook the trespass."

The warning was understood as the two men stared at each other.

My father finally nodded as Peter extended his hand to him, walking across the room. "I'm Peter Church, Logan's father. It's a pleasure to meet the man who sired my son's mate."

"Mitchell Rayne," my father said, shaking his hand. "May I ask why you allowed your son to take a male mate? It's the end of your house."

Peter nodded, releasing my father's hand. "I'll confess I was scared, very scared, at first, and then I realized that I'm not living a hundred years ago. I'm living in a time of adoption and surrogates, and more importantly, I am a man that has always wanted the very best for his children. My son has been blessed with a true-mate, a reah, and in finding him has become semel-re. I have met only two other semels in my life that have found reahs, and both had the largest, strongest tribes I have ever seen. The semel who finds his reah is unlike one who does not. I had forgotten that for a brief moment."

"So your son is a better semel than you were?"

"Oh, yes, absolutely."

"Better simply because he has a reah."

"Yes."

"But your son will not be a father."

Peter chuckled. "That is not for you to say. No one can see the future."

My father nodded. "I would like to meet your son."

That meant that Logan had not been in the room before Danny took his stroll and forced my father to follow him right to me.

"Let me show you to him," Peter said quickly, spreading his arms, herding both Danny and my father toward the door, giving me a quick smile over his shoulder, the warmth radiating off him just as it did his son.

"Well, that was fun," Crane muttered, headed toward the door, following.

"Where are you going?"

"If your dad can forget about the rules and barge in, then so can I. I'll be right back."

I was going to argue, but he was right. The day was getting weirder by the second. It took a turn for the worse when my father suddenly reappeared in the empty kitchen minutes later.

"Well, you certainly have your semel's father confused about what's truly important," he snapped. "How did you manage to do that?"

"What are you—"

"Jin!"

He wasn't treating me like a reah; he wasn't treating me like another semel's mate. He was still treating me like I was just his son, and not one he even liked much.

"Answer me."

The man would never change. I took a quick breath and tried to calm my racing heart. "How are Mom and Kei?"

"They're both well. I asked them to come with me, but neither of them wanted to see you."

One more dig for good measure. "Well, I'm sorry about that."

"Are you?"

"Yes," I sighed, and I realized, finally, that what I wanted and what would be were two totally different and separate things. My biological family would never accept me; my new family was the one that counted. I was so lucky to have found them, so lucky to have found Logan, most of all. My vision was suddenly blurred, and I looked down so my father would not see the tears that to him only ever signified weakness. I had never been so emotional in my life. It was almost funny.

"Jin." My father's voice dropped low as he stepped in close to me. "Why do you persist in this perversion? You know that a male reah is not a blessing, but an abomination, and when others ask where you came from and—"

I couldn't contain my gasp, because really, it was like he hit me. I had been so wrong. He had not made the trip to destroy my dreams, to take everything away from me by trying to talk Logan out of loving me. His intentions were much more insidious. He had come from Chicago to fill me with self-loathing, to spread his venom for the second time in my life, and to engulf me in fear and doubt in the hopes that I would run again. He could not have his gay son be the reah of a tribe. Just the thought was killing him.

"You're vile," he said coldly, his voice steeped in hatred, "and you bring shame to Logan and his tribe with your very presence and to me for being your father."

I nodded, rubbing my eyes, trying to stop the tears. I had to get myself under control, but it was hard. Letting go of something old was painful, and accepting something new was overwhelming. When the truth ambushed you, it was tough to get your bearings, especially with only seconds to work with.

"Get out of my house," I said, stepping away from my father, feeling gutted suddenly, like a building after a fire, utterly destroyed.

"It's not your house; it's not your home! You have no home, no place with any panther tribe. You were exiled."

The thing about burned buildings was that they could be rebuilt. And even though my father and his love for me were gone forever, I was still standing and my foundation was strong.

"You cannot think that Logan truly loves you," my father spewed as he advanced on me. "It is simply the power of a reah working on his senses. When he has his fill of you, when the spell is broken, he will drive you from his home and perhaps even butcher you in the process for your role in the seduction of his true nature."

He was so matter-of-fact with his threats of my demise. What had ever possessed me to hope for his love? But really, I knew the answer. This was still my father spouting his rage and hatred and lies. The blue eyes were still his, the dark brown hair now streaked with silver was cut as it had been forever, and his smell, his aftershave, remained unchanged. This was the man who had raised me, even though he no longer saw me at all.

"When Logan discovers what you have taken from him—his name, his pride, his reputation, his very standing in our community—he will hate you and may very well kill you."

I took a step back, but he grabbed my arm, his fingers digging into my bicep hard. His grip would leave marks.

"Jin, did you see where your dad went?" Crane asked as he walked back into the kitchen.

"Yep," I said sarcastically, taking a quivering breath.

Crane moved fast, and my father let me go, making room, seeing the look on my best friend's face. "What the hell is going on?" Crane roared, pointing an accusing finger at my father before pivoting around to face me. "And you!"

"Me?"

"Yes, you! What the hell are you doing in here talking to him like it's nothing! You never receive anyone without your sheseru, Jin. You know that. Everybody knows that. You gotta start acting like the reah you are!"

He was pissed at me? "Why're you mad?"

"Because you don't realize how important you are, and you gotta start. Without you, nothing works!"

And he was right. I had to realize who I was.

The air in the room that had felt old and stagnant moments before was suddenly moving again, like Crane had brought with him a refreshing breeze. I felt the tension draining out of me, melting away. How good to be reminded that I was loved.

"And what are you thinking, putting your hands on our reah?" Crane snapped at my father, shoving between Mitchell Rayne and me, his muscular frame forcing my father back. "You're just a sylvan; you can be punished for such a trespass."

My father saw me as the dirt beneath his feet, and Crane as merely the disowned son of the sheseru of his tribe. "Watch how you speak to me, boy."

"Watch how you speak to me," Crane thundered, and I watched my father take a step away. "I am beset of a reah, and as such command you to remove yourself from his presence or I shall be forced to call for my sheseru."

"Crane—"

But my friend's motion cut him off as he turned his back on my father to face me. "I know it goes without saying, but I want to stick around and join your tribe."

I was momentarily stunned. "Oh, I-I thought, I mean, I always just assumed you would. I don't want you to leave. Ever! Don't leave. Stay."

"Okay," Crane said, and the smile was luminous. Sometimes I forgot how great looking my best friend was, even more so because I could see his heart.

Turning back around, he faced my father. "As I was cast out by my tribe, I choose to seek sanctuary with another and herby renounce my place in the tribe of Anuket. I will become a member of the tribe of Mafdet."

"Crane," my father sighed, rubbing the bridge of his nose like my best friend was just so tiresome, "you shouldn't act so rashly. Our new semel, Archer Pike, is a much stronger semel than Gabriel ever was, and under his leadership, our tribe will—"

"I renounce my place," Crane said firmly, turning sideways, his hand on my shoulder, steering me around my father toward the door. He wasn't leaving me alone anymore. "You may tell my father when you see him."

"You should come home," my father told him.

"Jin is my home," he said. "He always has been."

"Because while a semel leads the tribe, a reah strengthens it, makes it whole," Logan growled as he stepped into the room, obviously having been right outside the door for several minutes. Yuri and Mikhail stood behind him. I had no idea all of what he'd heard. "You," he said, pointing at Crane, "are beset of my reah and belong to me as surely as he does. I will hear your testimony and oath at the next tribal gathering, but I already consider you a member of my tribe, Crane Adams."

My best friend nodded and left the room fast, brushing by me in his hurry to not show a flicker of the emotion he felt in front of either Logan or my father.

"You," Logan said, his voice low and husky as he pointed at me, "come here."

When I was close enough, he reached out and drew me with him out into the hall, leaving Mikhail to watch my dad. He held me close to his chest, his hands on my face, touching my skin, his breath ghosting over my hair. "Are you all right?"

I saw how dark and molten my mate's eyes were. I smiled quickly, licking my lips to distract him. Clearly he was not pleased with whatever part of my father's rant he had heard. "You left me in there on purpose," I told him.

"Yes." His voice was full of obvious pain.

"So I could make my own decision about what I wanted to do."

"Within reason," he agreed, smoothing my hair back out of my face, savoring the feel of my hair slipping through his fingers. "I will never let you go, but knowing that you can hear lies and not believe them, have faith in me before anything else… I'm very proud. Just looking at you gives me joy. You have no idea."

I couldn't contain my sigh. "I love you."

"I know." He nodded before he wrapped me in his arms and crushed me against his hard chest. And even though the man was a mountain of muscle, he was gentle with me, tender, because I was treasured, prized above all others, loved. Held in his arms, to his heart, I was the safest I would ever be.

"Did he hurt you?" he asked as he let me go, hands back on my face, lifting my chin gently, checking for damage. "Jin?"

I shook my head because my throat had closed up.

"You're gonna freeze like this," he said, hands on my arms, rubbing to try to warm me up. "Go put on some socks and a sweater and come back down. We'll wait right here."

"But you shouldn't be alone with—"

He gave me a look like I was out of my mind. Like my father could ever hurt him with anything he had to say. "Just go put something on already."

I nodded and smiled at him before I bolted. Yuri was at the bottom of the stairs when I reached them. "What are you doing?"

"I'm making sure no one follows you upstairs," he told me.

"But you should go stay with Logan and—"

"The sheseru is the enforcer of the semel, the guardian of the reah," he recited from a law we both knew. "Is that not so?"

It was so and we both knew it. When he smirked at me, I wanted to smack him, but anywhere I decided to jab him I would hurt my hand. The man was made of stone. Leaving him, I raced upstairs, grabbed a zippered cardigan and a pair of crew socks, and got back to Logan as fast as I could. What I found when I returned froze me in my tracks.

Counting my father and Danny, there were four men on their knees on the tiled floor of the kitchen. It was surprising for me; I had never seen my father kneel to anyone but his own semel.

"We beg your forgiveness, semel-re, for disturbing your home and for daring to speak to your mate without permission," one of the two men I didn't know said quickly. "Had I my own reah, I would kill any who dared to touch her, and I know that the life of my sylvan is forfeit to you for this breach. I will say that as my sylvan is your reah's father, I'm sure he was momentarily overcome with seeing his son again."

"The lies and hatred that were spoken make me doubt your words, but as I don't know you, I will assume you speak from a place of sincerity."

"Thank you, semel-re." He bowed his head to Logan.

"Rise," Logan said darkly.

"Will you forgive my sylvan his grave insult to your reah?"

Logan nodded. "This once, but never again."

The man put his hand on my father's shoulder before looking back at Logan. "May I address your reah?"

Just a slight dip of Logan's head, but it was enough. The man stepped forward, offering me his hand. "I am Archer Pike, semel of the tribe of Anuket, and it is a pleasure to meet you, Jinnai Rayne."

"It's just Jin," I corrected him, taking his hand, watching his jaw clench, his nostrils flare. "Only my mom calls me Jinnai."

Archer was a tall, gaunt-looking man, and his face was not kind, even when he smiled—or tried to—and there was a cold, predatory feeling that rose off him. The slate blue eyes, now fixed on me, held no warmth either. They looked instead like two pieces of colored ice.

"I have never seen a reah. No one told me that there had been one in my tribe. Had I been semel of the tribe when you revealed yourself, I can assure you that the treatment you suffered at the hands of my brother, your father, and the others would not have occurred."

"What treatment?" Yuri asked from behind me, and because he startled me, I instinctively tried to pull my hand free of Archer's grip. But he tightened his hold so I couldn't move.

"My sylvan told me on our flight here that his son was beaten and left naked on the road by my brother and the tribe."

I winced inwardly. I would have preferred Logan had gone his whole life without knowing that piece of information. Why did people always feel the need to share?

"You beat your own son?" Yuri growled, his voice rising as he advanced on my father, his hand on my chest as he moved by me. He pushed me gently backward, out of Archer's grip, back against Logan's chest. "Did you beat him until he bled? Was he conscious when you left him?"

Logan's arms wrapped around me as he drew me back against him, his stubbled cheek rubbing over mine as he bent to kiss the crook of my neck. "They beat you?"

I opened my mouth to say something, but my father commanded all the attention in the next moment.

"He's filth," my father spat. "He's a perversion, and your tribe will suffer if you call him your reah! Your semel is not blessed, he's cursed by a love that is sick and twisted and wrong. People will flee the tribe of Mafdet in droves."

"Actually, they're *coming* in droves, you ignorant ass." Mikhail chuckled, lightening the mood as he stepped forward. "Being a reah cancels out all else. Man, woman, it doesn't matter what a reah is. They're blessings, and our semel is semel-re because of your son. He found his mate, and your semel is weaker because he didn't. A mated pair leads the strongest of tribes, and you know that just as well as I do."

My father had no argument. There was none. The facts were indisputable. I was a reah, Logan, a semel, and we were a mated pair. It was truly a miracle that we had found each other, and I had to start treating it as such.

"I'm the reah," I breathed as Logan squeezed my shoulders and stepped around me to face the others without me between them. "I am the mate of the semel of my tribe."

All eyes were on me as I looked around.

Logan groaned softly. "Did that finally just sink in, right this second?" He was scowling at me.

"Pretty much, yeah." I grinned, not put off by the furrowed brows.

He rolled his eyes before he turned back to look at my father. "You, sir, are the abomination. A father loves his son no matter what. This is *maat*."

Mitchell Rayne would have spoken in his own defense, but Logan's lifted hand left no room for argument. My dad's time to speak was ended. "As for you, semel"—Logan's gold eyes moved to Archer Pike—"take your sylvan and go. Do not return without invitation. I have no use for the family or the former tribe of my mate, for they are blind to the gift that he is."

"Semel-re," Archer began.

"And do not seek to gain allies in hopes of somehow hurting me to in turn bring harm to my reah. I have sent my maahes to speak to Ethan Locke in New York, and if he accepts my asset, Simone, then he and I will share a covenant bond. And Martine Soto in Miami is a dear friend. I only warn you, because if you suggest to him any alliance to strike back at me… well, he's very dangerous, and his ideas about torture are somewhat antiquated."

I saw Archer blanch.

"Justin Cho is the semel of one of the largest tribes I know of, over two hundred, and he lives in San Francisco. Should you want to speak to him, please give him my regards. We've been friends for over fifteen years. He visits every summer."

"I understand what you're saying to me," Archer told him.

"I live on this mountain in this small place and bother no one, but do not mistake me for a man without friends or connections or resources. If you or your sylvan have any further contact with my mate without my permission, I will kill you. And if I cannot, I will send my sheseru in my stead."

All eyes went to Yuri, and I saw him as they did. He was scary. Big and scary, even bigger than Logan, and in him, there was the ability to separate what needed to be done from who he was. Guilt did not live in Yuri, and neither did mercy.

"Am I making myself clear?"

"Yes," Archer said softly, reverently.

"You cannot—" my dad started.

"The man is my mate!" Logan exploded, yelling, the fury finally boiling over. "Jin Rayne is reah of the tribe of Mafdet! I will present him to everyone, every semel, at the Feast of the Valley when we all meet in Cairo in six months' time." He pointed at Archer. "You will be there, as will every other semel, and when you present your yareah, I will applaud. When I present my reah, you will hear the difference. The sound will be deafening. There will be hundreds of semels there, Archer, and I can promise you that I will be the only one there with a reah at his side. Perhaps you don't truly understand how rare a reah is right now, but you will. You surely will."

"Again, Logan, I apologize. My sylvan and I meant no disrespect to you or your house. There are extenuating circumstances at work here, and I appreciate your patience in this matter," Archer practically groveled.

Logan nodded curtly. "And now my patience is done. When you and your sylvan see my reah and me at the feast, you will keep your distance."

"Yes," Archer said weakly.

"Now go. All of you, get off my land. My sheseru will show you to your cars. Mikhail, please escort them to the airport; call Christophe and make sure he knows you'll be in his territory on my orders."

"Yes, my semel."

"I would like to speak to my son," my father said to Logan, his voice strained, "with your permission, of course."

"No," Logan denied flatly, his tone icy and hard. He deliberately turned his back on all of them, turning to face me, blocking my view of anyone but him and his breathtaking golden eyes. He pointed to the kitchen door. "I want to talk to you now."

I turned and walked out of the room without another word, reaching the stairs and taking them in twos to the second floor.

When I reached Logan's bedroom, now mine as well, I realized how much I loved it and sighed deeply. It was a sanctuary away from the world. I loved everything about my new home, especially the man in it.

"He beat you?" Logan yelled from behind me, and I heard the bedroom door slam shut.

I turned to look at him, smiling as I looked my mate over from head to toe.

"Jin?" he said as he folded his arms across his chest.

My mate was waiting for answers, but I was having trouble concentrating. Everything was swirling around in my head. I had wanted to belong to a tribe again after my own had abandoned me, and now I did. Between Logan's patience and love, the acceptance of my new family and friends, and the closure of seeing my father for the evil he really was, it was like I was brand new, starting over with a clean slate. I felt like I could fly.

"Tell me everything that happened."

But it was a lifetime ago, and it no longer mattered. I wasn't a scared teenager anymore; I was all grown up with a mate who loved me and a tribe that wanted me… me! They wanted me! "Who cares?" I smiled at him, motioning him over. "Don't be mad. Just come kiss me."

"No. I wanna talk to you first."

"I'll make you a deal," I teased. "You take off that shirt, and we'll talk."

"Jin, I don't—"

I put up a hand to cut him off. "Shirt first, talking second."

His exhale was loud and irritated, but he pulled off the shirt, balled it up, and threw it on the chair next to the window.

"Better," I said, walking over and diving onto the bed, rolling over onto my back, making a snow angel on the covers.

"What are you doing?"

"I dunno," I said, letting out a deep sigh of contentment before I looked at him. "But you've still got too many clothes on. How 'bout you ditch the shoes."

"This is not a striptease. I wanna know what—"

"Shoes."

He growled, but he toed off his sneakers and then yanked off his socks. "Happy?"

"Almost." I grinned at him, loving that he was now walking around in jeans and nothing else. There was never a time that looking at him wasn't a pleasure, all that gorgeous golden skin over hard, rippling muscles. "Now come lay down."

He said something I didn't catch.

"What's that?" I asked.

"I said you're a brat."

"Is that all?" I pulled off my sweater before I unsnapped the top button of my jeans.

"No." He cleared his throat, his eyes all over me. "You're beautiful too."

"If I'm so beautiful, why don't you come lay down with me?"

He coughed once. "Because I wanna know what they did to you."

"But I don't wanna live in the past," I assured him, tracking him as he walked around the room.

"No?"

"No."

"So is that it, then?" he asked. "You got all your insecurities taken care of now?"

"What?"

"You heard me. Are you done with the 'poor me' martyr bullshit?"

I stared at him, holding his golden gaze. There was a flicker of mischief in his eyes, the beginnings of the wicked grin that could annihilate me.

"Well?"

"Yes," I said with conviction, and I felt the happiness just rolling off me. I might have been glowing. "I know who I am, and I know who I love, and I know where I belong."

"Finally," he grumbled, coming over to the bed and sinking down on it. I watched him crawl toward me, but when I reached for him, he grabbed my arm and flipped me over onto my stomach.

"What are you doing?"

His lips were on the small of my back.

"Everyone's still downstairs, Logan."

"No, they're not, but I wouldn't care if they were all in the room," he assured me, kissing and biting and licking up my spine to between my shoulder blades, each touch featherlight and scorching at the same time. "I will claim my mate whenever I want."

The possessive tone sent a ripple of heat through my entire body.

"And now I feel the need to mark what's mine," he said as he gently lifted me to my hands and knees.

"Oh yes," I murmured, loving the feel of his hands as they caressed my back and then smoothed down my ribs to my hips. My jeans were eased to my knees and each of my legs lifted slowly in turn as the denim was slid off me. The fingers that grazed my cock sent tendrils of pleasure pulsing through me.

"Claim you," he breathed, moving behind me, bumping the back of my head so I would let it drop forward.

"Yes," I barely got out, my body aching with my need for him. "Please, claim me."

"I will." His voice was like a caress sliding over my heated skin. "My mate, look how beautiful you are. You are irresistible to me."

"Which is lucky, since no one wants me but you, Logan. You're the only one who claimed me and loves me and gave me your heart."

"Because you're mine." He exhaled, and his warm breath made me shiver as he kissed down my spine. "My reah, my mate… I didn't give you my heart… you *are* my heart."

God, I loved this man. "Logan, please… put your hands on me."

He moved fast, one saliva-coated finger sliding between my ass cheeks and deep inside me, his teeth sinking into the back of my neck at the same time.

I couldn't breathe. It felt too good.

"Oh, he likes that," he said, adding another finger, pushing in and pulling out slowly, sensually, licking the back of my neck. "Look at you ready for me… anticipating."

It was torture, waiting for him to be inside me, and I told him so.

He bit my ass, and I shivered at the same time as I felt his cock against my hole. I tried to lean back into him, but he held me still with his hands on my hips, making me moan as he entered me in one long, slow stroke that let me feel every inch of him as he filled me.

"God, baby, the way your ass holds me and swallows me… you just open up and take me in and you're so hot inside… so hot."

I felt the burn as he stretched me, the quivering, fluttering spasms as my muscles contracted with every push, every driving thrust going deeper.

"Logan!"

He slid out just a fraction of an inch and then shoved back inside hard and fast. I cried out as he fucked me at the same time his strong hand worked over my shaft, sending me over the edge into bliss.

"I love fucking you, being buried inside you, having my cock balls-deep in your tight little ass and feeling your dick swell in my hand. Most of all I love to hear you scream my name… I will never tire of hearing that."

So I screamed for him as he nailed my prostate with a hammering thrust and jerked me off at the same time.

"But I'm the only one that will ever be inside you, ramming into you over and over, just like I'm doing now."

He was claiming me. I was his possession, and I wanted nothing else. My back bowed, and the muscles in my ass clenched tight around him as I came. Logan's yell came seconds later, he, too, having found his release. His arms wrapped around me as he collapsed, pinning me to the bed beneath him, impaling me on the end of his shaft.

"You belong only to me, and it's just going to be me, forever, holding you like this."

I was weightless, and even though I could barely breathe, it didn't matter. I craved the man, body and soul. I was content to keep him inside me as long as he wanted.

"You're mine."

"Yes," I sighed deeply, happily, my body sated, my mind at ease, my soul content. "I'm your mate. I belong to you."

The satisfied male grunt let me know he was just as content as I was.

Check out this excerpt of

Trusted Bond

By Mary Calmes

Sequel to *Change of Heart*
Change of Heart: Book Two

Jin Rayne is having trouble adjusting to the new life he's supposed to love. Instead of adapting to being the mate of tribe leader Logan Church, Jin can't get past the fact that his lover was straight before they met. He's discovered the joy in belonging to Logan but fears his new life could disappear at a moment's notice, despite Logan's insistence that they are forever, end of story.

Jin wants to trust Logan, but that desire will be put to the test both by a rival tribe leader and by a startling revelation about Jin's existence. At stake is Jin's life and his place in the tribe. If he's going to survive to see Logan again, he'll have to release his fear and freely accept the bond, for only then can he truly trust.

Available at
http://www.dreamspinnerpress.com

Chapter One

EVERYBODY has a favorite season. Mine is summer. Certainly our love affair first began when I was a child, and three months of vacation with nothing to do but get into trouble was irresistible. But as I grew, I realized that during those long hot days of June, July, and August, there were no expectations of me. There was always time, when summer was over, to get my life in order, prepare for school, the new year, whatever was to come. In summer anything was possible.

Lifting my head, I stopped a minute from crossing the parking lot to savor the warm night breeze as it danced over my skin. The town where I lived, Incline Village, north of Lake Tahoe, was never too hot, and that was just one of the many reasons I loved my home.

Six months ago, I would have never thought that I would be calling any place home ever again, but that was before I met Logan Church. In such a short time I had gone from being an outcast to being the mate of a semel, or tribe leader, and being part of a tribe again.

I was born both a werepanther and a reah. Had I also been born a woman, then my life would have made sense, but as it was, my road had been a rocky one. Reahs only mated with semels, and as semels were only ever male, the only mate I could conceivably have would be a man. While what I was had always made sense to me—men, not women, had always been what mesmerized me—the tribe I grew up with, as well as my family, had quickly decided I was an abomination.

Having been cast out at sixteen, it had been me and my best friend, Crane, alone without a place to call home until I had met Logan Church, my mate.

Now, as a recognized reah, my life was no longer simply me and my best friend, but instead about my mate and his family and my new tribe. I was still reeling, still overwhelmed, buried under a landslide of obligations and protocol and demands on my time. It was daunting and had become even more so in the past week. I had no idea how I was even going to begin to explain events to my mate.

I let the scent of wildflowers, the faint trace of the lake, and the charcoal burning close by distract me from my thoughts. The smells drifted around me as I resumed my walk. Lazy days of summer were aptly named; I wanted to lounge in a hammock somewhere and forget all about the recent events. I waved when my name was called by different members of my team yelling good-night. It was nice that they had all missed seeing my face. Managing a restaurant was hard work, but what made it worth it was the people, and mine were some of the best. When my phone rang, I debated whether to answer it, seeing that the call was from home, but went ahead anyway.

"Hello?"

"Jin."

My heart skipped a beat, and I stopped walking, frozen there beside my Jeep, just the sound of the man's voice sending a wall of heat through me.

"Jin?"

"Logan… you're home." I exhaled, my voice quavering. "When did you get home?"

"You don't sound pleased."

I was and wasn't all at the same time. "No, I'm glad. I'm just surprised; I thought you said it would be ten days, but it's only been seven."

"I can't come home early?"

"That's not what I meant."

"So you're glad I'm home." He sounded uncertain.

"Of course I am," I said quickly, "but when did you—"

"Just a few minutes ago. Mikhail and I, we…." He was distracted; something he was looking at was drawing his attention. "Where are you?"

What to say?

"And where is everyone? The house is empty. Mikhail and I get home and there's nobody around? How is that even possible?"

With twelve people living in one place, eleven now that Simone had officially moved out to get married—mated—the expectation was that at least one person would be there when Logan got home from his weeklong trip to New York. That there had been no one there to greet him had to have been weird.

"I want to see you."

There was the underlying command in his voice, but he had not phrased it as an order, which, thankfully, allowed me to ignore it. I was relieved, because there was no way I could see him in the state I was in. "Okay."

"Okay?"

"Yeah."

"What does that mean?"

"It means that I can be home in a couple of days, but—"

"A couple of days?"

"Yeah. You said you were gonna be gone, so I wanted to make sure I was too, and now I'm locked into plans I can't get out of."

"Why would you want to leave home? You love being at home."

And he was right—I did. Having been homeless for so long, outside of work, it was where I could normally be found.

"Jin, what's going on?"

"With what?" I asked lightly.

"What plans do you have that you can't change?"

"Logan—"

"Who are you with?"

I cleared my throat. "No one."

His silence was long, like he was thinking. "Jin."

I had planned to think up my story that evening; I wasn't prepared yet. I was toying with telling him I had to go to Vegas for my boss or something along those lines. The idea of lying to my mate hurt to consider, but the alternative, the truth, was no better.

"Jin?"

"I'm here."

"What the hell is going on? Where is everybody, and why the hell don't you want to see me? I've been gone for an entire week; didn't you miss me at all?"

I had missed him way too much, which had basically been the cause of the entire problem, from what Abbot had said.

"Jin… love." Logan's voice softened, husky with feeling. "Why don't you want to see me?"

"I do… I so do," I hedged. What was I supposed to say? "I just don't want you to see me until I look good." Which was basically the truth, just not the whole truth.

"You always look good."

It was nice that he thought so, but I didn't always look good, and now, even worse, I was battered and bruised and still healing. As I was a werepanther, I strengthened after being hurt much faster than an average person, but there had been a lot of blood and cuts, and I still looked pretty bad. I had told everyone at work that I'd been in a car accident, and when I had showed up at the restaurant just to post the schedule and pass out paychecks, they were not sure I should have been out of bed. Had I told them the truth, that I was breaking up a fight between two werepanthers, they would have looked at me like I was crazy.

"Are you at work?"

"I'm actually just leaving," I said, because I was, in fact, going to be driving away from the restaurant where I worked in the next few seconds. "I'm going to my friend Eddie's to—"

"Jin." He cut me off. "I—what is going on?"

I was silent, because the conversation was headed in a bad direction. I could not be ordered home.

"Jin?"

Crap. "I thought I had more time."

"More time for what?"

I couldn't say that I was trying to save a man's life.

"Jin?"

I let out a deep breath. "You're gonna be really pissed."

"I'm already pissed," he snapped, "because you're not talking to me and you're trying to hide things from me. I'll ask again—what the hell is going on?"

"See… it's not Abbot's fault."

"What?"

"I mean it is but—"

"I don't—Abbot George? The sheseru Yuri's training from Kellen's tribe?"

On the request of Kellen Grant, another semel, the leader of a werepanther tribe, Logan had agreed to have his own sheseru, his enforcer, Yuri Kosa, mold another. Kellen's sheseru had been killed during a menthuel, or honor challenge, and so his brother, the next in line, became the new tribe enforcer. Abbot George had been with us a month when Logan left to attend Simone's mating ceremony in New York.

"Jin?"

"Sorry, what?"

"Focus."

I was trying to, but it was just hard. I was too worried about what was about to happen, and Logan's voice was doing things to my stomach. Fluttery, rolling, twisting things that were not altogether bad. I had missed him like crazy.

"Jin!"

I moaned because he'd yelled and reminded me that he was the dominant in our relationship. He was the semel, leader, and I was his mate. The ache of need pooled in my groin.

"What's wrong? Tell me."

His voice was deep and growly, and my thoughts roamed to the last time I had been in bed with him. He had wanted to tie me down, and I had let him. The bindings had been his silk dress ties, but they had held me because we allowed them to, both of us wanting the fantasy.

"Jin?"

"Missed you," I whispered.

"Me too," he told me gruffly, his voice deep and low. "Honey, what's going on?"

Lost in the sound of his voice, my body's yearning for him, the craving I felt down deep, I almost tipped my hand. I cleared my throat, pulled myself together. "Logan, I—"

"You're talking about Abbot George, right? The guy Yuri is training?"

Was training.

"Jin?"

"Yeah," I said solemnly.

There was a pause as understanding hit him. "What did he do?"

"It was a mistake."

"What was?"

"Just keep in mind that it was a mistake."

"Jin, so help me if you—"

"I'm fine."

"Why wouldn't you be fine?" His voice hardened. "What are you try—"

"It was a mistake."

"You said that already. What the hell happened? Just tell me."

I winced because I heard how icy his tone was. "Okay, so I guess because I was missing you and because I'm your reah and—"

"Christ, this is like pulling teeth! Just tell me what the fuck happened!"

He wasn't mad at me, and I knew that, but still, he was irritated. "The pheromones," I sighed. "I didn't even realize I was… but Abbot said it was like I was in heat."

"Abbot said." His voice dropped low, going deadly still.

I made a noise in the back of my throat.

There was a shuffling noise, muffled, and then, "Jin."

Mikhail's calm voice washed relief all over me. Him, I could talk to. The sylvan of our tribe, the teacher, the counselor, he was a constant source of sound reason and strength. Confessing to Mikhail was something everyone did, and I was no exception. "Hi." I smiled widely, the deep sigh coming up out of me. "How was your trip?"

There was a deep male grunt. "I will tell you all about New York when I see you, but first I need to know what went on here. My semel demands it, and so do I. Why are you not in your home, my reah, and where is your sheseru?"

I thought a moment about what to say.

"Just tell me."

But it had all happened so fast. One minute I was in the kitchen making spaghetti, and the next I had turned to find Abbot George, the sheseru in training, a panther from Kellen Grant's tribe of Selket, standing in front of me. He should not have been allowed to be alone with me, the reah of my tribe, the mate of our leader, but in my own home, my rules were lax. If you were in my house, I trusted you.

"Hey." I smiled at him. "How's the training going with Yuri? You think you still wanna be a sheseru, or you gonna give up?"

His eyes narrowed as he closed in on me. "My semel, Kellen Grant, he took for his mate a yareah, a woman he picked himself, not a reah that was destined for him from birth. He does not have a true-mate. He doesn't have a reah."

"Sure," I agreed, tipping my head back at the stove. "The spaghetti's not as good as Logan's mom makes, but it's okay. You want some?"

He didn't answer, instead moving in closer, pressing me back, crowding up against me.

"Abbot?"

"A true sheseru is meant to be the enforcer of the semel and the protector of a reah, is he not?"

"A sheseru does as his semel demands," I clarified for him. "Could you maybe step—"

"I read the law. A sheseru is a reah's champion."

"If the tribe has a reah," I corrected. "If there is no reah, then—"

"A sheseru is lost without a reah."

"No, they just guard the yareah instead...." I couldn't concentrate; I was wary and on edge. "Could you maybe... could you step back just a little," I suggested, certain that he had no idea how uncomfortable he was making me.

"A sheseru is meant to be the protector of a reah," he said flatly, encroaching further.

"Stop," I said gently but firmly.

"I thought it was the same," he said, his voice dropping low, his fingertips grazing the side of my neck. "Reah or yareah... I had no idea there was any difference until I came here."

"Abbot." I said his name as two men I had never seen in my life walked into the kitchen.

"What are you—"

"It's not the same. A reah is... a miracle, and after being here, with you, a true reah, I see and feel the difference. I must remain here, at your side; Logan must accept me and banish Yuri."

He was out of his mind, and before his hand could close around my throat, I stepped back the final amount of room I had, bumping into the counter behind me. "Yuri is Logan's sheseru and will be for as long—"

"Since Logan's been gone, it's like you're in heat," he whispered, and I saw how huge his pupils were, marked the shudder that ran through him. I wondered vaguely where Yuri was. "I think a sheseru cares for their reah in all ways when the semel is gone."

There was almost no white at all, just big dilated eyes swallowing me. It was creepy, almost scary, and what the hell did the *all ways* comment mean?

"I think you need me.... Your body cries out for mine."

Who talked like that? "You should go watch some TV in the living room," I suggested softly, watching him, the hair on the back of my neck standing up as I glanced at the other two men. "And take your friends with you, unless they want something to eat first." I was working hard to keep my tone neutral, calm, and upbeat.

"I have never wanted a man before," Abbot confessed, his voice dropping low. "But neither have I ever seen a man who looked like you, Jin Rayne."

I went cold. And not because I was scared. I was furious. How dare he treat Logan this way? How dare he violate the sanctity of Logan's home? I was the mate of the semel, completely untouchable, and now this man thought to claim me? My mate was the strongest male panther I had ever come across, and this man thought he could usurp him? Take me? He presumed to think I needed anything more than my mate? It was obscene.

"Get out of my house," I ordered, my voice cold, hard.

"Reah." He cut me off before he lunged at me, knocking the plate from my hands as he grabbed my face and yanked me forward. His mouth was on mine, his tongue forced between my lips as he bent me backward over the counter.

I pushed and fought, but he was so much bigger and stronger than me, his hands everywhere as I managed to dislodge his mouth from mine. "Stop," I rasped out, trying so hard not to yell, terrified for him, for the transgression he was committing. I had gone from anger to fear for his life in seconds. I could have shifted and gotten away easily, but if anyone saw me they would wonder why I needed to be in my panther form in my own home. What would prompt me to shift into my animal? Why would I need to fight? And as soon as the question arose, my sheseru, Yuri Kosa, would kill them. So I didn't want anyone else to see us or hear us. But the second the others put their hands on me, though, I forgot about their safety.

The kitchen table was cleared and I was slammed down onto it face-first, my arms stretched out, held tight. Strangers held my wrists firmly as Abbot shoved his groin against my tailbone, his hands on my belt buckle, fumbling to get it off. I had originally thought there were only three men, but now, clearly, I realized my error. There were four.

I had no choice. Like liquid I shifted through their fingers, my body transforming in the blink of an eye from man to panther. Gasps filled the room as I rolled to the floor, tangled in my jeans and shirt, freeing myself in seconds, happy that I had been barefoot. I had missed when Abbot's reverence became obsession, but he had apparently missed my speed. I was so much faster than he thought, as evidenced by the fact that I was across the huge kitchen before any of them could track me with their eyes.

"Reah," Abbot breathed even as he began tearing at his clothes in a frenzy to get them off, to shift to his panther form.

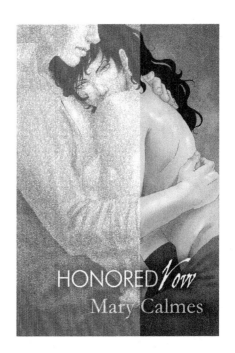

Don't miss

Crucible of Fate

By Mary Calmes

A Change of Heart Novel

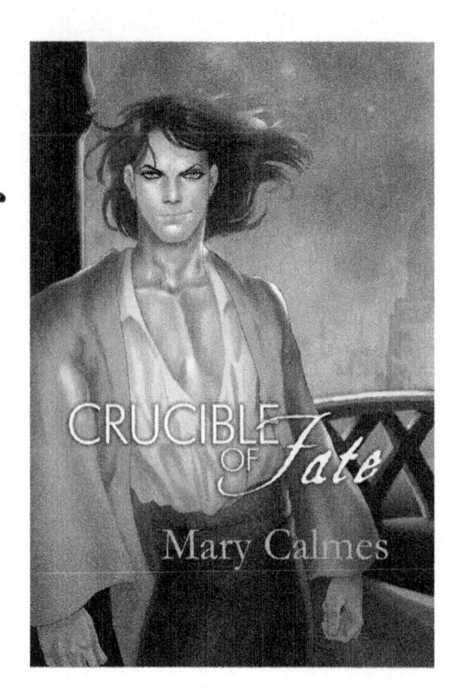

In the secret city of Sobek, Domin Thorne is making his way as the newly chosen semel-aten, the leader of the werepanther world. He aspires to make sweeping changes—he's set goals for himself and the people he chose to bring with him, modeling his reign after that of his friend, Logan Church. But Domin may have set too lofty a goal: his normal leadership style isn't working.

While juggling a homesick Crane, a moody Mikhail, a bullwhip-wielding Taj, servants with murderous intentions, a visiting ex, and a mate on a dangerous goodwill mission, Domin has to figure out his new role alone. He also must determine how to deal with a conspiracy, all the while falling hard for a man who, for the first time in Domin's life, reciprocates that love. Whether Domin is ready or not, Fate has stepped in to teach him a lesson: internal threats are just as dangerous as external ones.

Available at
http://www.dreamspinnerpress.com

Don't miss

Forging the Future

By Mary Calmes

A Change of Heart Novel

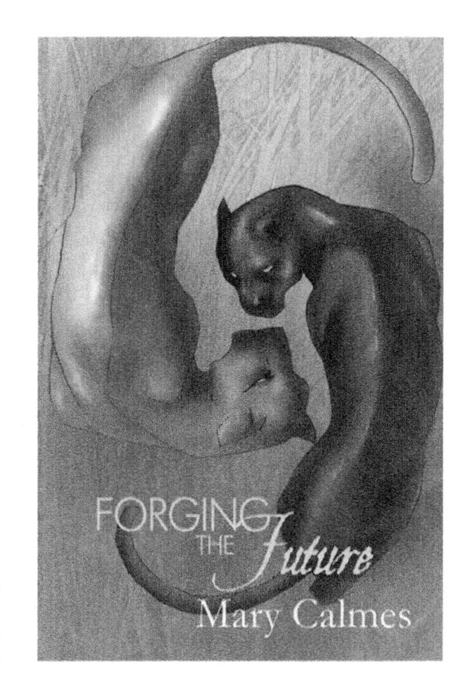

Jin Church is back where he started, alone, wandering, and uncertain of his path. It's not by choice but by circumstance, as he remembers he's a werepanther… but not much else. He knows one thing for sure—he needs to find the beautiful blond man who haunts his dreams.

Logan Church is trapped in a living hell. His mate is missing, his tribe is falling apart, and he's estranged from the son he loves with all his heart. His world is unraveling without his mate by his side, and he has no one to blame but himself.

If Jin can regain his memory and Logan can overcome the threats to his leadership, then perhaps they can resume their lives. The question is: Is that what they want? Back to the same house, the same tribe, the same troubles? They can choose from various roads leading to their future… or they can forge their own path.

Available at
http://www.dreamspinnerpress.com

MARY CALMES lives in Lexington, Kentucky, with her husband and two children and loves all the seasons except summer. She graduated from the University of the Pacific in Stockton, California, with a bachelor's degree in English literature. Due to the fact that it is English lit and not English grammar, do not ask her to point out a clause for you, as it will *so* not happen. She loves writing, becoming immersed in the process, and falling into the work. She can even tell you what her characters smell like. She loves buying books and going to conventions to meet her fans.

http://www.dreamspinnerpress.com

PARTING
SHOT
Mary Calmes

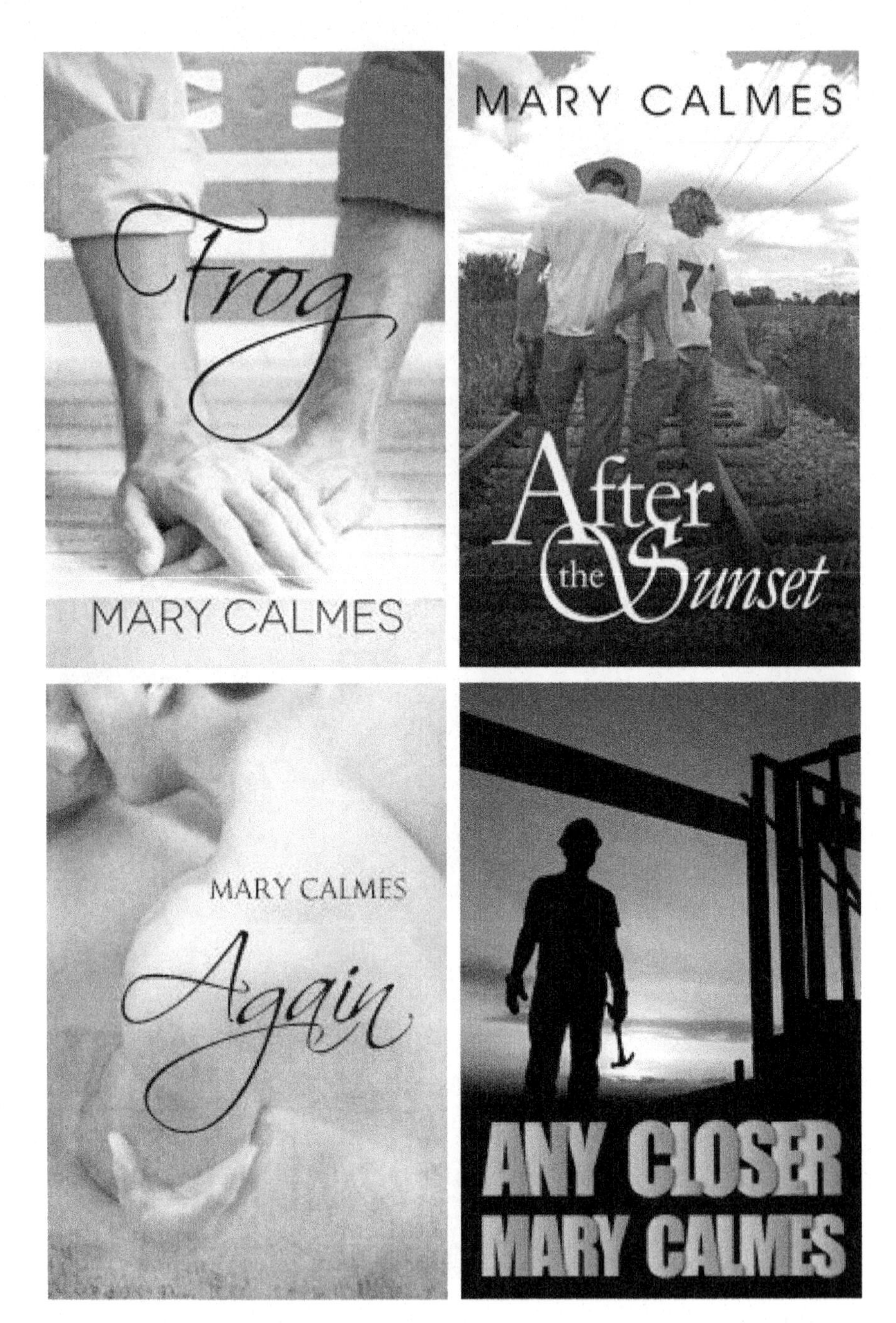
Frog
MARY CALMES
MARY CALMES
After the Sunset
MARY CALMES
Again
ANY CLOSER
MARY CALMES

Mangrove Nights from MARY CALMES

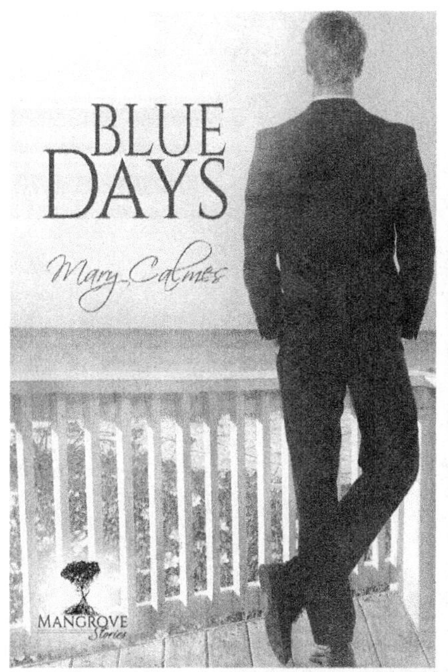

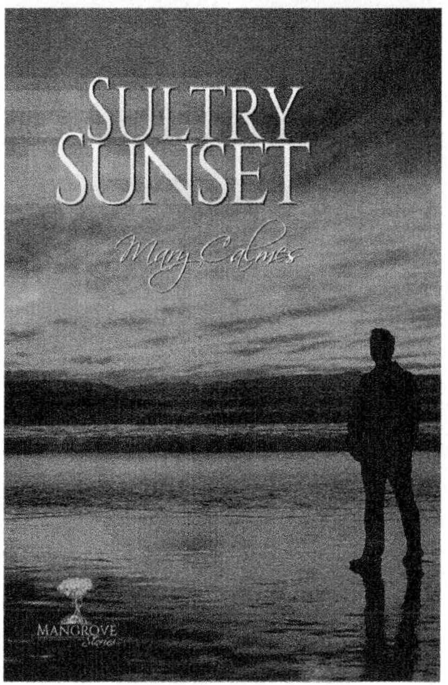

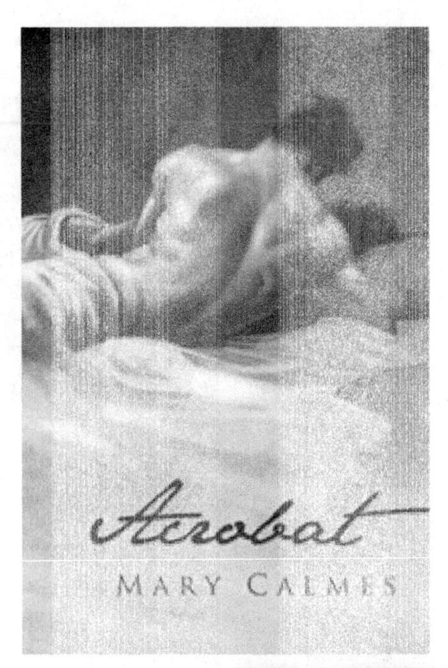

http://www.dreamspinnerpress.com

http://www.dreamspinnerpress.com

http://www.dreamspinnerpress.com

HIS
HEARTH
MARY CALMES

HEART
IN HAND
MARY CALMES

SINNERMAN
MARY CALMES

http://www.dreamspinnerpress.com

http://www.dreamspinnerpress.com

FOR
MORE
OF THE
BEST
GAY
ROMANCE
DREAMSPINNER
PRESS
dreamspinnerpress.com

CPSIA information can be obtained at www.ICGtesting.com
Printed in the USA
BVOW06s0201310715

411282BV00009B/71/P